Dear Reader,

For many years Harlequin Books has been a leader in supporting and promoting causes that are of concern to women and celebrating ordinary women who make extraordinary differences in the lives of others. Through Harlequin More Than Words, we annually honor women for their compassionate dedication to those that need it most, and donate $10,000 to their chosen causes.

We are proud to highlight our current Harlequin More Than Words award recipients by telling you about them and, with the help of some of the biggest names in women's fiction, creating wonderfully entertaining and moving fictional short stories based on these women and their causes. Within these pages, you will find stories written by Carly Phillips, Donna Hill and Jill Shalvis—and online at www.HarlequinMoreThanWords.com you can also access stories by Pamela Morsi and Meryl Sawyer. These two stories are free and we hope you'll read them and pass them on to your friends. All five of these stories are beautiful tributes to the Harlequin More Than Words award recipients who inspired them, and we hope they will touch your heart and inspire the real-life heroine in you.

Thank you for your support; all proceeds from the sale of this book will be returned to the Harlequin More Than Words program so we can assist more causes of concern to women. And you can help even more by learning about and getting involved with the charities highlighted by Harlequin More Than Words. Together we can make a difference!

Sincerely,

Donna Hayes
Publisher and CEO
Harlequin Enterprises Ltd.

NEW YORK TIMES and *USA TODAY* bestselling author

Carly Phillips
Donna Hill
Jill Shalvis

More Than Words

VOLUME 7

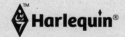

Harlequin®

TORONTO NEW YORK LONDON
AMSTERDAM PARIS SYDNEY HAMBURG
STOCKHOLM ATHENS TOKYO MILAN MADRID
PRAGUE WARSAW BUDAPEST AUCKLAND

Recycling programs
for this product may
not exist in your area.

ISBN-13: 978-0-373-83763-2

MORE THAN WORDS: VOLUME 7

Copyright © 2011 by Harlequin Books S.A.

Carly Phillips is acknowledged as the author of *Compassion Can't Wait*.
Donna Hill is acknowledged as the author of *Someplace Like Home*.
Jill Shalvis is acknowledged as the author of *What the Heart Wants*.

This edition published by arrangement with Harlequin Books S.A.

For questions and comments about the quality of this book please contact us at Customer_eCare@Harlequin.ca.

® and TM are trademarks of the publisher. Trademarks indicated with ® are registered in the United States Patent and Trademark Office, the Canadian Trade Marks Office and in other countries.

www.eHarlequin.com

Printed in U.S.A.

CONTENTS

STORIES INSPIRED BY REAL-LIFE HEROINES

VALERIE SOBEL

∽ Andre Sobel River of ∽
Life Foundation

It was a phone call like so many others Valerie Sobel
receives: a desperate mother on the line, stumbling
over her words and barely making sense. The
woman was emotionally spent, physically exhausted
and unsure who to turn to in this darkest hour.

After speaking with the mother for a few minutes,
Valerie understood her plight. The woman had just received a letter signed by her family saying that although
they loved her and her son, they could no longer look
after "a cripple" while the single mom worked to pay
the bills.

The eight-year-old boy in question, Benjamin, was
dying of a malignant spinal tumor.

"Tell me, what would it take for you to stay home
and care for him?" asked Valerie.

The woman didn't miss a beat.

"You don't understand—I *have* to work," she answered. "I'll need to pay for Benjamin's caregiver."

It took Valerie, founder of the California-based Andre Sobel River of Life Foundation, a few more minutes of prodding before the mother finally understood that perhaps Valerie was offering her a solution she never could have imagined—a way to be with her dying child.

In the end, Valerie's charitable organization cut through the red tape and immediately paid for the family's COBRA insurance as well as the difference between unemployment and the single parent's salary. And while, sadly, Benjamin did eventually pass away, he had his mother with him for the last days of his journey.

"I am humbled every day that I can say yes to people whose needs are so great," Valerie says. "But they should never be in this situation, because to me, it's the elemental right of a human being to be where they need to be when they have a dying child."

When compassion can't wait

Giving human life dignity, both for the sick child and the parent, is what ASRL's Compassion Can't Wait project is all about. Founded by Valerie in 1995 with a seed donation, ASRL is now a public charity supported by hundreds of donors across the United States.

Its mission? When compassion can't wait and single-parent families are in despair, the organization helps with urgent expenses to allow caregivers to stay at their child's side.

Knowing there is no emotional room left for dealing

with bureaucracy when a little one needs so much time and attention, Compassion Can't Wait ensures that the parent does not spend precious hours filling out endless forms for aid when they would rather be with their child. Instead, the family's social worker determines how much financial aid is needed, develops a plan for the family and contacts ASRL on its behalf. If all other resources have been exhausted, ASRL pays the bills and lifts the financial burden.

The organization has given money to pay for insurance, save homes, put groceries in the fridge—and Valerie has given her heart.

It started with Andre

When Valerie holds a grieving parent's hand, or strokes the head of a critically ill child, she does it out of compassion that only those who have faced tragedy can truly understand.

On Thanksgiving Day in 1993, she received news that her beautiful teenage son, Andre, had an inoperable brain tumor. He fought the deadly disease as hard as he could, but passed away on January 12, 1995. Valerie held her son for three hours after his death, wondering how she would ever go on, but knowing she had to find some way to change the world to make up for her son's terrible absence.

"There are some things that can never fade," she concedes. "I don't even remember the person I was before. It changes you at the cellular level."

The year turned out to be cataclysmic. Soon after

Andre's death, Valerie's mother died—the same woman who ushered the family to safety after they fled their native Hungary during the 1956 uprising against the Soviet regime. Valerie still remembers carrying her younger brother on her back while walking eight miles with her parents through marsh to cross the border into Austria. Months later they left refugee camps behind to settle in Toronto and eventually moved to California.

Then, one year to the day of Andre's death, Valerie's husband took his own life in despair.

It took four more years of grieving, forgiving and opening herself back up to life before Valerie's vision to help families with critically ill children could take shape. But it did. She simply could not forget witnessing other children who were by themselves for hours in the hospital, having to face their fears, pain, treatments— and at times even their deaths—alone.

Haunted by what she saw, Valerie kept asking herself how she could have managed Andre's illness without financial and emotional support. How would their journey have been different if she had been a single parent? She admits her initial ways of trying to honor Andre did not give her the sense of grace his life deserved.

"Honoring his life is about how I can help others who are going through what I went through," she says. "It started with him and ended with me."

Making change happen

Today Valerie is a force of nature. Her innovative work includes convening a think tank of leading doctors and social workers to document how single parents with critically ill children can cope. She can also be found on the phone with landlords, negotiating past-rent forgiveness, matching it with ASRL's own rent payment, and working with utility and credit-card companies to remove late fees and penalties.

"Valerie is an exceptional woman," says Anne Swire, the organization's CEO, who left a job in Washington, D.C., to work in partnership with Valerie on the West Coast. "Her visionary idea has brought urgent assistance to thousands of grateful families, but most will never know her name."

Valerie is not in the caring profession to win personal accolades. Her greatest hope is to see real societal change that would embed services like Compassion Can't Wait right into the health-care system. At present, ASRL tries to accommodate over two thousand freestanding children's hospitals, and eighty percent of its funding comes from private sources—a challenging way to raise money, especially during tough economic times.

Until that change happens, Valerie, who seems to have lived at least eight lives (she once won roles in Jimmy Stewart and Paul Newman movies when the acting bug caught her as a teen) keeps moving forward.

When she's not working fourteen-hour days, she vacations with friends in Istanbul, writes poetry and connects with families who need her support.

"It reminds me that a sad time in my life is over and now I can help someone else," she says. "How fortunate am I to do that?"

CARLY PHILLIPS
~ COMPASSION CAN'T WAIT ~

◦— CARLY PHILLIPS —◦

Carly Phillips started her writing career with the Harlequin Temptation line in 1999 with *Brazen*, and she's never strayed far from home! In 2002, Carly's book, *The Bachelor*, was chosen by Kelly Ripa for her Reading with Ripa book club, making it the first romance to be chosen by a nationally televised book club. Carly has published thirty books, and, among others, she has appeared on the *New York Times*, *USA TODAY* and *Publishers Weekly* bestseller lists. An ABC soap-opera addict, Carly lives in Purchase, New York, with her husband, two teenage daughters and two frisky soft-coated wheaten terriers who act like their third and fourth children. Carly loves to interact with readers!
You can find Carly online at www.carlyphillips.com and blog with her at www.plotmonkeys.com. Carly is also on Facebook:
www.facebook.com/carlyphillipsfanpage and Twitter:
www.twitter.com/carlyphillips.

⌒— DEDICATION —⌒

Thank you to Marsha Zinberg for thinking
of me for this special project, to Brenda
Chin for your persistence and faith in me,
and most of all to ASRL and especially
Valerie Sobel for your inspiration. And to
Anne Swire for your help and dedication.
I admire you all.

CHAPTER
⤗ ONE ⤗

Smack. Smack. Smack.

Julia Caldwell listened to the familiar sound of a ball hitting the center pocket of a baseball mitt. It echoed through the hospital corridors, as routine as the monitors beeping at the nurses' station in Miami's Caridad del Cobre Children's Hospital. For the last month, the Cortez family, mother and fourteen-year-old twin sons, had been a fixture at the hospital; Michael Cortez and his baseball obsession were a welcome break from sickness and pain.

Michael and his brother, Manny, were twins, alike in so many ways except for a cruel genetic twist. Manny had leukemia. Michael did not. Manny had his mother at his side day and night. Michael did not.

As the healthy child in a single-parent home, baseball was the only comfort Michael Cortez had. Nobody, from the nurses to the doctors to other patients or parents, would ever ask him to stop the repetitive sound.

Every afternoon, Michael walked to the hospital from school and took up residence in either his brother's room or the family lounge. Not wanting to be a burden to his mother, he'd do his homework without being reminded, bring his mom coffee and then turn to the comforting routine of tossing the ball into the glove.

Smack. Smack. Smack.

From her small office near the nurses' station, Julia filled out the Request for Assistance forms for the Andre Sobel River of Life Foundation. As the social worker responsible for the pediatric wing of Caridad del Cobre, Julia had already been in contact with the program manager at ASRL and the foundation was expecting the formal request. Within twenty-four hours, ASRL would cut a check to Anna Cortez's landlord, electric company and phone provider. The rent for their apartment and other essential expenses would be taken care of while Anna sat by Manny's bedside, willing him to live. Anna had already lost her job because, as everyone at the hospital understood too well, a child's illness was all consuming. ASRL's motto was Compassion Can't Wait.

And the foundation always stepped up immediately.

Before Julia faxed in the Request for Assistance, she said her usual prayer of thanks to the people at ASRL, grateful she'd contacted the foundation almost two years ago for another single parent of a teenage girl with a brain tumor. Since then, Caridad del Cobre routinely applied to ASRL for funding for families who met the criteria—single caregivers who needed to be with their sick children.

Julia leaned against the wall and sighed. But who would make sure the needs of Michael Cortez, the healthy child, were met?

Smack. Smack. Smack.

She listened to the sound, as familiar to her as the number 22 emblazoned on the fourteen-year-old boy's jersey. Number 22, Kyle Hansen, star pitcher for the Miami Suns, the city's three-year-old expansion team, which had made it as far as the playoffs last year. Kyle was their multi-million-dollar boy, their marquee player and their captain.

He was also Julia's high school sweetheart and first love—before life choices got in the way. The fax machine beeped loudly, letting her know the message had gone through. Shaking off the past, she headed down the hall to tell Anna Cortez that everything would be taken care of soon.

Smack. Smack. Smack.

Drawn by the sound, Julia paused by the family waiting room and glanced at the dark-haired boy sitting alone in the lounge, rhythmically smacking the ball into his glove.

"Hey, Michael."

"Hey." He didn't take his eyes off the ball. With hard work and a guardian angel, the boy's focus and concentration could take him far.

Just like his idol.

"What time is today's Suns game?" she asked him.

"Seven."

Julia nodded. Her paid day ended at five. "Want company?" She didn't have plans for the night and she could just as easily watch the game here as at home.

The boy shrugged. "Don't care."

Smack. Smack. Smack.

"Good. That settles it, then. I'll pick us up burgers for dinner and be back in time for the game. It'll be like we're at the stadium."

"Burgers from Burgers, Shakes and Fries?" he asked, showing the first sign of eagerness.

Julia grinned. "Yeah. I can go to Burgers, Shakes and Fries." Even if it was fifteen minutes in the other direction. Michael's smile was worth it.

Her heart swelled and she felt an overwhelming empathy for the boy who was losing his childhood along with his brother. She'd once been there, the healthy sibling with a sister dying of leukemia, and she knew exactly how Michael was feeling.

Alone, lonely, resentful and afraid. She also knew that whether Manny recovered or not, Michael's life would never be the same. His relationship with his mother, his sibling, even the rest of the world, would be forever altered. As hers had been.

If someone didn't step in and acknowledge that he was important too, his already rioting emotions would change him from just a teenager with attitude to one who found validation elsewhere, in crime or, worse, in one of the street gangs prevalent in the downtown area where he lived. Julia knew it would take a special person with unique skills to get past the teenager's well-honed defenses and impress him. Someone like the man Julia hadn't seen in nine years and who she'd never had any intention of contacting again.

She ran her hands up and down her arms as she traveled down memory road. Kyle had signed a letter of intent to play baseball for the University of Miami, but turned down the scholarship when he was selected in the first round of the amateur draft to play for the Seattle Mariners right after graduation. He'd asked, actually he'd expected, her to go with him.

She'd refused. For more reasons than she could think about now.

Could she just resurface in his life all these years later and ask him for help? And even if she was willing to step up and do that, she couldn't easily find a way to contact him now that he was a celebrity.

But she had resources. Illness didn't discriminate, and thanks to her work at Caridad del Cobre and her association with ASRL, she had met people from all walks of life.

With all sorts of connections.

As always, Kyle arrived at the newly built Suns Stadium way before game time. Usually he stretched and hung with the team, and on a pitching day, he used the time to get into the zone. Today wasn't his day on the mound, so he could relax his focus somewhat. He parked his Porsche in the private team lot, grateful for the reprieve from the female groupies who never stopped believing the star players would single them out for attention.

It wasn't that Kyle didn't appreciate the fans who filled the seats and helped pay his hefty salary. He definitely did. But he could do without the hangers-on who wanted a taste of fame, fortune and whichever ballplayer would toss some kind of interest their way. He used to revel in that kind of attention and indulged in whatever the willing females had to offer.

No longer.

He hadn't been that desperate—or interested—in a while. Restless and edgy described him a lot better. Not that he knew why, when he'd achieved his dream. Lessons learned were often painful. Back in the days when he'd been a staple at the bar scene, running far from memories and himself, he'd had something to prove. He'd taken his aggression out on the mound and the players at the plate. Off the field, he'd dared anyone else to try to mess with him, shoving his up-and-coming star status in everyone's face.

He'd always known he was more talented than the average ballplayer and that he'd have to work his way out of the gutter in which he'd been born. A lucky break got him noticed by a pastor at Westminster Academy, who'd wrangled him a scholarship to the school. That's where he'd met Julia Caldwell. But after she'd wished him luck in the minors and kissed him goodbye, he'd lost his focus. After one drink and one fight too many, Kyle had ended up behind bars. His mentor in the minors bailed him out, sobered him up and shoved his face in the mirror, forcing him to realize the path to success wasn't strewn with alcohol and bimbos.

Kyle shook his head and shoved his sunglasses onto

the bridge of his nose. There was no reason those days should've come back to him now. He'd behaved and worked hard ever since, and he was finally living his dream as the marquee player of Miami's newest expansion team.

He swung his duffel bag over his shoulder and walked through the stadium doors, waving to the security guard as he passed.

Before he could turn down the long corridor leading to the locker room, a familiar female voice called to him. "Hansen, I need a word!"

He cringed at the commanding tone. Macy Kroger, the Suns' publicist, had a stronger voice than any man he knew and an iron will. When she wanted something from someone, she usually got it.

As the captain and face of the team, Kyle went out of his way to play nice with Macy, but he had one rule he expected her to obey.

"Business after the game, not before," he called over his shoulder as a reminder. Whether or not he was pitching, he demanded his concentration be on the game.

Macy's stilettos clicked as she ran down the hall, catching up with him just as he rounded the corner. "Kyle, wait."

He turned to face her. "What?"

She'd tucked a pen behind her ear, and her fiery-red hair fell over her shoulders, but to her credit she wasn't winded from her sprint down the hall.

Macy was about thirty, tough as nails and as gorgeous as they came. The Suns' owners had lured her away from their crosstown rivals with the promise of a six-figure salary and complete access to the players, which she needed to make her job a success.

"What's so important that it can't wait?" he asked.

"A mission of mercy." She pulled out a folder and began to read him sad statistics on single parents and the effect of catastrophic illness on families, along with a host of other issues he was way too familiar with.

Once again, thoughts of Julia tried to come flooding back.

He glanced at his gold watch and tapped the face. "Get to the point," he told Macy. "Game's in three hours."

She shot him a smirk. "Fine. Twin brothers. One has leukemia. The other doesn't. Healthy twin could use a mentor of sorts."

Kyle's gut tightened at the word *leukemia* and the notion that it was the *other* sibling who needed help. Julia had once been that other sibling. Back when they'd met, he'd needed her to tutor him in Spanish. She'd just plain needed attention and he'd been only too happy to provide it. His days with Julia represented a time in his life he didn't like to revisit. She'd hurt him badly and he hated going down that road.

Too many *what-ifs* and *could-have-beens*.

So, as he always did when random thoughts of Julia arose, he squelched them. "Put Ryder on it," Kyle told the publicist. "He could use some exposure and I've seen him with the manager's kids. He's your guy."

In the year since Macy had been on the job, she'd made stars of their rookies and garnered the team a reputation for charitable good deeds. Children were the

Suns' most passionate cause. Ryder would make a great mentor for the kid.

"I wasn't asking for suggestions. I already have my man." Macy met his gaze with a determined one of her own and stepped closer.

That was Macy—she talked in circles until he finally understood her point. Which was usually a good one.

"Let me backtrack so you'll have a clear picture," she said, unaware of his thoughts. "Dave Granderson's new wife has a teenage daughter from a previous marriage. The daughter was diagnosed with a brain tumor two years ago, when the current Mrs. Granderson was a single parent. Are you with me so far?"

Granderson was the team's co-owner, and if he was involved with this request, Kyle understood why it would be given top priority. "Go on."

"The hospital that treated her daughter, Caridad del Cobre Children's Hospital, referred Mrs. Granderson to the Andre Sobel River of Life Foundation, ASRL for short. ASRL stepped in and made sure her rent and electric bill were paid, they put food on the table when she couldn't work because she was by her daughter's bedside. In short, Mrs. Granderson would do anything for ASRL."

"Understandable," Kyle said. Forget that the order came from ownership. He respected what ASRL did for single-parent families. He'd only suggested Ryder to avoid old memories, but if he was the best man for the job, so be it.

"You don't need the hard sell," he told Macy. "I'll meet the kid."

She smiled in obvious relief. "Good. Because Michael Cortez, the boy whose twin is dying, idolizes you. ASRL told the hospital's social worker to contact Mrs. Granderson, who in turn promised you'd be happy to get together with him."

He nodded. "Now that I've agreed, we can talk details *after* the game." He turned toward the locker room.

Macy stopped him with a hand on his shoulder. "Not so fast. You need to take a meeting. Now."

"With who?"

"The social worker in charge of coordinating your meeting with the boy. She's waiting for you in my office."

Kyle shook his head in frustration. "Seriously. Doesn't *business after the game* mean anything to you?"

Macy smiled. "Well, normally I insist anyone who wants to meet with my players abide by my rules, but this woman said she knew you."

"Does *she* have a name?" Even as he asked, the hair on the back of his neck stood up and every nerve ending in his body prickled with unease.

"Julia Caldwell."

The name hit him like a fastball to the head. No wonder he'd thought of her earlier. Call it premonition or just a plain old gut feeling, somehow he'd sensed her presence.

"You can find her in my office, but I'll give you some time alone first," Macy said. "You look like you need it."

She turned and walked away, leaving him to digest her news.

Julia Caldwell had come back. *For business, not for him*. Man, she had a knack for bruising his ego, he thought as he strode down the hall toward Macy's private office.

He passed life-size photographs of the Suns' current roster lining the walls of the stadium, including one of number 22—Kyle Hansen, Team Captain captioned beneath. But not even the reminder that he was no longer the kid with one pair of jeans and just a minor-league contract to his name helped make Kyle feel like the superstar he'd become. The prospect of seeing Julia again had brought him back in time and he didn't like it one bit.

Kyle paused outside the wooden door to Macy's office to regroup. Julia needed something from him, which meant he was the one in control this time. Even if ownership insisted he fulfill her request, he could at least act as if he had the upper hand. That meant not letting her know she still held any power over him or his emotions.

And maybe she didn't.

He rotated his shoulders, forcing himself to relax. Almost a decade had passed and a lot of things had changed. For all he knew, there'd be no attraction left between them at all.

CHAPTER
∽ TWO ∽

Julia waited for Kyle in the team publicist's luxurious office. The plush carpet and mahogany furniture reminded her of her father's office in her childhood home. A place that had been her sanctuary, where she'd do her homework and hang out with her father, until Meghan's illness had altered everyone's world. There were times she'd resented the hell out of her little sister for being sick. These days, she wished she had a sister to resent. That's why she was here. So Michael Cortez would have fewer days to look back on and feel guilty about. So he'd have some joy during this painful time.

Nobody had seen to Julia's happiness. At least, not until Kyle entered her life. She stopped pacing and admired the team photos on the wall in Macy's office, capturing the individual players in various stages of public-relations activities. She leaned in for a closer look. A picture showed Kyle and a group of teenage boys in junior Suns uniforms smiling at each other, seemingly unaware of the camera. Kyle's smile was wide and genuine as he gripped the ball and hung out with the kids. That he already worked with teens eased her mind. Convincing him to meet and coach Michael Cortez might not be difficult after all.

She'd kept up with Kyle's stats and watched the games. She couldn't help but read the columns featuring the Suns' star player and the rumors about which lucky woman would land the wealthy eligible bachelor. He was never linked to just one woman, nor was he a purported player. He appeared to be a man who kept his private life out of the papers as best he could, allowing the gossips to speculate.

Even Julia wondered whether there was a special woman in his life. In fact, he was so private, this photo was the first time she'd seen him in what looked like an unguarded moment. He was relaxed and at ease, and she almost didn't recognize the intense, bad-boy teenager she remembered.

"See something you like?" a familiar male voice asked.

She jumped and turned at the sound of that deep voice. She hadn't even heard the door open.

She met his steady gaze, immediately struck by how large a presence he'd become. "I was just...killing time until you got here. I mean, looking at pictures while I waited." Nerves had her rambling.

She clamped her mouth shut and drew a deep breath.

She'd dreamed of this moment over the years. She'd had more than twenty-four hours to get used to the idea of facing him.

But she was completely unprepared now. She dragged in another breath. "Hi, Kyle. It's good to see you again." She felt much more composed.

On the outside.

Inside, her stomach was churning like crazy.

He eyed her steadily, singeing her with the intensity of his blue-eyed stare.

"Julia." His voice was lower, more masculine.

Warmth seeped through her veins and suddenly she knew. *This* was what had been missing with every man she'd encountered over the last nine—almost ten—years. No one had ever made her feel as alive and aware, as important, with just a simple look.

But there was nothing simple about Kyle Hansen. There never had been.

"So." He inclined his head, his gaze unapologetically raking over her. "You look good."

She bit the inside of her cheek. "So do you."

He was taller, if possible, his shoulders broader. His sandy-blond hair brushed his forehead and hung longer in the back. Even high-definition television hadn't done the man justice. He was beyond handsome.

She cleared her throat. "Thank you for seeing me on such short notice." She attempted to keep things to the point and professional—the only way she'd survive the meeting.

He stared her down. "I would have met with *you*, Julia. You didn't have to go through formal channels."

She shrugged, unsure if she believed him. "I wasn't so certain."

A flash of something akin to hurt crossed his face, but the brief look was gone too quickly for her to analyze.

"Even if I wanted to, do you think it's easy to find you?" she asked. "Unlisted number, guards at the stadium and I have no idea where you live now—" She ticked off the list on her fingers.

"Star Island." Kyle couldn't believe he'd blurted out the private, secluded location.

Julia's big brown eyes widened in surprise. "Nice area," she murmured.

"You have a place nearby?"

She let out a laugh, an easy, free sound that took him back to the first time he'd heard it, sitting in the library, Spanish book open between them.

Their teacher, Señor Fuentes, had recruited Julia to bring up Kyle's grades. Kyle had agreed only to ensure his enrolment at the private school and his position on the team. He thought working with the uptight brainiac would be torture. He'd cracked a bad joke to ease the tension and then she'd laughed. The librarian had threatened to throw them out if they weren't quiet. Julia had met his gaze, a twinkle of amusement in her eyes, and giggled once more. And Kyle had been instantly hooked on his new tutor.

He forced his mind back to the present. "What's so amusing?"

She cocked her head to one side. "Not amusing as much as ironic. I couldn't afford Star Island in three lifetimes. Social workers aren't as well paid as major-league ballplayers."

"In other words, our positions have changed," he said, unable to suppress a grin.

She inclined her head in a nod. "I bet that's something you never imagined would happen."

"Can't say that I did." When he'd dreamed about baseball, his focus was the game, not the fame or fortune success might bring.

Julia had always understood that for him, playing baseball was about the game…and the escape he found only on the field. She'd been able to look beyond the surface and really *get* him. That obviously hadn't changed.

Neither had the instant attraction he'd experienced all those years ago. Being in the same breathing space with her got his adrenaline pumping, and his body came alive with yearning. He looked her over again, noticing how achingly familiar she was. Her light brown hair had the same streaks of gold and she still preferred a ponytail to any sort of elaborate time-consuming style. Even her brown eyes still provided a wide-open window to her compassionate soul.

But there were changes, too. Beneath the black slacks and simple peach blouse, her curves were more womanly, her face more expressive with the passage of time and those beautiful eyes held a lifetime of knowledge—and sadness, he was forced to acknowledge.

He wasn't surprised she'd become a social worker. Caring for others was a part of her nature.

"Look, I know this is awkward," she said into the

silence. "So I'll explain why I'm here and then you can get back to playing ball." She gestured toward the field, visible through the large plate-glass windows behind them.

Oddly, he was in no hurry to leave. "Macy already gave me a summary. She said there's a child at the hospital you want me to meet?"

She nodded. "Michael Cortez is fourteen years old. He's obsessed with baseball and he idolizes you. He wears your jersey, brings in magazines with you on the cover, doesn't miss a game on TV and he's constantly tossing a ball in his mitt." Julia's eyes misted a bit. "Like it's a distraction from what's really going on in his life."

"His brother's leukemia." Kyle said the word before she had to.

Julia nodded. "Exactly."

His chest hurt as her past settled over him. "How is your sister?" He forced himself to ask the difficult but necessary question.

Julia glanced away, but not before he caught sight of her damp gaze, her long lashes suddenly fringed with moisture. "Meghan died a few months after you left."

"I'm so sorry." For more than her sister's passing, he thought as he forced the words past the lump in his throat. Although Julia's family had always held on to hope, the prognosis had never been good.

Guilt and pain sucker punched him hard. When Julia had refused to come with him for his stint in the minors, he hadn't been able to leave town fast enough. He'd deliberately not kept in touch, wanting to distance himself from the pain she'd caused him, never once thinking of her.

"I didn't know." The words sounded as inadequate as he knew the feeble excuse to be.

"There's no way you could have." Her voice sounded accepting and resigned, as if she hadn't expected any more of him.

And that stung.

She turned and walked to the wall of photographs she'd been checking out when he came in.

He let her go, needing time to regroup, figuring she felt the same way.

While she studied the pictures, Kyle took a long hard look back. He hadn't spoken to anyone from his childhood in years, and for good reason, but he should have somehow kept up with Julia.

He hadn't because there were times when longing for her had nearly suffocated him, so he'd ruthlessly pushed aside those feelings. He hadn't wanted to think about her. Hadn't looked beyond himself and his own pain.

As the kid of an alcoholic father and a mother who'd run off before he turned five, Kyle had had his hands full making sure he and his father had food on the table, juggling baseball practices and keeping his grades high enough to be allowed to play. In between, he worried about dragging the old man to bed after one of his binges, and trying to get him up in the morning on the odd days when he held down a job.

Kyle had stopped having anything to do with his father when it became apparent the old man only cared about his son's ability to buy him more booze. Enabling the old man was a distraction Kyle didn't need in his regimented life and he'd been forced to set down a new rule between father and son: no rehab, no relationship.

But unlike *his* family dysfunction, Julia had come from a stable home, at least until her sister's illness struck, isolating her from her parents, who spent all their time at the hospital. It was during that time when they'd met and formed their strong bond.

He could see now that he'd been young and stupid, assuming she'd give up her life for his. Selfish. He'd known what she'd been dealing with at home, yet he'd expected her to leave it all behind. And when she hadn't, he'd gone off to follow his dreams, holding on to his anger as if he'd been the only one hurt.

At the realization, he felt the weight of the responsibility he'd never accepted, and any lingering anger disappeared.

This was Julia, his Julia.

For him, the years had melted away. For her, the distance clearly remained. Her body language—her rigid shoulders and tight expression—told him in no uncertain terms that she didn't expect any more of him now than she did then. She was here for the boy and hoped Kyle would give some of his precious time to the child she'd taken under her wing.

He strode to her side, his hands curled into tight fists to keep from reaching for her, the urge to do so strong. "When can I meet Michael?" he asked, broaching the safest subject he could think of.

Julia pivoted toward him. "As soon as possible!" Her

eyes were alight with excitement and gratitude—the first sign of happiness he'd seen yet.

"Tomorrow's a day off. I can stop by the hospital later in the day."

"That's perfect. Thank you! I wonder if I should tell him? Or let him be surprised?" She spoke more to herself than to Kyle as she picked up the purse she'd left on a chair, getting ready to leave.

He wanted to catch up, to ask her to dinner, but he refrained. She was clearly uncomfortable around him and he wasn't sure how to deal with his sudden one-eighty when it came to her. Besides, thanks to a boy named Michael Cortez, Kyle knew for sure he'd be seeing Julia tomorrow.

CHAPTER
⟿ THREE ⟿

K nowing she would be seeing Kyle again tomorrow, Julia barely slept. She woke up cranky, exhausted, and though she hated to admit it, excited too. And not just because she couldn't wait to see Michael's reaction when he came face-to-face with his idol. Julia wanted to see Kyle.

She was curious about the man he'd become, intrigued that his larger-than-life persona still held hints of the boy she'd once known.

The morning hours dragged by and the afternoon ones seemed even longer. By her four-o'clock break, she headed for the cafeteria, taking her usual seat and nursing a cup of coffee because she didn't need the caffeine to make her any more jumpy than she already was.

"Mind if I join you?"

She glanced into the handsome face of Dr. Richard

Montoya. "Of course not." She waved a hand toward the empty chair across from her.

He sat down, somehow looking elegant in his scrubs from a surgery earlier that morning. "So the hospital grapevine is buzzing. Is it true you arranged for Kyle Hansen to come meet Michael Cortez?"

She nodded. "It's true."

"Then why don't you sound more excited? You're giving the best medicine to that boy." Richard smiled, approval and admiration in his gaze.

Because in fulfilling the young boy's dream, Julia had also brought back a whole host of feelings she thought she'd put behind her forever. She didn't know how to deal with them, but she wasn't about to admit as much to Richard.

"I'm just tired," she said instead. "How are you?"

"The same. Manny's latest bloodwork wasn't as good as I'd hoped. We may have to change protocols for his treatment."

Julia shook her head, not surprised that when she asked Richard about himself, the subject turned to his patients. It was just one of the reasons she'd consistently refused to go out with him. She'd been out with enough doctors and paramedics who had shared dinner and graphic stories of anonymous patients. She no longer dated men who didn't know how to separate their personal and work lives. At work, she was surrounded by illness on a daily basis and she'd had plenty of it in her past. In the little free time she had in her personal life, she wanted fun, not sadness.

But that didn't make her unsympathetic. Especially

for this patient. "I'm so sorry," she said to Richard. "I know how much you were hoping this protocol for Manny would do the trick."

He reached out, covering her hand with his. "That's what I appreciate most about you, Julia. Your compassion and understanding. That and your beauty."

She smiled. "Thank you."

She appreciated the compliment, but she didn't want him to get the wrong idea about them. Of course she'd been tempted to go out with him. What woman wouldn't be? Richard was a handsome man, his olive skin made darker by the Florida sun, and her mother would be thrilled because he was a doctor. A doctor who was looking for the right woman to be his wife.

Even if he wasn't obsessive about his work, Julia had no intention of getting involved with any man who wanted something serious. She was the first to admit she had issues with the opposite sex. Both her father, the first man in her life she'd ever loved, and Kyle, the one she thought she'd given her heart to forever, had abandoned her in different ways. She wouldn't trust another man that intimately ever again.

Richard thought she was playing hard to get and the man was persistent, hoping to wear her down, joining her for lunches and breaks.

She treated him to a smile. She was about to respond to his remark when the normal cafeteria chatter suddenly stopped and all eyes turned toward the entrance.

Without looking, Julia knew what caused the awed silence and her stomach jumped in anticipation. Before she could fully prepare, Kyle joined them, his powerful presence sucking up the oxygen in the room.

"The nurse on the pediatrics floor told me I could find you here," Kyle said by way of greeting.

Richard's hand remained on hers, a fact Kyle didn't miss, if his narrowed gaze was any indication.

"You're early."

"I didn't think you'd mind since we still have a lot of catching up to do." His silky voice rippled over her with all the warmth of a long kiss.

Richard rose to his feet. "Kyle Hansen? I'm a huge fan."

Julia gathered her wits and stood up to introduce them. "Kyle, this is Dr. Richard Montoya. Richard is the head of pediatric oncology here at Caridad del Cobre." She turned toward Richard. "Obviously Kyle needs no introduction," she said.

The two men stared at each other long after the greeting had ended. Julia had the distinct impression they were sizing each other up. Male posturing at its finest.

She rolled her shoulders in a futile attempt to relax. Not happening, she thought, her stomach still churning.

"I didn't realize you knew the Miami Suns' star pitcher personally," Richard said, treating her to the perceptive stare she'd seen him use on residents and nurses alike. The look that had them shaking in their Crocs and admitting to all sorts of errors and mistaken judgment calls.

"Kyle and I go way back," she said, deliberately vague.

"High school sweethearts," Kyle supplied ever so helpfully.

She shot him an annoyed glance. If she'd wanted Richard to know their personal business, she'd have told him herself.

"Well." Disappointment etched the doctor's features. His brow furrowed, and his lips formed a definite frown. "Now I understand why I never stood a chance." The normally confident Richard was beating a retreat.

"I never said you didn't stand a chance! And he's not the reason I wouldn't date you." She jerked a thumb toward Kyle, hating the way she was screwing things up even more. "What I mean is…I don't know what I mean," she said, resigned to leaving things a mess between them.

And furious at Kyle Hansen for getting in the middle of her life again.

Ignoring her, Richard turned to Kyle. "I think it's a great thing you're doing for Michael Cortez. He needs special treatment right now."

"Thanks. I intend to see that he gets it," Kyle assured the other man.

"And I need to return to my patients." For a brief moment, Richard's gaze settled on Julia. "I'll leave you two alone to…*reminisce*."

Regret filled her. Even if his assumptions were wrong, she'd obviously hurt him. "Richard…" Her voice trailed off.

He'd already walked away.

"Well, that was unnecessary," she said to Kyle.

The corners of his mouth tilted in a sexy grin. "What? Telling him the truth?"

The man had a point, much as she hated to admit it. But Richard had read more into said truth—and that bothered her. Unfortunately she couldn't say as much to Kyle, who looked pleased with himself for having driven the other man off.

Julia glanced at the clock on the wall. Instead of giving him the satisfaction of *catching up,* she decided to get directly to business. "Do you want to meet Michael? He should be here by now."

Kyle didn't miss a beat and extended his hand to let her go first. "Lead the way."

She headed out of the cafeteria and followed the familiar route back to the children's wing.

Kyle slipped a hand against the small of her back. An intimate gesture and one so very adult, it took her off guard. For the first time, she responded as a woman and not the young teenager head over heels with the idea of first love.

Kyle's presence had knocked her routine existence right out of the ballpark. Or in her case, the hospital. And she wasn't the only one affected by the man. Every person they passed, male and female alike, turned to stare at the superstar. Nurses, patients, family members and doctors nudged each other, pointed and whispered. A bold few stopped him for an autograph.

Kyle smiled, made small talk, signed one person's magazine, another one's arm, and never lost patience. He drew a crowd and ultimately Julia got nudged out of the way.

She leaned against a far wall and waited for him to finish, giving herself far too much time to think. This was a major part of the reason she'd never have agreed to go with him to Seattle. He'd had a big future ahead of him and she hadn't wanted to live hers in his shadow. That, and she'd held on to the futile hope that her sister would recover and she'd get her family back the way it used to be.

The one thing she'd never counted on was her sister dying and her parents falling apart. While Julia had been left to grieve alone, missing her sister and her parents, they'd coped by withdrawing even more. They didn't need her. Even after Meggie died, they hadn't turned to Julia. They'd barely turned to each other. Then Julia had gone to college and they'd sold the house—too many memories, they'd said—and moved to Georgia. After college graduation, Julia had opted to return to the familiar in Florida, not the distant parents she barely knew in a state that didn't feel like home to her.

So as she waited for Kyle to part from his fans, she was grateful for the reminder that their differences had grown exponentially in the intervening years.

"Sorry about that." Kyle came up beside her, bursting into her thoughts.

She forced a smile. "Comes with the territory, huh?"

He nodded. "The fans fill the stands and that pays my salary." He shrugged. "You get used to it."

She didn't see how she ever would. "Do you enjoy it?" she asked, curious how he really felt about the attention.

"I used to." He met her gaze with an unexpectedly serious one of his own. "Now it's a necessary evil."

The admission surprised her. It eased the anxiety that had been building inside her since she'd been pushed aside. Which was ridiculous, since how he felt about his fame had nothing to do with her.

"Shall we?" She tilted her head in the direction of the lounge where Michael waited.

He nodded and they strode back down the hall.

Smack. Smack. Smack.

She heard Michael before she saw him and paused outside the entrance to the visitors' lounge, the rhythmic sound never stopping.

"Baseball gives Michael comfort," she explained.

"Something he can count on in a world where nothing else is certain," Kyle said, his voice suddenly thick. "I remember."

Julia's own throat had filled. "I'm sure you do." He'd never had anyone he could count on.

They'd had that in common. She'd gone from having parents who'd attended every art show she'd been in, every game when she was a cheerleader…to parents who'd had no energy or emotional support left to give.

But Kyle, he'd never had anyone. And suddenly she wondered how he'd managed all these years. Whether he'd kept in touch with his father, an alcoholic who'd never cared about his son, only his next drink. Unlike Kyle, who'd been the man of the house before he even knew what that meant. He'd had a protective instinct that she'd always admired, even for the parent who'd abandoned him in every way except for being physically present.

She could wonder, but she wouldn't find out. She might have told Kyle she wouldn't go with him, but he'd walked away and never looked back. The only reason he was here now was for Michael. He'd come for the teen. Not for her.

They were finished almost a decade ago.

"Michael's a great kid, but he's got attitude," she warned him.

Kyle laughed. "He's a teenager. I get it. I can handle him." He met her gaze and brushed a strong knuckle over her cheek.

She trembled at the unexpected touch, feeling his warmth from the tips of her toes to the pit of her stomach. She knew Kyle could handle the teen.

What she didn't know was whether *she* could handle Kyle.

"Do you want to prepare him?" Kyle asked. "Let him know you're the one who made it happen?"

She shook her head. "This isn't about me. It's about him."

As if by unspoken agreement, she and Kyle silently peered into the visitors' room.

Michael sat on the couch, knees bent, tossing the ball into his mitt, over and over. His dark hair fell over his face. He wore his number 22 jersey, his expression sullen.

She wondered, as she often did, what he was thinking as he smacked that ball into the glove. Did he have an imaginary target in that mitt? Or had he just numbed out, trying to remain oblivious to disappointment and pain? She remembered doing both, expressing her emotions in her drawings and venting them in her diary, while maintaining a stoic mask.

She eased back out of sight.

Unnerved by the reminders of her childhood, she cleared her throat before speaking. "I think the element of surprise would be fantastic."

He grinned. "You're the boss."

Julia stepped back so Kyle could work his magic.

He knocked once on the door frame and strode inside. "I heard there's someone in here who loves baseball as much as I do?"

Michael didn't look up. He didn't break the monotony of pounding the ball into the glove.

Undeterred, Kyle continued into the room, stopping short of the couch where the young boy sat. "I also heard you're a pitcher."

Michael merely grunted.

Julia leaned against the wall and gripped the door frame hard in her hand. Michael was a tougher nut than she'd thought. Kyle's words hadn't even piqued his interest.

Kyle must have sensed her distress. He glanced back at her and winked.

With that one simple gesture, he guaranteed her that he'd have Michael in the palm of his hand. Heaven knew he had her right there already.

"Maybe I could give you some pointers?" Kyle offered the boy.

"What makes you think you can?" Michael asked, all attitude and arrogance. He never once glanced up.

"One Cy Young and a ninety-five-mile-an-hour fastball, that's what."

The commanding voice, the confident tone and the words themselves caught Michael's interest. His dark head snapped to attention, his gaze settling on Kyle's broad chest and familiar face.

"Kyle Hansen! Cool!" He jumped up from the couch, his precious ball hitting the floor with a thud.

Michael's initial curiosity changed to shock, awe and finally total admiration. Julia's heart completely melted at the sight. Her instinct to bring Kyle here had been on target. But in the end, it was Kyle's willingness to meet the boy that made all the difference. And it was Kyle's help that might change the course of Michael's life.

Julia eased out of the room and left the two alone to get better acquainted.

Her job here was done.

CHAPTER
∾— FOUR —∾

Julia headed to her office where she buried herself in paperwork. Not a difficult thing to do when there were piles everywhere she looked. Working for the hospital brought her joy, sadness and plenty of administrative duties. But today, not even the stacks of work could hold her attention for long. Her focus was on the two people in the other room—the teenager who silently cried out for attention and the big bad baseball player who still held a part of her heart.

Yeah, that hurt to admit. She'd spent years convincing herself she was over him, only to discover it wasn't that simple.

"Knock knock. Mind if we come in?"

The sound of Kyle's voice startled her and Julia jumped in her seat. "I guess I got lost in my work after all," she said to herself. "Come on in."

Michael stepped in first, followed by Kyle. His massive presence took up her entire office, which wasn't all that large anyway.

He stood with his back to a Georgia O'Keeffe print, and though his masculinity should have overpowered the more feminine flower, Julia realized that the oversize floral was like Kyle himself, big, imposing and extremely compelling.

"What can I do for you two?" she asked, aware that Michael's eyes had a light and life she'd never seen before.

"Kyle said I could hang out at the stadium tomorrow since it's Saturday and I don't have school!" Michael blurted out.

"Yes, I said that, but we have something more important to discuss first." Kyle lightly nudged the boy. "Well?"

"Right." Michael stepped closer to Julia's desk. "I didn't know you and Kyle were once a thing! But thank you for gettin' him here. For me."

Julia blushed, the heat flushing her cheeks. "We weren't... We didn't... You're welcome." Once again she shot Kyle a glare.

Kyle shrugged. "Just giving credit where credit was due."

"Thank you," she said, oddly touched. And still embarrassed. "Now, what's this about a day at the stadium?"

"Well, that can only happen if you come along because I have to be in the dugout and I can't very well keep an eye on him." Kyle gestured toward Michael, who looked at her with big, imploring eyes. "I'm going to try to get him in as a batboy, but even then it'll be a help to have you there."

Julia felt stunned. First, because Kyle's generosity was staggering. Macy, the publicist, had promised a meeting. That's all. And second, because the man had actually made promises to the boy dependent on *her* agreement. And the unrepentant man stood there grinning as he stared her down.

"Come with me, please?" Michael practically hopped up and down with excitement, begging her.

"Unless you have other plans?" Kyle asked, *his* laughing blue eyes begging her, too.

"He said you can sit in the owner's box! But I can't go without you cuz my mom has to be here with Manny." Michael's voice dropped at the reminder of his brother and the potential disappointment that might be heaped on him if Julia said no.

Not that she would. She'd never turn Michael down. As for Kyle…

Julia shook her head at the two ganging up on her.

"Well, what's it gonna be, sweetness?"

Kyle used his old nickname for her and everything inside her melted. Danger signals pummeled every part of her body, even those that enjoyed the sensual onslaughts caused by the sound of that name coming from his sexy lips.

Somehow she forced her stare away from Kyle and looked at Michael. "Of course I'll take you," she told him. "*If* your mother says its okay."

"Yes!" He pumped his fist in the air, letting loose all the joy he'd been withholding for the last few months.

"You said you wanted to meet Manny, right?" Michael asked Kyle, the teen obviously in hyperdrive. "So let's go now and I'll ask my mom."

Kyle shook his head and laughed at the boy's enthusiasm. "I'll meet you there, okay? I want to talk to Ms. Caldwell."

"About what?" Michael asked, sticking his cute, curious nose where it didn't belong.

"Yes, about what?" Julia asked him, curious herself.

Kyle rolled his eyes. "I was going to ask her over for dinner tonight. I'll even cook."

The teenager grimaced. "Hey, real men don't cook!"

"If they want to eat they do," Kyle assured him.

And Julia knew that knowledge came from years of painful experience. But she didn't think being alone with Kyle was a good idea. Too many unresolved feelings were involved, at least for her.

And all the reasons she wouldn't have gone along with him almost ten years ago, even if she hadn't had a terminally ill sister, still remained. Magnified now by his status and success, and her own inability to trust.

"Scram so we can discuss this in private," Kyle said lightly. He turned from Michael to Julia. "Unless you want to answer me right now so I can walk with Michael to his brother's room?" He sounded teasing, yet was deadly serious. She saw the determined intent in his gaze, the same intent that had gotten him this far in the major leagues.

He wasn't above using his new young friend to get her to agree, either. Dirty pool, Julia thought.

"What is this?" she asked them. "Tag team?"

"Is it working?" Kyle tipped his head endearingly.

Oh, she had it bad. Again.

"Is it?" Michael mimicked. "Say you'll have dinner with him, please?"

She wondered if Kyle had put him up to this or if they just played off each other naturally. If so, Kyle Hansen would make a great father. She shivered at the thought and knew she had to get him out of here.

"Well?" Michael pushed.

"Okay. I'll go to dinner." The words were out before she could stop them.

The gleam in Kyle's gaze told her how pleased he was that she'd agreed, while the butterflies in her stomach told her this was a really bad idea.

Kyle wasn't accustomed to using a kid to get what he wanted from a woman. Most women would throw themselves at his feet for the opportunity to have him cook them dinner at his home. He liked that Julia made him work for it. She'd always stood out from the other girls and she was still unique. Worth any effort he had to put in.

He wanted to get to know her again, and Michael had been the catalyst to make that happen. He was a good kid, Kyle thought. Whether he was as talented as he was passionate remained to be seen. He'd bring him on the field, hit some balls, let him pitch and see what he was made of. Kyle saw a lot of himself at fourteen in

Michael Cortez. The sullen moodiness that was a cover for lack of attention at home, the arrogance barely kept in check and the all-encompassing love for baseball.

One look at Michael's brother, Manny, and Kyle knew exactly how consumed their mother had to be with the other boy's illness, how left out Michael was and how much emotional pain he was in. If Kyle could give him this one day out of time, away from the awful reality of his life, he would. Whether or not Julia had been able to join them. It was to his benefit that she could, even if it had taken a little arm-twisting.

Right now, he had a home-cooked meal to worry about. One that was less about impressing her with his skills than invoking old memories. And since he'd insisted on picking her up at her apartment instead of having her drive to his place, he didn't have all that much time left to prepare.

Good thing his plan wasn't complicated. It just involved simple food, some catching up and a whole lot of seduction afterward.

A few hours later, with everything at his house under control, he drove over the bridge connecting the island where he lived to the MacArthur Causeway and the rest of Miami Beach. Her apartment was fairly close to the hospital, an up-and-coming neighborhood, far enough from the bad areas to keep her safe. It was way different from the suburban neighborhood in which she'd grown up, though, with large houses on spacious lots, reflecting both an upper-middle-class mind-set and wealth.

To his surprise, Julia met him outside her building, not waiting for him to come ring the bell or even step out of the car to open the door for her. He wondered if this was her way of making sure he knew they weren't on an official date.

Little did she know.

"You look beautiful," he said, taking in the floral sundress that bared her tanned skin. A nice change from the more conservative pants and top she wore to work.

A light blush stained her cheeks. "Thank you."

He pulled onto the street and headed back to his place. He'd already decided not to let silence reign. "So where did you go to college? And how long have you been working at the hospital?" He figured the best way to relax her was to talk about the present.

"Well, let's see. I went to the University of Florida and did my graduate work at Nova. I did certification work at Caridad del Cobre, and of all the places I interviewed, it was the one that really made me feel needed."

"I can see why. I met Michael's brother today." He caught her somber nod before refocusing on the road and felt compelled to ask, "How do you do it?"

"Work with sick children?"

Nothing so simple, Kyle thought. "No, work with them and not revisit your own memories every single day?" He couldn't imagine it was easy.

She set her jaw and he could tell this wasn't a subject she wanted to discuss. "I don't," she said tightly. "I mean, I do revisit the memories, but the truth is I'd do that whether I worked in the hospital or not."

"You think about her often?" he asked gently.

"Every day. But at least I'm doing something to help

kids who are sick like she was, parents who have to learn to cope and even siblings like Michael."

"I really admire you," he said, surprised at how gruff his voice sounded.

"You, Miami's favorite son, admire *me?*" She let out a laugh. "Now, that's some pickup line. You should add it to your arsenal." She folded her arms over her chest and leaned back in the plush leather seat.

He shook his head and grinned. "What makes you think I need pickup lines?"

She raised an eyebrow. "Oh. So all it takes is your charm and good looks for women to fall at your feet?"

He gripped the steering wheel tighter in his hands. "Actually, all it takes is my seven-figure contract," he admitted, and not without embarrassment.

It had gotten to the point where it was hard to tell a woman who wanted and accepted *him* and those who wanted what his income could buy and his status could gain them. He'd all but stopped trying to figure it out and had taken himself out of the game altogether.

"Sucks to be you," she muttered.

He laughed, but recognized the hollow sound. "You'd be surprised."

She seemed about to reply, when they reached Bridge Road and the view captured her attention instead.

They were having a late dinner and the sun had begun to set on the water. He knew how the myriad colors must be affecting her. The incredible orange, red and yellow bursts against the darkening sky still left him in awe.

"I've never seen anything this beautiful!" she murmured.

He glanced at her profile and knew he could argue the point, but he doubted she'd believe him. She was more reserved with him than she used to be and he didn't think it was just the years that caused the distance. Julia was different now. More introspective and somber. He still had a lot of work to do and trust to rebuild.

Trust that needed to go both ways. He hadn't forgotten that she'd abandoned him. He merely understood that her reasons for staying were far more compelling than his for leaving. But they'd both let something solid and good go without trying to make it work long-distance. That they'd never attempted to understand the other's reasons spoke to their immaturity at the time, and he hoped that was something they could talk about, work through, and see if anything remained.

Julia had grown up not lacking for anything. She supposed she'd belonged to an upper-middle-class family. Probably closer to upper class, if she really had to give it thought. She rarely did because what her parents owned had nothing to do with the life she led except for the minimal amount of money they'd insisted on giving her so she could stay in Miami and move into a safe neighborhood.

But now, as she walked into Kyle's easily ten-thousand-plus-square-foot home on three acres of Star Island real estate, she was forced to acknowledge he was way out of her league. Not even their differences way back when could compete with the stratosphere that separated them now.

The lush greenery of the island itself had been spectacular, and she'd admired it on the drive here.

But his home was unbelievable. Immense beyond her imagination.

They'd entered through an arched doorway to soaring ceilings and enormous living areas that seemed to stretch as far as the eye could see. The color scheme was neutral, but there was nothing simple about the place. She could barely take it all in.

"Your home is…surreal," she said, knowing she sounded as if she was in awe.

She was.

"I liked that it had enough room to put in a batting cage and a hitting machine. The pool is good for my workouts and the sauna helps ease the aches and pains." He spoke lightly, as if his needs were simple.

"Makes sense." She supposed.

She glanced at him standing in the marble entryway, breathtakingly handsome in khaki pants and a black T-shirt that accentuated his broad chest and muscled arms. Except for the greater definition added to his physique, and the maturity in his face, he looked the same as she remembered. And though his voice was a little deeper, he even sounded the same. But everything else about him was different.

Had to be different, given that he lived in this massive but hollow house. The Kyle she'd known had wanted out of the poor, dangerous neighborhood in which he'd grown up, and he'd wanted to play baseball. She'd sensed it wasn't just about the sport, but needing someplace to belong. The field and the camaraderie of being on a team gave him that. But in all their talks about his future, he'd never mentioned material things, or status. In fact, he'd disdained the trappings of wealth that her parents valued—the luxury cars, the country club, the yacht. Yet the four-bedroom, three-and-a-half-bathroom home she'd grown up in could fit into a corner of Kyle's mansion.

She shook her head. Then again, maybe he'd just been jealous of what he couldn't have. Maybe he'd secretly yearned for all this. But all *this* made Julia uncomfortable.

"Are you ready to go into the kitchen?" he asked. Unaware of her thoughts, he grasped her elbow, obviously intending to take her there.

"Wait." Before they headed to the other room, she had more questions that she needed answered.

"What's wrong?"

Julia glanced up the winding circular staircase that seemed to disappear into the ether. "How many bedrooms are up there?" she asked.

He paused a beat before answering. "Ten."

"Bathrooms?"

Once again, he hesitated. "Eight," he finally said.

"Ten bedrooms and eight bathrooms… And you live here alone?"

"Yeah. Unless you count Mrs. Watkins, the housekeeper—I knew her from the neighborhood where I grew up. She needed a job so I brought her to work here."

Julia nodded. That sounded more like the Kyle she knew.

"And there's the staff that it takes to come in and out and keep this place running," Kyle added. "But other than that, it's just me."

"Then I just have one more question."

He shoved his hands into his back pockets, eyeing her warily. "Okay...ask away."

"Why?" The question had burned inside her since the enormity of the house and the wealth it represented had sunk in.

Kyle dragged in a deep breath, meeting her gaze with his stunning blue eyes. "At the time I purchased it? Just because I could."

CHAPTER
᠗ FIVE ᠗

K yle would have been embarrassed if it were
anyone else he was answering. But from the
minute he'd pulled his SUV into the four-car
garage and Julia had stepped into the house, he'd sensed
her discomfort. The more he revealed, the more her
unease had grown. If he'd given her any answer but the
truth, she'd have known.

And bolted without a second thought.

"Look, can we at least talk about this in the kitchen?"
he asked.

"Just tell me you don't have a five-course meal
planned and staff ready to wait on me," she said, obviously trying for a lightness she didn't feel.

He sensed the seriousness behind the joke. Good
thing he'd been sure he still knew her well. "No staff,
no courses, just you, me, pasta and garlic bread."

Awareness crept into her eyes and her tight expression eased. "You're kidding, right?"

"Come see for yourself."

She grinned and her lips lifted in a genuine smile. The burdens she seemed to carry suddenly fled. "You remembered!"

"Do you really think I could forget?"

He'd always refused to bring her to the run-down apartment where he'd grown up. But there was one night when he'd changed his mind. Her parents had been too busy at the hospital and missed one of Julia's awards ceremonies at school and his father had left to visit a relative out of town. Kyle had gone to the ceremony, standing in the back until it was over, just so she had someone in the audience. Then he'd brought her back to his place, cooked her spaghetti and garlic bread to celebrate her award and slept with her for the first time.

"I wasn't sure before," she admitted, her gaze sweeping around the house he'd bought as a statement to himself and to the world.

I am somebody, he'd thought as he signed on the dotted line. It might have been the smallest house on the island, and he might have gotten a foreclosure deal because of someone else's misfortune, but last year when he'd signed his three-year thirty-million-dollar contract and bought this place, he'd felt like a king.

For a little while. Until reality set in along with the emptiness of the huge house. Then he realized he was stuck with a big parcel of real estate and nothing else. This place had never felt like home.

Until Julia had stepped inside.

"But I'm sure now." Her voice cemented that thought. "You haven't changed in here…where it counts," she said, pressing her hand to his heart, which pounded hard and fast inside his chest.

"You're sure about that?" he asked, needing to know that someone still knew *him,* not the marquee player expected to perform.

"That you're still you? That this house doesn't mean you've lost the things I loved—liked most about you?"

His breath caught. Even if she'd changed her mind about saying the word, something strong and important still existed between them.

She nodded. "If you cooked me spaghetti and garlic bread again, then yeah, I'm sure."

And just like that, the wariness and distrust she'd been feeling faded and she stepped toward him until he was enveloped by her fragrant, sensual scent. The years melted away and suddenly she was in his arms, his lips coming down on hers and taking him to the only place that had ever felt like home.

At one time Kyle's kiss was the answer to every dream Julia had ever had. Every hope, every wish and every fear. That had changed, but for the moment, she wound her arms around his neck and gave in to the familiar feelings.

It had been so long since she'd experienced this kind of need, desire, and she welcomed the sensual assault on her body. The shared kiss was a duel that merged the past and the present, until nothing mattered but the here and now. And when he paused, her stomach flipped, because she was sure he meant to stop. Instead, he tilted his head for a better angle, a tighter fit, and slid those delicious lips over hers once again.

He kissed her, long drugging kisses that melted her will and resistance until she curled her fingers into the back of his shirt, urging him closer. He complied, his body aligning with hers, his mouth never once releasing her own. She leaned into him, feeling every hard plane and defined muscle.

Was she ready for this? With the man who'd been her first? Who she'd also once thought would be her only? Her last?

He broke the kiss and she wondered if he'd sensed her sudden uncertainty. "After that, I hope you're still hungry for dinner."

She met his gaze, his eyes a stormy hue of conflicted emotions. So she wasn't the only one. Good.

"I'm still hungry," she assured him, well aware of her double meaning.

In surprisingly comfortable silence, Julia worked beside Kyle in his huge, state-of-the-art kitchen. She put the garlic bread in the oven and heated the water on the stove for the spaghetti. He opened a bottle of wine. They sat next to each other in the cozy eating area of the kitchen, and while they ate, he told her stories about his early days in the majors, making her laugh more times than she could count.

Dinner was delicious, reminding her of the night he'd cooked for her in high school. Their first night together. And while she was thinking about that, he leaned back in his seat and nailed her with his deep-blue eyes.

A wary tremor rippled through her.

"I think it's time to catch up, don't you?"

She swallowed hard, so not ready to go there.

But apparently he was. "What happened after I left?" he asked, going right for the jugular.

Julia felt her emotions closing up all over again. She stiffened and forced out a reply. "Life went on."

He rolled his eyes at her deliberate evasion. "Can you be more specific?"

She could if she wanted to. She didn't. "My sister got worse and eventually died." Man, that word still tripped her up and she forced down the huge lump in her throat.

Though he placed a hand on her shoulder, he didn't offer her a reprieve. He wanted answers and obviously would wait until she gave them.

She expelled a harsh breath. "Fine. I went to college a semester late, wanting to be around for my family. I thought my parents would turn to me, but they didn't. They barely turned to each other." She clenched and unclenched her fists, uncomfortable speaking the truths she lived with. Even to Kyle.

"Not even your father leaned on you?" he asked softly.

She'd confided in Kyle how close she and her father had been before her sister's illness.

She shook her head.

"So it was like losing him twice."

She managed to nod.

But it was so much more than that. She'd already lost Kyle a few months before, and then what remained of her world had crumbled around her. It had taken all the strength she had to pick herself up and simply live.

These days, she recommended therapy for the survivors. Back then, nobody had suggested the same for her.

He brushed his knuckle down her cheek. "I'm so damn sorry," he said gruffly.

He should be, she thought. He'd left without looking back. But that was in the past and she knew she had to let it go if they were going to be friends now.

"So what about you? What happened to you in the intervening years?" She turned the tables, finished discussing herself. "You told me the fun stories. Now tell me about your hard times."

Turnabout was fair play, she figured. And she wanted to know everything that had happened to him in the years since she'd seen him.

He cleared his throat before speaking. "When I went into the minors, I reverted to the guy you met when you started tutoring me. I was nothing like the one who'd mellowed out from being with you." His eyes were murky as he delved into his memory.

The admission didn't surprise her. She'd been devastated at his reaction when she'd refused to come with him. He'd shut down, barely looked at her. She'd known then she wouldn't hear from him again.

"You were still angry I didn't come with you?"

He nodded. "But I was also angry at the world and felt like I had something to prove. I mean, every guy who comes up in the farm system has attitude. A guy wouldn't make it into the minors without a good amount of arrogance, but I took mine off the field, too."

He paused and she didn't push him. He'd continue when he was ready.

"Luckily, I had a good mentor who bailed me out— literally—and he stopped me from blowing my one shot."

"Jail?" she asked, horrified it had gone that far.

"One night in a holding cell until I sobered up. The other guy declined to press charges and the cops let it drop. Roger Carstons made me take a hard look at myself and told me to make a choice right then and there because he wouldn't be bailing me out a second time. I got it together after that." He sat, arms folded, back stiff, obviously waiting for her to react.

"It would have been a huge waste if you hadn't." She knew how much internal strength he possessed, considering no one had looked out for him before.

Whoever this mentor was, Julia was grateful he'd come along. "You moved up pretty quickly after that, right?"

"Good guess?" he asked.

She shook her head. "Once you started hitting the news, it was easy to follow your progress. I never forgot about you." Even if he'd never followed up on what had become of her.

It didn't matter that she'd refused to go with him. He should have known she couldn't have left her family. He could have come back for her. Kept in touch. She tried not to let the truth come between them now, but it still hurt. And she was unwilling to open up her heart to him by admitting it.

"You became a name pretty quickly," she said,

keeping her focus where it belonged and was safe. "I was still in college and you'd already had a shot in the majors."

"I got lucky when their pitcher blew out his elbow and needed Tommy John surgery. Sucked for him, shot for me. The powers that be in Seattle called me up and gave me a chance."

"And you made the most of it."

He nodded. "I did. I went from earning a hundred and fifty grand to millions within three years." He shook his head, as if he could barely believe it himself.

"And this house was the proof?"

"Yeah." He let out a dry laugh. He rose and began collecting the dishes and taking them to the sink.

She stood and helped in silence, giving him the space to tell his story his way.

"Can you imagine what it was like, a kid who had to make a package of hot dogs last for weeks when my father was on one of his binges? I had money to buy whatever I wanted, whenever I wanted. I bought this place among the biggest stars in the country and thought, I have arrived." He patted his chest with pride.

But there was no self-respect in his eyes. "I signed, I moved in and I realized something important." He turned, his back to the sink, and faced her.

"And what was that?" she asked, almost breathless in anticipation.

"I was still alone."

Despite the pain she'd experienced because of him, her heart ached for him now. "What about your father? All these rooms, does he ever—"

"No." He slashed his hand through the air. "I never heard from him until I signed that contract. And before you ask, yeah, he knew where to find me. He chose not to until I had money to keep him in alcohol for the rest of his life."

"I'm so sorry." It seemed they were both saying a lot of that.

"I'm not. Not about him. And not about the rest of it, either. It's a pretty damn good life. Yes, I may live alone in this big house, but I'm not exactly suffering."

She grinned, laughing at his summation. "Good point. I do get why you bought this place. It's just that for a minute, I thought you'd become someone else. Someone I didn't know." And not knowing him anymore scared her, she realized now.

"Oh, you know me. Intimately." He paused. "And if you don't want to know me that way again, it's time for me to take you home," he said, his eyes raking over her, devouring her with his hungry gaze.

When he looked at her that way it was so easy to put the past away and let herself forget, but she couldn't. She'd had enough pain and heartache for a lifetime.

Still, his pleading yet hungry look shook her to the core.

"You're shameless," she told him.

"Does that mean you're staying?" His teasing tone told her there was no pressure.

And she wanted to stay.

Desperately.

But she couldn't simply open herself up to him that way again. She could never just have sex with Kyle. If she let herself get that kind of close with him again, it would destroy her when the relationship ended.

And that's what men did. They left her. Kyle had left her. And now that she knew how far from reality his life really was, she couldn't go back. For Kyle, a reunion would be fun for a little while and help break up the loneliness he experienced from time to time. But eventually, his big glamorous life would pull at him and he'd leave her again.

She shook her head, regret filling her.

"I didn't think so."

She caught the disappointment in his tone. Saw the sexual frustration they'd both be dealing with tonight in his taut expression.

But there was also understanding in his eyes.

"I'll see you when you bring Michael to the stadium tomorrow?"

She grinned. "Like I said. Shameless. Yes, I'll see you tomorrow."

He strode over to the counter and grabbed his keys. "Nothing but the best," he promised. "VIP treatment all the way."

"I'm sure Michael will love it. I have to say, it's way more than I expected when I asked ASRL to put me in touch with you." They walked toward the garage that housed his cars.

She'd seen a Porsche, driven in his Escalade. How many cars did one man need? As many as he could afford, she thought, understanding his need to fill the void in his life.

He flipped on the garage light. "What I'm doing for

Michael has nothing to do with trying to impress you," he said, clearly offended.

"Did I say that it did?"

"You implied it. You said it's more than you expected. I work with kids all the time. Ask Macy. Read the press. This weekend is about Michael." He spoke in a defiant tone. "But *this* is about you."

He turned, pulled her into his arms and into a heart-melting kiss.

One that tormented her through the long night alone in her very empty bed as she counted down the hours until she would see Kyle again.

Kyle dropped Julia off at her apartment. He walked her to the door and left her with a long kiss. One she allowed, but one that left him colder than the previous kiss. Ever since he'd coaxed her—make that forced her—to discuss her past, she'd put up definite walls to keep him out. He realized now that he'd screwed up royally by wallowing in his own pain and disappointment and never going back for her.

She'd been a daddy's girl and had never apologized for it. One day her father was there for her, the next he was gone, consumed by his other sick child. Then Kyle had stepped into her life and they'd filled each other in ways their younger selves could never have understood.

And he'd abandoned her, too.

No wonder she'd closed off. The question was, could he break through those barriers?

Or had he really lost her forever.

CHAPTER
⤚ SIX ⤜

VIP treatment.

If not for Michael, Julia didn't want or need special handling. Her idea of going to a ball game was sitting in the stands, listening to the vendors yell as they walked up and down the aisles selling popcorn, peanuts, soda and Cracker Jacks. A hot dog under the hot baking sun. That was her idea of the perfect baseball game. Not sitting in an air-conditioned, luxury box, with big screens showing the game on two separate walls. But she had to admit, with the outside temperature plus ninety, she appreciated the A/C.

She'd been looking forward to seeing the stadium and the game through Michael's eyes. Kyle had insisted on picking them up so they'd get there early, allowing Michael time with the team beforehand. The teen fairly bounced in the car on the way to the stadium, filling the Escalade with questions and excitement.

When they arrived, Kyle handed Julia over to Macy's assistant and he took the boy to the locker room, where Kyle explained he'd dress in a team uniform and be a batboy for the day. From that point on, Kyle was elevated from idol status to a god in Michael's eyes. Kyle had really gone all out for the teenager, showing a whole other side that Julia had never seen before.

And though she was thrilled Michael would have this experience, his absence left her alone in the luxury box with over a dozen strangers. Everyone smiled and nodded in her direction, but they migrated into private groups who knew each other and had things in common. And when a particularly young group of women arrived, their giggling took over the room, making Julia uncomfortable.

With fifteen minutes to game time, she focused on the field, looking for glimpses of Kyle or Michael, and tried not to appear as out of place as she felt.

During the "Star-Spangled Banner," the team publicist slipped into the empty seat beside her. "Whew," Macy said. "First game I've made it to on time in over a week. I see you got here okay. Are you having fun?"

Though Julia didn't know the woman except for their brief meeting in her office, she was grateful to have a friendly face beside her now. "Yes, I am. Thank you for helping to arrange all this. I've never seen Michael so animated or excited. I'm so grateful to you and to ASRL for making this happen."

"I'm happy to help," Macy said. "So tell me, just how far back do you and Hansen go?"

"High school."

"Aha."

"Frankie and I met in high school." A pretty brunette who looked about Julia's age joined them.

"Do you two know each other?" Macy asked.

Julia shook her head.

"Julia Caldwell, this is Lisa Banks, the wife of our first baseman, Frank Banks," Macy said, handling the introductions. "Lisa, this is Julia. She's an old friend of Kyle Hansen's." She tapped on her blinking BlackBerry. "Look, I need to handle some things. Mind if I leave you two alone?"

"I'll keep her company," Lisa promised.

Julia smiled. "I'll be fine."

"Great!" Macy ran off to do her job.

Julia turned to Lisa. "You really don't have to babysit me, you know."

"I'm not babysitting. Frankly, you look more my type than some of the other women here today." She leaned in closer and explained. "This box is for the players' families and friends. Sometimes it's a great group up here. Other times, the rookie players wrangle special favors from Macy and get tickets for their girls. Then we end up with that." She subtly tilted her head in the direction of the young women Julia had noticed earlier.

While Lisa and Julia wore jeans, short-sleeve shirts, little makeup and had pulled their hair into loose ponytails and plopped baseball caps on their heads, the others had primped and made themselves up like life-size Barbie dolls. Not to mention their cleavage-popping tube tops, and stomachs with belly rings.

"I'm actually very happy to have the company," Julia said, trying not to think too hard about the girls in the corner.

She had already seen similar-looking females crowding the entry to the private lot where Kyle had parked, craning their necks for a look at the players, hoping to get noticed.

He'd shrugged it off as no big deal.

These were obviously the lucky ones who'd gotten beyond the hopeful stage. She wondered how many of Kyle's women had occupied her very seat. Clearly she wasn't being successful in ignoring their presence in the scheme of Kyle's life.

"You'll keep me from ogling the scenery," Julia said.

Lisa laughed. "I wish I could say you get used to them, but you don't."

"It's a good thing I don't have to worry about it then. Kyle and I are just old friends."

Old friends who'd kissed like about-to-be lovers, she thought, her mind immediately going back to last night.

The other woman raised an eyebrow. "Mmm, hmm." Her tone conveyed complete disbelief. "Okay, well, you should know that you're the only friend he's ever gotten box seats."

"Really?" Julia asked, so hopeful she gave herself away.

"Truly." A satisfied grin settled on Lisa's face. She'd

obviously seen through Julia's lie and liked being proven right.

Kyle, with his honesty, his generous spirit and the connection that still remained between them, meant much more to Julia than just a friend.

Uh-oh.

"Frankie and Kyle are good buddies. They're the same age, the young guys look up to them and they joined the team the same year."

Lisa chatted throughout the game, telling Julia stories about the individual players, both good and bad. She talked more about how she and Frankie had been together since high school and married the same year he was called up to the majors. They had no kids— yet—and had weathered some serious storms during their time together. The traveling took its toll on their relationship, but they'd both worked hard to keep it together. In short, Frankie and Lisa were the couple Julia and Kyle could have been.

She glanced out the huge window just as the batboys were running onto the field. Julia jumped up and cheered for Michael, thrilled beyond belief that he'd been given this opportunity.

"Are you two related?" Lisa asked.

Julia shook her head. "No, he's just a very special boy." She went on to explain her relationship to the teenager and how he'd brought Kyle back into her life again.

"Life works in mysterious ways. Kyle's great with kids. Every fundraiser the team has, he's the first one out there, hands on, hanging out with them."

Lisa was giving her insight into a side of Kyle she didn't know—hadn't had the chance to know.

"I saw him throwing balls with the boy before the game."

"That's great! Validation from Kyle will mean everything to Michael." Julia didn't know how to thank him. This was so much more than she could have hoped for.

She realized she was taking Michael's situation to heart and was getting way too close, both to the boy and to Kyle. Julia knew better than to get emotionally involved with patients at the hospital or their families, but she couldn't seem to help it.

With Lisa by her side, Julia relaxed and enjoyed the game. Not only did Kyle pitch a phenomenal seven innings, but while in the dugout, she saw him rallying his team and fulfilling his role of captain. To the delight of the fans, the middle relief pitchers and then the closer held on to the win Kyle had handed them and the day was a huge success.

Since Michael was with the other batboys and Kyle would bring him to her later, Julia remained in the box and watched the press conference that followed on the big-screen television. Kyle fielded the reporters' questions like the pro that he'd become. He joked with the press, addressed many of the sportswriters and columnists by name and was at ease with himself and the world around him.

When the questions turned from today's win to the upcoming schedule, she discovered the Suns were about to embark on a ten-day road trip to the West Coast. Ten days. She didn't know why the length of time surprised her. She was aware baseball players spent huge amounts of time on the road. That had been one of the many reasons she wouldn't have gone with Kyle way back when, even if her circumstances had been different. She knew they'd end up living separate lives. The reminder that he'd be gone for ten days confirmed for her that they lived in parallel worlds. And his world had no place for her in it.

But she wasn't ready to walk away from him just yet. She could have tonight, said a small voice in her head. And maybe she *could* revisit the past and survive, as long as she knew ahead of time it was just one night.

Her breasts tingled at a possibility she found extremely appealing. As long as she separated her body and her heart, she'd be fine. Unfortunately it was her heart that took a huge leap an hour or so later at the sight of Kyle, his arm around Michael's shoulders, as he strode out of the locker room to meet her.

"Hey there!" She forced a smile and waved as the two of them walked up beside her. "So? Good day?"

"It was so freaking cool!" Michael's eyes lit up. "I watched the game from the field. I caught balls and washed the players' cleats after the game. And Kyle says I have talent. Real talent. He wants me to have a chance to learn, so he's going to find out about getting me a permanent batboy job." The teen was more animated than Julia had ever seen him.

"That's fantastic!" she said, her heart expanding by the minute at the change in the sullen boy she was used to seeing at the hospital.

And she had Kyle to thank.

She met his gaze, hoping he could sense the gratefulness and admiration she felt for him at this moment.

He winked at her and her knees went weak.

"Are you hungry?" he asked Michael.

The boy shook his head. "I can't wait to get home and tell my mom!"

"She said she'd be at your place after the game, so we'll drop you off and you can fill her in," Kyle said. "How about we pick up some drive-through on the way home?"

"Burgers, Shakes and Fries?" Michael asked.

Obviously he felt comfortable enough with Kyle to suggest his favorite. Another testament to the man: he was a superstar, but could still put a child who looked up to him at ease.

"You really think that's the best takeout?" Kyle asked.

"Ms. Caldwell brought it back special for me when we watched the game at the hospital the other night," Michael said, playing the Julia's-better-than-you-are card.

Kyle caught on immediately and grinned. "Well, if Ms. Caldwell eats Burgers, Shakes and Fries while watching me play, I'm all for it."

"That's not what he meant."

"I know. But it's what I *heard*."

"Shameless," she muttered under her breath.

He laughed. "I heard that, too."

CHAPTER
⤔ SEVEN ⤕

K yle dropped Michael and his hamburgers—plural—at his place with his mom and left them alone for what Kyle knew was very rare private time. There was much in the boy that Kyle could relate to, but not the desire to share things with the one parent who'd stuck around.

Grateful for time alone with Julia, he slid an arm across the back of the passenger seat and glanced her way. "You've been quiet."

"I think Michael did enough talking for all of us," she said, laughing.

"What about you? Did you have fun today?" She was a great sport, being at the game as Michael's chaperone if needed, but essentially she'd been alone most of the day.

"The box was nice. And I met Lisa Banks, your first baseman's wife. We hit it off."

"I'm glad. Frank's a great guy. I like his wife, too."

"There were other women in the box with us," she said.

From the tone of her voice, he knew exactly which women she meant. The rookies must've wrangled tickets from Macy, he thought in disgust.

"Who were they?" he asked, in case he was wrong.

"The type of women we passed on the way into the stadium. Big hair, bigger chests, painted-on jeans."

"The rookies' bimbos," he muttered.

"Is that what you call them?" she asked lightly. "Must be nice for you guys to have such easy access all the time."

He burst out laughing. "Is that what *you* call it?" He pulled into an empty space near her building and cut the engine.

"Come on, Kyle. It's not a bad life if you can get it." She turned to meet his gaze straight on.

The last thing he wanted was for Julia to believe he'd ever be interested in that kind of woman.

"What makes you think I want it?"

She cocked an eyebrow. "Um, you're a man?"

He placed his hand over his heart. "I'm insulted."

"You're telling me those women don't interest you?"

"Not anymore." He trailed his fingers along her shoulder. "In fact, not for a very long time. And definitely not right now."

Her eyes opened wide. "You're serious."

"Dead serious."

A slow, dare he say sensual, smile tilted her lips. "In that case, do you want to come inside?"

Only an idiot would say no, but he had one question. "As long as you tell me what changed your mind. Just yesterday, you weren't ready."

"Yesterday I was overthinking. Today I'm not."

He didn't know what to make of that. But he also knew the only way back to each other was to jump in with both feet and other willing body parts.

"Then let's go upstairs—and not think." He helped her out of the car and let her lead the way to her apartment, his heart pounding in his chest as if it was his first time.

She hadn't been his first, but he'd been hers, and he'd really thought she'd be his last. Talk about young and stupid.

She unlocked the door and walked inside, flipping on a light. "This is it," she said, spreading her arm, gesturing around.

He meant to look at where she lived. Instead, he only saw her—his first love, her face flushed, her gaze intent on his. She drew her tongue over her lower lip and that was all the invitation he needed.

He pulled her into his arms and lowered his lips to hers. Things moved quickly after that, kisses turning frantic, the heat exploding between them into an inferno.

Her top went flying, his shirt came next.

He barely had a moment to take in her womanly body before she reached for the waistband of his pants and all rational thought fled. "Julia, I think—"

"You said we wouldn't think," she reminded him, peppering his neck with soft, nuzzling kisses.

"Not thinking, just suggesting we might want to move it to the bedroom?" The hard wall and floor would be fun, but not what he wanted for their first time in ten years.

She grinned. "Okay, that kind of thinking is allowed."

He lifted her into his arms and followed her directions to the bedroom. And from the time he lowered her onto the bed and they stripped off the rest of their clothes, neither one of them thought at all.

Kyle woke up at six as he always did, no alarm, just his internal clock. The warm female body snuggling against him told him immediately something was different—in a very good way. Unlike him, Julia had never been a morning person, often making it to school just as the bell rang.

"Hey, sleepyhead." He kissed her cheek.

She didn't stir.

He grinned, liking that some things hadn't changed. Not that he'd ever woken up beside her before. But she was still not a morning person.

And she still rocked his world. Completely. Unlike any woman ever had. Or would. They had a connection that went beyond years, beyond the physical.

Kyle showered and dressed before waking her to say goodbye. He eased down on the edge of the bed and kissed her awake.

"Mmm. This could potentially make me a morning person," she murmured against his lips.

He sat up and grinned. "Glad to hear it."

She blinked, still sleepy, and pushed herself up against the headboard. Realizing she was still naked, she pulled the covers over her. The show of modesty was a little late as well as unnecessary, but he let it go.

"I've got to go home and pick up my things. Team has to be at the stadium for a meeting, then we leave for a ten-game road trip." One he hated taking right now, when they'd just gotten started. That was the main reason he'd decided to wake her and not let her think he'd just walked out.

At the reminder of his trip, her eyes grew shuttered. "Good luck." Her smile was forced.

He decided to just push past her resistance by ignoring it. "Thanks. I'll be fine. I've got you as my good-luck charm." He winked and leaned in for another kiss.

She wasn't as soft and giving this time.

His gut tensed, but he had to go. "I'll call you from the road."

"Safe trip," she said and snuggled back under the covers.

He bit the inside of his cheek and rose to leave. They might have a long separation ahead of them, but they had a lot to discuss when he returned.

Julia rose and made herself a cup of her favorite herbal tea, soothing in smell and taste, but not the least bit healing. She spent the day cleaning her apartment and doing errands she normally accomplished on the weekends when she wasn't at work. Then she met a friend for dinner at her favorite sushi place, and though grilled mercilessly, Julia refused to admit anything was bothering her.

Why tell a single living soul she'd allowed Kyle Hansen back into her bed...or her heart? For all his talk about her being his good-luck charm and calling her from the road, she refused to believe it meant anything more than an easy way to get out the morning after. He wasn't just on the road, he was gone from her life.

Monday morning, Julia headed to work, and by the time Michael arrived after school, the entire hospital knew about the teen's experience at Suns Stadium. The buzz about Kyle Hansen grew louder. As loud as the *smack, smack, smack* of Michael's ball in the mitt. A sound that struck her now as one of joy, not frustration, and Julia wondered if her imagination had gone wild.

Monday night she climbed into her bed, a place that held memories of Kyle. His scent lingered on her pillow and she sensed his presence on the other side of the mattress, making her wish she'd slept with him at his place and not hers.

Annoyed with herself, she fluffed her pillow and turned off the lamp, when the telephone rang. She fumbled in the darkness and finally answered on the third ring.

"Hello?" she snapped, her foul mood finally coming out.

"Is that any way to greet a man who's only at the beginning of a long trip?"

"Kyle?" She sat upright in bed, surprised to hear his voice. Surprised and extremely happy.

"Is there another guy in your life I don't know about?" he asked, his tone suddenly wary.

"No! It's just...I didn't expect you to call." She gripped the phone harder.

"You're kidding, right?" He expelled a harsh breath. And probably a curse she couldn't hear. "Never mind, don't answer that. You really had so little faith in me?"

"It wasn't about faith. It was about reality."

"And in your reality I'd make love to you and not call?" His voice rose, his disappointment traveling through the telephone lines. "Well, thanks for the vote of confidence," he muttered.

Julia winced. Put like that, he had every right to be hurt. "I'm sorry."

"Don't apologize for your feelings."

Silence descended.

She swallowed hard. "How was the flight?"

"Long, and we have a game tonight. It's always rough playing on West Coast time." He spoke, but she could tell she'd offended him and he wouldn't quickly forget it.

"Well, good luck," she said softly.

"Thanks."

When he didn't say any more, she took the hint. "Bye," she said, disconnecting the call and letting the phone slip to the floor.

"Way to go, Julia." He said he'd made love to her, but how could she let herself believe that was anything more than a nice choice of words?

What did he expect her to think? That after all this time apart, superstar Kyle Hansen suddenly wanted his old high school girlfriend back in his life?

That she belonged there?

Kyle's bad mood permeated every phase of the team's West Coast trip. The Suns went on a losing streak and Kyle blamed himself. It might be a team effort, but his lack of enthusiasm affected the mood in the dugout and all the guys reacted accordingly. He tried to pull it together, but he couldn't get over the simple fact that Julia hadn't thought he'd call her.

She'd really been so badly scarred by her past that she believed he'd use her for sex and not contact her after. Even when he'd said he would.

If he thought it would help, he'd call her every day, but he knew better. She needed to see him in person to gauge his sincerity. And that wouldn't be happening for five more long and very frustrating days.

CHAPTER
∽ EIGHT ∽

Six days had passed since Kyle left on his road trip. Five since he'd called her, Julia thought. Apparently it wasn't so hard to scare him off after all. Not that that had been her intent. But at least now she knew she'd been right. At the first sign of conflict, he backed off.

Her stomach cramped at the painful truth. She turned her attention to the mail on her desk, when someone knocked on her door.

"Come in." She looked up, surprised to see Michael waiting to speak to her, as always, in his number 22 jersey.

"Hi there!" She put down her papers and focused on the boy. "What's going on?"

"Nothin'." He kicked at the floor with his sneakered foot.

She wasn't buying that for a second. "Did you just

come by to say hi?" She rose and walked to the door, gesturing for him to step all the way in, and led him to the chairs in front of her desk.

He didn't answer.

She sat beside him. "So you're here because nothing's up."

"There's a father-son breakfast at school," he muttered without looking up.

"Aha." Her heart twisted for the boy. It couldn't be easy for him.

It was too bad schools were still so insensitive about the change in family dynamics. As for Michael, his mother had to be at the hospital anyway, which left him alone. She searched for the right words, not wanting to ask if he had an uncle or someone else who could attend, only to lead him right into more disappointment if he said no.

"But Kyle gave me his cell-phone number," Michael said, his tone perking up.

"He did?" Julia asked, surprised. She doubted Kyle Hansen shared his cell-phone number with every kid he met.

Michael nodded. "He said if I needed anything, to just call. So I left a message telling him the exact day, time and place of the breakfast. I know he'll be back in town by then and I know the Suns don't have a game until that night. And it's a really early morning breakfast. Like before school starts, so he'll be able to make it."

Julia opened her mouth and closed it again. She didn't know what to say. She couldn't make promises for Kyle.

But Michael was looking at her with big brown, *hopeful* eyes.

"I'm sure he'll do his best," Julia said. "Has he answered you yet?"

Michael shook his head. "Nope. But he doesn't have to. I know he'll be there. He said if I need *anything* to just give him a call."

The naiveté of youth, she thought, looking into the eyes of a child who had already experienced so much pain and heartache.

She was afraid he was in for more. Kyle was just a stranger to Michael, one the boy had put on a pedestal. For all Julia knew, he'd forgotten he'd given the teenager his cell number. Maybe he wouldn't remember about the breakfast once he returned home from this disastrous road trip and the losing streak the team was on. Or maybe the breakfast was just too much of a hassle. Like Julia herself.

"I'm sure he'll do the best he can," she hedged. "What's the date?"

Michael told her.

She realized immediately that the Suns were due to arrive back in town late the night before. Who knew if Kyle would be up to an early breakfast, let alone remember to call if he couldn't make it?

"So you think Kyle will show up, too?" Michael asked.

Julia drew a deep breath. "I think you'll have someone at that breakfast with you," she assured him, deliberately vague.

Reaching out, she ruffled his hair.

He scowled and ran his hand over the top of his head. He jumped up from his chair, eyeing her as if she'd committed a cardinal sin.

She stifled a laugh.

"See ya later," he said before running back into the hall.

"Slow down," she called out.

As soon as he was gone, she sat at her desk and jotted down the date, time and place of the breakfast. Michael might have unwavering faith in Kyle, but she couldn't afford such blind trust.

She'd been disappointed too many times by people she loved. By family. And yes, by Kyle. So just in case, *just in case,* Julia decided to make sure the teen had a backup male to be with him at that father-son breakfast.

The team charter took off late due to an unexpected storm that had backed up the flight schedule by hours. Kyle arrived in Florida exhausted and still pissed the team had managed only one win on the road. He fell into a dreamless sleep and the alarm he'd set to accommodate jet lag went off too damn early. But he forced himself into the shower, standing under the hot spray long enough to make sure he was really awake and functioning. He hopped into his truck, drove over the bridge and stopped at the nearest coffee place before making his way to Michael Cortez's school.

He never gave his cell-phone number out to anyone he met through charity work. He knew better than to make promises he couldn't keep because of his crazy schedule. Besides, he never knew what kind of request someone might ask of him. He gladly did whatever charity work the Suns arranged and some on his own, if an organization was important to him. But he never got involved beyond the event itself. Yet something about this boy struck a chord with him.

Kyle didn't kid himself that the teenager's connection to Julia made him more important to Kyle than the tons of other underprivileged kids he met. That and he'd really bonded with the teenager, saw so much of himself in Michael's yearning to play and desire to lose himself in the game.

Michael had left a message telling Kyle when to be at his school and informing him why the father-son breakfast fit into Kyle's schedule. The kid hadn't asked. He'd just trusted Kyle to show up and sit in as his dad—because no one else would. When he'd gotten the message and again now, a lead weight settled on Kyle's chest. He'd been that kid whose father hadn't shown up more times than he could count. And Kyle's father had been around. He'd just cared more about booze than his son.

Kyle was proud he could stand in today so Michael wouldn't experience the pain and humiliation Kyle had felt. And he was humbled that the teenager had asked it of him at all.

He parked the truck in the crowded parking lot and walked toward the school, scanning the groups of kids and parents, looking for Michael. Kyle finally found him, only to discover the teenager wasn't alone.

Dr. Feelgood, the same guy who'd been with Julia in the hospital cafeteria that first day, stood by Michael's side.

Confused, Kyle stepped up and forced a smile. "Hi, kid."

"Kyle! Awesome! I told Ms. Caldwell you'd come!"

Kyle narrowed his gaze. "Of course I'm here. Did you doubt it?" The kid wore Kyle's jersey so he must have had some faith.

"Nah. I knew," he said, smiling ear to ear.

"You just thought two dads would be cooler than one?" he asked, turning to the other man. "Dr. Montoya." Kyle forced himself to extend a hand in greeting.

He still remembered the man saying something about not standing a chance with Julia. Which meant he was interested. The thought had acid flowing in Kyle's gut.

"It's Richard. And it's good to see you again, Hansen. Sorry about the rough trip you and your team had."

"We'll turn it around." At the reminder, Kyle set his jaw, wondering if this man was going to be a jerk and if he'd make it through the morning without wanting to deck him.

"I'm going to go get my friends and tell them to come check you out. They didn't believe you'd be here as my dad." Michael dashed off, leaving the two adults alone.

Kyle hoped he could act like one.

"Actually, Michael wasn't the one who doubted you'd show," the good doctor said. "It was Julia."

I told Ms. Caldwell you'd come! Michael's words

came back to him. Kyle cocked his head to one side. "So she asked you to back me up?"

The other man nodded. "Just in case."

"Well, there was no need, but since you're here, two dads are much better than one. Or none," Kyle added under his breath.

"I can see why you have such a decent reputation around town. I'd like to hate you, but since I can't, I wish you luck. She's a tough nut to crack," Richard added, referring to Julia.

Before Kyle could reply, he was swarmed by teenage boys with paper and pens, demanding an autograph. He settled onto a picnic table with Michael by his side, assigning the kid the important job of telling Kyle his friends' names before he signed their papers.

All the while, he tried not to think about the fact that a teenager he barely knew trusted him more than the woman who owned his heart.

Midmorning the day of Michael's breakfast, Julia caught sight of Richard coming out of a patient's room and waved. "Can we talk?"

He inclined his head and they walked down the hall where they could have some privacy. She'd been curious about how his stint as dad went at Michael's father-son breakfast.

"Listen, I have to thank you again for agreeing to go with Michael. I know you didn't owe me any favors, but I really appreciate you stepping up that way."

Richard studied her with his appraising gaze. "No, I didn't owe you, but I agree with you that the healthy child is as important as the sick one. I was happy to attend."

She smiled. "That's why I asked you. I know you don't leave your work at the hospital. You take it home with you. Anyway, thanks for going."

"As I said, my pleasure. But it wasn't necessary. Michael had his first choice there after all."

Julia's stomach lurched. "Kyle showed up?"

Richard nodded. "And he wasn't too pleased to see he had company. Especially when he realized you'd arranged for me to be there if he was a no-show."

Julia broke into a cold sweat. "You told him that?" she asked, horrified.

"I didn't have to. Michael informed Kyle that *he'd told Ms. Caldwell Kyle would show up.*"

She leaned against the wall for support and Richard eyed her warily. "Are you okay?"

"Just a little dizzy," she admitted. And caught off guard.

"Do you mind if I offer you some unsolicited advice?"

She waved a hand. "You might as well. I'm not doing so well relying on myself."

"In all the time you've been at this hospital, even when you were still in graduate school, you rarely dated, and when you did, it never lasted."

"You've been keeping track?" she asked wryly. Strangely, she wasn't offended.

"I was always biding my time and trying to understand what made you tick. And you were always an enigma to me. Until Kyle Hansen walked into the cafeteria a couple of weeks ago."

Julia tried to swallow, but her mouth was dry and parched. "And?"

"And when you looked at him, I saw an entirely different woman than the one I knew. For a few seconds, before you caught yourself, you were like a teenager, carefree, and happier than I've ever seen you."

Now she really couldn't swallow, or speak, either.

"I don't know what your issues are, I don't know what you're hiding from, but it shouldn't be from him." He shrugged. "That's my two cents, for what it's worth."

"It's worth a lot." She smiled.

He leaned over and kissed her cheek. "Good luck, Julia. Whatever you decide." Richard strode away, ever confident no matter what obstacles life placed in his way.

She could learn from him, she thought, watching him go.

Alone, Julia retreated to her office, where she shut the door, locked it and sank to the floor. Then she lowered her head between her knees and prayed for the dizziness to subside. Once she started breathing evenly, she forced herself to deal with what was making her so upset.

Kyle had shown up for Michael's event when she'd been convinced he wouldn't. She'd even asked another man to attend in his place.

Kyle had said he'd call her from the road and she'd been positive he wouldn't. Even after they'd shared a spectacular night that had rocked her world. And from the way he'd looked at her before, during and after, he'd felt the same way.

But instead of facing her feelings and acknowledging the powerful connection still between them, she'd run far and fast. Worse, she'd made him feel as if he wasn't worthy of her faith, or her trust, or even her love.

And hadn't he had enough of that to last a lifetime?

Almost ten years later and she was still wallowing in the pain of being neglected by her parents, putting barriers up against the one thing she wanted more than life itself because she was afraid of losing it—afraid of losing him—again.

But what was worse? Losing him after trying her best to make it work? Or knowingly throwing away a second chance because she was too afraid to even try?

She rose, and as she pulled herself together, Richard's words came back to her, loud and clear. *I don't know what your issues are, I don't know what you're hiding from, but it shouldn't be from him.*

Well, she knew what her issues were and it was time to get over them. No more hiding from herself or from life. She was going after what—make that who—she wanted.

Whether or not he would still be there was another story.

CHAPTER
∾ NINE ∾

Kyle stood by his locker stretching and trying to get in the zone. He was pitching tonight, coming off not just a loss in the last game he'd started, but a humiliating road trip the fans probably wouldn't let the team forget. Hell, *he* couldn't forget. But he couldn't concentrate either.

How the hell could Julia think so little of him she'd send that uptight doctor to Michael's father-son breakfast on the assumption that Kyle wouldn't show? Did she honestly believe he'd let the kid down? After the way he was let down every damn day of his life?

He slammed his locker door closed, rattling the walls. Every last one of his teammates steered clear.

"Hey, Hansen!"

Macy.

"Go away. I'm pitching in an hour."

She came up to him, standing toe to toe, in his personal space. "I've got a meeting for you to take. Now."

What little buzz had been going on in the locker room came to a halt. Everyone knew his rule.

"You're kidding me?" he asked.

"You're in a fine mood." She placed her hands on her hips. "No, I'm not kidding. I'm serious."

"Then you must have a death wish," he muttered.

"No, I have a wish to *win,* like everyone else in this organization, including you. So take the meeting and then get yourself on the field and pitch like you're being paid to." She paused to draw a breath. "In my office. Now." She turned and strode away, red hair flying behind her.

Kyle stormed out after her.

Not one player got in his way.

He walked down the hall, not in the mood for ownership to berate him for his attitude before a game—no matter how valid their complaint.

At Macy's office door, he blew out a harsh stream of air before letting himself inside, where he expected to find the general manager or owner, ready to chew him out.

Instead, he found Julia.

Julia, in her tight jeans and *his* jersey, standing in front of the wall of photos she'd been admiring the first time he saw her here.

She glanced up.

He speared her with a look and turned to walk out.

"Kyle, wait."

Her soft voice tripped him up. "I can't do this before a game. I need to focus."

And she was as big a distraction as he could get. Macy ought to know better.

"I know. And I wouldn't be here unless I thought I could give that back to you. Your focus, I mean."

He wasn't in the mood for riddles, but he knew he wouldn't get rid of her unless he listened. And now that he'd seen her—glossy lips, breasts full beneath *his* number—he wouldn't be concentrating on a pitch unless he found out why she'd come.

He turned around to face her, crossed his arms over his chest and waited.

She blew out a puff of air. "Okay, here's the thing. I know you believe I don't have faith in you. You think I don't trust you and I've done nothing to make you believe otherwise. But it's not you. It's me."

More riddles, he thought in frustration. And the clock was ticking down to game time. Still, he waited.

She clenched and unclenched her fists in a nervous gesture he remembered well and he fought with himself not to soften toward her.

"Look, unlike you, I had the perfect childhood," she said. "Well, as close to perfect as you can get, at least as far as families are concerned. And then my sister got sick and my parents forgot they had me. I was all alone. I woke myself up, got myself to school and then home from school. I cooked my dinner and did my homework…"

Nothing any different than what he'd done every

day of his life. Except she hadn't been used to it. She'd known love and attention and then she'd lost it.

She rubbed her hands on her jeans and met his gaze. "And on top of all that, I worried about whether my sister would live or die."

He felt like an awful human being for being so angry, but what he'd experienced had to count too, he thought, struggling between feeling petty and wanting to pull her into his arms and hold her tight.

She turned and walked to the wall of photos before facing him again. "And sometimes I was jealous she had their attention. Can you imagine that?" she asked. "And when I wasn't jealous, I was resentful that she was sick. I mean, I was a mess. And then I got stuck tutoring you." For the first time, the beginnings of a grin tilted her lips, making them sexier because she was smiling.

And he felt the first real crack in his armor. Because he remembered that time too and it also made him smile.

Turning, she stepped toward him. "You were my everything, Kyle. And when you asked me to go with you—well, actually you expected it—I just…couldn't. My sister's life was in limbo. I had to stay. Just like you had to chase your dream. I understood that in a way you didn't."

"You're right about that," he admitted. He hadn't understood or forgiven. Not until he'd seen her again. He shook his head, fighting the shame.

"The thing is, you could have called or come back for me, or checked on me. But you didn't." Her voice broke.

And he wanted to apologize and bury his face in her soft hair and kiss her lips, but she kept on talking. He let her, listening and battling his own pain, and his own memories of that time.

"So my life went on." A tight smile pulled at her mouth. "My sister died and I thought maybe my family would pull together, grieve together. That I'd get something back to compensate for the huge gaping loss. But that never happened, either. I was really well and truly alone with one big lesson learned— People leave. People who say they love you can't be trusted to act like they do. And from then on, I was going to protect my heart because I never ever wanted to feel that way again." Her brown eyes were big, damp and open to him for the first time in almost ten years.

He knew in that moment she'd come here and risked her heart. For him.

He couldn't love her any more than he did right now.

"Julia—"

She held up one hand. "I'm not finished."

He suppressed a grin. "Okay."

She swallowed hard. "You need to know that I think you're an amazing man. You're a stand-up guy. Honest and trustworthy and I should have known that. But the reasons I didn't know that have nothing to do with who you are today."

"No, they have to do with who I *was*. A selfish, immature kid who expected you to leave your dying sister and grieving parents and come with me for an uncertain future. And when you wouldn't, I decided I was the wronged party and it was all your fault. You're right. I should have come back for you, and if I'd looked inside my heart and beyond my overly inflated ego, I would have."

"So we both share some of the blame. Good to know." She laughed and wiped a tear from her face. "Anyway, I came to tell you that. To apologize and hopefully take away enough of the hurt and anger so you can focus tonight. And win."

"Because that's what matters to me, right? The game and winning."

"It's what has to matter tonight, anyway. You're due on the mound soon."

He glanced at the clock on the wall. His manager and the pitching coach were probably ready to kill him by now. Unless Macy was soothing their tempers.

He shook his head. "No. From this minute on, *you're* what matters most to me. Always and forever. Promise me you won't forget it?" He opened his arms.

And she flew right in, burrowing into him as if she'd never let go. He separated them enough to tip her head with his hand and seal his mouth over hers in a kiss that meant everything to him.

"I love you," he said between kisses.

"And I love you," Julia murmured, putting everything she had, was and would be into the kiss.

She wanted to spend the rest of her life proving to him that she did indeed believe he was trustworthy and honorable and a man she wanted by her side now and always. They'd wasted ten years. She didn't want to lose another minute.

When someone banged on the office door, Julia wanted to pull back, but Kyle kept his arms solidly around her waist. "Come in," he called, not letting her go.

Macy peeked her head in. "Um, I'm getting reamed for dragging you out of the locker room so close to game time. You about ready?" she asked hopefully.

"Do we look ready?" he growled, obviously hoping to scare her into backing out the door.

Macy's gaze darted from Julia to Kyle. "You look satisfied enough to focus and win. Just think what you have to come back to afterward," the publicist added, stepping into the room and physically separating the two of them.

"Let's go. You—on the field," Macy said, commanding Kyle with her tone and a pointed finger. "And you—up in the box," she ordered Julia. She clapped her hands. "Now! Move!"

Kyle stole another kiss from Julia and ran out the door.

But not out of her life. Julia believed that now. She believed in him.

∽EPILOGUE∽

MIAMI SUNS
FOR IMMEDIATE RELEASE
Contact: Macy Kroger, Miami Suns, Publicity

Suns Pitcher Weds

Miami Suns pitcher and captain, Kyle Hansen, married childhood sweetheart, Julia Caldwell, a social worker at Caridad del Cobre Children's Hospital, on December 1, 2012, in a sunset ceremony at the athlete's exclusive home. The wedding follows the Miami Suns' 2011 World Series win. The couple were joined in a small ceremony attended by friends and teammates. The best man was, to quote the groom, "an up-and-coming star pitcher in his own right," fifteen-year-old Michael Cortez. In lieu of gifts, the couple asked that donations be made to the Andre Sobel River of Life Foundation, an organization they credit for their reunion. For over ten years, ASRL has provided funding *when compassion can't wait:* within twenty-four hours, ASRL helps with urgent expenses to allow single parents to stay at their children's bedside during catastrophic illness. More Information on ASRL can be found at: http://andreriveroflife.org/.

* * * * *

Dear Reader,

We all lead very busy lives and, as authors, we have deadlines. When first approached to write a story for *More Than Words,* I was honored to be asked but I wasn't certain I could find the time in my schedule. Luckily for me, the people at Harlequin who are involved with the More Than Words philanthrophic initiative were persistent and I agreed. I never imagined what a gift writing this story would be. Through More Than Words, I was introduced to the Andre Sobel River of Life Foundation. Within twenty-four hours of a request, ASRL helps with urgent expenses to allow single parents to stay at their child's bedside during catastrophic illness. What greater need can be filled? What greater gift can an organization give?

As a writer, I am honored to bring you my story, "Compassion Can't Wait," in honor of the Andre Sobel River of Life Foundation and the selfless work of Valerie Sobel, Anne Swire and everyone else at ASRL. I urge you to visit www.andreriveroflife.org and read about this truly inspiring organization and consider them when choosing where to make your charitable donations. In the meantime, I hope you enjoyed social worker Julia Caldwell and star baseball player Kyle Hansen's reunion. Theirs is a story of love, loss, hope and possibilities for the future—and that is what ASRL provides each and every day.

I wish you all health, happiness and as always, happy reading.

Best wishes,

Carly Phillips

www.carlyphillips.com

NANCY ABRAMS
‹— Family Reconnect Program —›

Imagine a teen—your teen—huddled in a doorway overnight. A dusting of snow covers her thin sleeping bag and forces her to cram her shivering body deeper into its meager warmth. She is afraid, hungry and homeless.

That night she tells herself she is finished living in fear on the street. She wants to go home and be with her family again. Only one problem: she has no idea how to make it happen. There's no money, but even more important, she's worried that if she returns, nothing will have changed. She'll still feel like an outsider. Her parents will still act exasperated by everything she does.

So she stays on the street, a target for violence, a vessel of despair.

Now imagine that Nancy Abrams, supervisor of the groundbreaking Family Reconnect Program offered by Eva's Initiatives in Toronto, is there to offer a hand. Since 2002 her job has been to help homeless youth, from sixteen to twenty-four, reestablish supportive relationships with their families, allowing them to return home or live in the community with family support.

Dedicated to helping all marginalized young people find safety, she also introduced an Early Intervention Program for youth at imminent risk of living on the streets. Sound tough? Nancy waves the thought away, instead focusing on the positive.

"When I look at my career I have no regrets about what I've chosen to do," says Nancy, who has more than thirty-five years of experience as a manager, counselor, child and youth worker, college instructor and volunteer. "It's really a privilege to be part of this journey with people. It truly is."

Working with abused women and their children, youth in correctional facilities and children in mental-health settings has taught Nancy to be pragmatic about the situations she helps people climb their way out of. She talks not about changing lives, but "shifting lives to a more healthy place." She does that by offering respect and by refusing to judge the youth and families she meets.

Safe communication

Housed in a wing of the organization's shelter, Eva's Place, the Family Reconnect Program was launched after workers overheard heartbreaking telephone conversations between youth and their families. The kids wanted to go home, the parents were still angry, or vice versa. With communication skills lacking or too much anger driving a wedge between them, there was no easy way to reconnect children with their homes.

Now, with the help of two other family intervention counselors, Nancy meets with the youth, listens to their stories and is there in the room with them making that first important phone call home. They try to set a face-to-face meeting with the family if all goes well.

"That first meeting with family is a celebration," she says. "Parents and youth are interested in working things out. I find families so remarkable during such difficult times."

Nancy knows some people worry that kids are being sent home to less than ideal situations, but with proper support and family therapy, nearly all home situations can be improved, she says. In fact, since 2002 when the program started, she and her team have seen only three families they did not feel comfortable sending the youth to. That's an incredibly small number considering that in 2008, the program worked with more than a hundred and fifty homeless youth.

Even when families are not prepared to open their hearts again to their daughter, son, granddaughter, grandson, niece or nephew, and take them back in, Nancy remains optimistic. She knows that "no" can sometimes mean "not yet."

"To them we say, 'We're here. We'll try again when you're ready,'" she explains.

Full of hope

Nancy remains hopeful, even when endings are not happy ones. She thinks back to a young man she helped who struggled with an addiction problem. When he was clean, she says he was warm, loving and kind. But when on drugs, he became aggressive, stole from his single mother and challenged everyone. Nancy knew the family well. His mother never turned her back on her son and leaned on Nancy to help her find ways to turn the situation around.

Although Nancy had helped the young man get treatment, he was still mixed up with dangerous peers and was eventually murdered.

The following Christmas, Nancy received a phone call from the boy's mother. She and her son had received holiday gift baskets through Eva's Place in the past, and the woman decided this was the year she would donate to the people who'd helped her through her darkest hours. She made a beautiful Christmas bag to give to another family being helped by the Family Reconnect Program.

"Here was a woman who was having her first Christmas without her son, who wanted to give back. It was quite amazing," says Nancy now. "But this is the experience I have all the time. People are very giving, kind and caring. Family therapy and counseling helps give them the language they need to share these qualities with their children."

Getting it done

Whether she's trying to get a teenager a hospital bed so a specialist can diagnose and treat his debilitating obsessive-compulsive disorder, or finding help for another youth challenged by mental illness, Nancy is known for being tenacious. She cuts through bureaucratic objections as forcefully as she cuts through red tape. She badgers if necessary, writes letters, schedules meetings and never gives up.

She does it all because she knows the alternative: placing a phone call in the middle of the night to tell a family their child is injured, sick or dead.

She admits there is a huge gap in the mental health and hospital systems where teens and youth fall through. Yet with Nancy's care, understanding and dedication to helping families reconnect, that gap is becoming filled with families who understand their youths' lives better and demand services that will turn those lives around.

"Every morning I wake up and I'm excited about the work I do," says Nancy. "It's more than work, though. I feel blessed in my life and I'm so proud of the youth and families I meet."

DONNA HILL
∽— SOMEPLACE LIKE HOME —∽

∽ DONNA HILL ∽

National bestselling author Donna Hill began her career in 1987 with short stories, and her first novel was published in 1990. She now has more than fifty published titles to her credit, and three of her novels have been adapted for television. Donna has been featured in *Essence,* the *New York Daily News, USA TODAY, Today's Black Woman, Black Enterprise* and other publications.

Apart from her writing, Donna served for many years as the Site Coordinator for Kianga House in Brooklyn, NY—a residential facility for teen mothers and their babies. The wonderful work done at Kianga House and Eva's Initiatives are very close to her heart and the inspiration for "Someplace Like Home." She is also co-founder and publisher of InnerVision Books, an ebook publisher.

Donna lives in Brooklyn, New York, with her family. Find out more about her at www.donnahill.com.

⚛️ PROLOGUE ⚛️

"**D**id you hear about the Harris family?"

Verna Scott glanced up from the mountain of case files on her desk. It seemed that the more she worked, the higher the stack grew. One wrong move and the files would go tumbling to the floor. Files containing the most intimate details of broken lives.

Nichole Graham, her longtime coworker, was standing in the doorway.

Verna took off her black-framed glasses and gently massaged the bridge of her nose. She wasn't sure if she could handle any bad news today. They'd gotten a report earlier in the week that two children who had been placed in separate foster homes had run away and still not been found. It had been in all the newspapers and on television. Everyone was pointing fingers. Verna was the director of the division. Thankfully, her staff was cleared. They'd followed protocol to the letter and the assigned social workers had been to see the families in question at least two days before the kids ran away. She could only pray they would be found quickly and unharmed.

Verna had been a certified social worker for nearly a decade. She had her doctorate in child psychology and was passionate about her work. There was no greater satisfaction than seeing a family reunited, a runaway teen get the kind of loving care he or she needed or watching the countless foster children placed in homes with people who loved them. Unfortunately in her line of work, the tragedies often outnumbered the triumphs. There were days, like this one, when she didn't know if she could keep working. That's why she'd been carefully and slowly formulating plan B for the past two years.

"Do I want to know?" Verna asked with a tired smile.

Nichole stepped inside, lifted some overstuffed files from the one wooden chair and plopped down. She crossed her long legs at the knee. "They got burned out last night."

Verna lowered her head and covered her face with her hands, then looked across the desk at Nichole, her own anguish reflected in her coworker's blue eyes. "How bad?"

"They lost pretty much everything. We have them in a hotel for the time being. The Red Cross is helping. But, of course, we had to remove the children who were with them."

Verna nodded at the inevitable and clenched her long

fingers into fists. "Of course. We just placed the sister and brother with the Harrises. It was so difficult finding a family willing to take them both, and now this."

"I know."

"Those poor kids." She banged the table with a fist as she looked off into the distance then around the room, which was nearly bursting with files of other children. The ache inside her rose in a wave, leaving her feeling helpless. Rare tears pricked her eyes.

"Verna...we'll manage—" Nichole's brow creased. "Are you okay?" The two of them had worked together for the past five years, and even in some of the most dire situations, Nichole had never seen Verna crack. She got up and came around the desk to sit on the edge. Reaching out, she covered Verna's tight fist. "Talk to me," she coaxed.

Verna looked up, and the worry in Nichole's expression propelled her out of her seat and across the room to where her purse hung on the wobbly coatrack. She unzipped the bag and took out a Dunkin' Donuts napkin. She dabbed her eyes and pushed away the countless images of hurt and confused children, before turning toward Nichole. She sniffed, cleared her throat and tugged on the hem of her navy blue jacket. "Allergies," she said, forcing a smile.

"How long have we been friends—or at least coworkers?" Nichole asked. "We're both trained to see beneath the surface. Whenever you want to talk, I'm here."

Verna swallowed over the tightness in her throat and nodded.

"Thanks, Nikki. I appreciate that."

Nichole stood. "I'm going to start looking at some options for the kids."

"Try to keep them together," Verna said, but her tone reflected the reality of what they faced: red tape and not enough families willing to take two adolescents into their home.

"I'll keep you posted," Nichole said before walking out.

Once the door closed, Verna squeezed her eyes shut, mentally berating herself for her lapse. She prided herself on her professionalism and objectivity, at least on the surface. For the most part, Verna was all about business. It was the only way she'd managed to get through the thousands of cases over the years. To become attached would be detrimental to the child, the family and the caseworker.

She'd earned the directorship of the New York office of the Agency for Children's Services nearly eight years earlier. She was a career social worker with multiple degrees and certifications. She could easily open her own office, set her hours and decide on her cases. But she'd stayed in the trenches, digging through the debris of human heartache and trying to fix it. During the last few years, though, she'd begun to feel more and more that she was swimming upstream with no shore in sight. The several handfuls of successes were no longer enough. She wanted—no, needed—to be hands on, and so she'd started making plans. She'd visited Canada several years earlier and connected with people running an organization called Eva's Initiatives in Toronto. She'd particularly been interested in the Family Reconnect Program that worked with young people and their families to help them rebuild relationships after family breakdowns. When she'd returned from that trip she was determined to use it as a model for her own program one day.

She turned and looked out her fifth-floor office window onto the gray concrete below. She knew it was time. She'd done all she could do here.

CHAPTER
∾ ONE ∾

"Someplace Like Home is a model project that comprises several successful programs," Verna said into the microphone.

She looked out at the sea of faces—some eager, some open, many jaded. Most of these high school guidance counselors wanted to do more than just help kids fill out forms. These men and women were on the front lines, and often saw problems certain students were having before anyone else did.

"Our facility is structured with a small residence for up to five youth, as well as a twenty-four-hour service center, counseling services, fully equipped recreation room, tutoring, emergency intervention specialists, a nurse, a small library and a yard for outside activities. Our goal is to provide an anchor, a sanctuary for kids who are being shuffled through the system, and provide them with the nurturing, resources and support that they need to survive. But most important, we create a home for them. A place that they can come to no matter what or when.

"We welcome visits and we're always looking for volunteers," she added, her smile filled with invitation. "Thank you all for listening. I've left literature on the tables."

Verna moved away from the podium, walked down the three short steps and headed to the table where she'd placed her coat. Several of the conference participants came up to her and handed her their business cards. Others came to say thanks for the presentation.

She checked her watch and slipped into her gray wool three-quarter jacket, digging her hands into her coat pockets to retrieve her gray leather gloves. The temperature had dropped significantly throughout the day and the weather report predicted snow. It was March. Go figure, she mused as she walked to the exit.

"Dr. Scott," a voice called out.

Verna turned. One of the conference attendees walked quickly toward her. She recognized him from the front row.

"I was wondering if you have a minute," he said. He stuck out his hand. "Ronald Morris."

"Sure. Would you mind walking and talking at the same time?"

"Not a problem." He pushed open the swinging door and held it for her to pass through.

Once they stepped outside, the biting wind almost

whipped their breaths away. They both reeled with shock then started to laugh.

"Maybe the weatherman is right for a change," Verna said, knotting her scarf around her neck as they crossed to the parking lot.

Ronald glanced skyward. "Too cold for snow."

Verna looked up at him in the waning afternoon light. Six foot two, she surmised. He stood a good head above her, even in her heels. His dark hair was cut close, but still held a hint of gentle waves. He had what the old folks would call an easy face, one you could get real comfortable looking at.

"I was wondering if I could make an appointment to stop in for a visit," Ronald said, halting her assessment of him.

The brisk wind caused them to hasten their steps and inadvertently they drew closer.

"That's not a problem. Did you get one of my cards and the packet of information?"

"Sure did."

"Give us a call and we'll set something up." She paused. "Teacher or guidance counselor?"

"Guidance counselor at Lexington High."

Verna nodded. "The school in Clinton Hill. Charter, right?"

He grinned and she noticed how the corners of his eyes crinkled.

"You're good."

"I try to keep up." She lifted her chin. "That's my car over there. The blue Honda."

Ronald looked to where she indicated. "I'm right behind you in the silver Honda."

They laughed at the coincidence.

"Seems we have a few things in common—looking out for kids and driving Hondas," Ronald quipped.

Verna wasn't sure if his comment was a friendly observation or a come-on. Rather than guess wrong, she chose to ignore it. She pressed the red button on her key ring and deactivated the car alarm with a soft chirp. An airplane roared overhead. She turned to him. "It was nice talking with you. I hope to see you at Someplace Like Home."

"I'll give your office a call and set something up."

"Great. Take care." She reached for the door handle, but Ronald got to it first. They stood barely a breath apart and Verna caught a whiff of his warm scent.

He opened the car door then shut it for her while she fastened her seat belt.

"Thanks," she mouthed through the glass.

He waved goodbye and went to his car.

Verna watched him through her rearview mirror while the heater warmed up. He was a good-looking man. A gentleman and someone who cared about what he did. She smiled to herself. Not bad, not bad at all.

CHAPTER
∽ TWO ∽

Verna was in the middle of drafting a grant proposal when Nichole, who'd joined the team the moment Someplace Like Home opened, tapped on Verna's office door.

"Still at it?" she asked, poking her head in and stepping inside.

Verna leaned back in the comfort of her chair.

The office was small but cozy and looked more like a mini living room. Instead of a traditional desk, Verna had opted for two circular tables, and cushiony club chairs replaced standard swivel seats. Files were stored in built-in wall cabinets that went up to the ceiling. She preferred a laptop to a desktop computer so she could easily tuck it away or take her work with her. Paintings hung on the cream-colored walls, and drapes adorned the windows. Someplace Like Home was located in a four-story brownstone in the heart of Brooklyn's Fort Greene district. Verna had been determined that when the place was redesigned to suit her needs, she would maintain as much of the original architecture as possible. She'd searched for months for just the right building and finally found one that had been taken over by the City of New York and left abandoned for years. When she presented her proposal for a residential and therapeutic program to the Homeless Housing Unit of the city, they were more than happy to get rid of the albatross. She'd purchased it for a steal and used much of her own savings, along with donations and government grants to get it into shape.

The doors were heavy inlaid oak. The floors were the original parquet, shined to a high gloss, and many of the windows still displayed the priceless stained glass. Chandeliers hung in the hallways and main rooms and there was even a working fireplace in the gathering room.

"Have a seat and relax for a minute," Verna said. She placed her glasses on the tabletop and absently ran her fingers through her short hair.

Nichole sat down and stretched her legs out in front of her. "This sure is a change from the Agency for Children's Services," she said. "You've come a long way, Verna."

"I had a lot of help. You included."

"You know I was never one to pass up an opportunity." She laughed lightly. "Besides, we do good work here. There's nothing else like this in the city."

"Well, if we get this new grant I'll be able to make

some improvements. The backyard needs an overhaul. Plus, I want to get a van or two so that we can pick up the kids and drop them off. And—"

"Whoa!" Nichole interrupted. "Are you going to take over the world while you're at it?" she teased.

Verna lowered her eyes. "I know, I know. I get carried away sometimes. But I want so much for these kids, Nikki."

"No one works harder than you do, and the kids appreciate it. But you need more in your life than just work. When was the last time you took a vacation? Or for that matter, took a day off? You've been working nonstop for two years."

Verna sighed. "We're not going to have that discussion again. This is my life, plain and simple."

Nichole pursed her thin lips. "Fine." She threw up her hands in mock defeat. "But just remember, all work and no play makes Verna very boring."

Verna snickered. "I'll keep that in mind. How many do we have in the house today?"

"Hmm. Let's see. Felix and Alexander and Shawn are in the game room. Lynn, Stacy and Carmen were in the library. April is in her room. Carol and Yvonne haven't gotten in yet. And Leslie is helping in the kitchen."

With each name Verna registered a face and a story. They'd all been in and out of the foster-care system since middle school or younger, having been removed from their dysfunctional homes by court order. Carol and Yvonne were seniors in high school and lived in the residential section of the building on the top floor, along with April and Carmen. All of them had entered the program unwillingly, angry and wary. But in the months that they'd experienced the magic of Home, Verna had seen marked improvements. Their school reports and their foster parents concurred. She drew in a breath of satisfaction. This was her calling.

"I never got a chance to ask you how the conference went last week. Any takers for the volunteer slots?"

"I thought it went well. But as far as I know we haven't gotten any new calls." She'd thought she would have heard from Ronald Morris. He'd seemed genuinely interested. But she was fully aware that once people reviewed the material and the time required to volunteer, it was more than many were willing to handle. That's why she needed this grant. It would allow her to at least offer a small stipend to the volunteers.

"We'll manage," Nichole said.

"Yes. We always do. But with spring break coming we'll be swamped. The 'come back anytime' policy is a crowd-pleaser." When school was not in session, many of the previous program participants came back to Home to hang out, see old friends and simply return to someplace nurturing and familiar. "We'll need to make sure that we have plenty of supplies. I'll give Vinny a call and see if he has any more game boxes to donate." Vinny was an old friend and game store owner. He refurbished used gaming systems and was always willing to donate.

"We could use another television in the rec room. It's about on its last leg."

"Hmm." Verna made a note. She might have to go into her own pocket for that, something she did more than she let on.

Nichole pushed up from her seat. "How long are you staying?"

"About another hour. I'll do my last rounds and then head home."

"Promise?"

Verna smiled. "Promise."

"Okay. I'll see you in the morning."

"Oh, did Phyllis get in yet?"

"Yes, she's been here about an hour. She was checking on April and then she was going to do some inventory."

"Great. I'll be sure to see her before I leave."

Phyllis Warren was the housemother and stayed overnight at the residence. To the teens who lived at Home, she was often the mother they never had. Everyone adored Phyllis.

"Okay, see ya."

"Night."

Nichole closed the door behind her.

Verna stretched her arms high above her shoulders and slowly tilted her head from left to right. The tight muscles began to unwind. She checked her watch. It was almost seven. The aroma of beef stew drifted into the room, and her stomach rumbled in response. Gail, the cook, was up to her fabulous cooking. If it wouldn't look so obvious that she had nothing else to do, no one to go home to, Verna would stay for dinner. Instead, she'd probably warm up some leftovers and watch the news.

She switched off her laptop and tucked it away in the cabinet, checked around the office then walked out, locking the door behind her.

* * *

Ronald hung up the office phone. His frustration level had reached its threshold. For weeks he'd been trying to reach Dayna's family—mother, father, anyone—to no avail. He was worried about her. He'd seen the change in her over the past few months: missing classes, arguing with teachers, getting into altercations with other students. She'd started to look different, too. Dayna had always been well-groomed. Lately she'd come to school unkempt and tired, as if she'd slept in her clothes. She was smart enough not to miss consecutive days of classes or get picked up for truancy, and when he'd called her down to his office to talk, she was sullen—slouching in the chair and refusing to meet his eyes. She insisted that she was fine, and that's about all she would say.

If it were up to him he would pay a visit to her house, but that was against school policy. His hands were tied and he didn't know what else to do.

He opened a file folder on his desk and began working on reference letters for two of his college-bound seniors. There was some good that he was able to do, but it was cases like Dayna's that made him question his effectiveness as a counselor.

Ronald completed the letters, made copies for the files and put the originals into the college packets for mailing. He leaned away from his desk and massaged the back of his neck with the tips of his fingers, sighing as the tense muscles relaxed. It had been a long day. Classes had been over for a couple of hours and he'd been at his desk since seven that morning.

He stood and took his coat from the hook on the back of the office door and headed out.

"Long day, Mr. Morris," Cliff the security guard said when Ronald reached the exit.

Ronald chuckled. "That it has been." He buttoned his coat. "Have a good evening."

"You, too." He gave a mock salute as Ronald walked out into the encroaching evening.

When Ronald reached the faculty parking lot, his car was the only one left. A regular occurrence, he mused. Most days he didn't leave much before five, often later. He enjoyed his job. He enjoyed working with the kids, helping them. But the question always nagged him: Was he doing enough?

He stuck his hand in his jacket pocket to pull out his car keys and a white card floated to the ground. He bent to pick it up. *Someplace Like Home*. He palmed the card. Since the conference he'd had every intention of contacting Verna Scott and setting up an appointment. But the days seemed to get away from him. He made a mental note to call the next morning without fail.

As he got behind the wheel and started the car, a crystal-clear image of Verna materialized. He recalled the warm welcome of her light brown eyes, the smoothness of her honey-toned skin and the direct way she spoke—confident and assured. He liked that about a woman, someone who knew who she was and was not afraid to show it. He smiled to himself as he drove off. Yes, tomorrow he would give Verna Scott a call.

* * *

Verna had a restless night and awoke edgy and achy. She'd had that dream again. It had been several months since she'd seen herself in that room, waiting for a decision, listening to her heart pound. The door would open. A shadow would fill the doorway. She could never tell if it was a man or a woman that would beckon her to the door.

On the other side was a nondescript bus that would take her from one house to the next. At each house she would ask, "Do you want a little girl?" And each time a door would slam in her face with a resounding no.

The dream was repeated over and over in some kind of macabre loop until her alarm clock went off at five. It usually took her a couple of hours to shake off its effects, and today was more trying than usual.

Verna stood by the sink watching the percolating coffee drip hypnotically into the pot. She yawned loudly as she took a mug from the cabinet. That's why her work was so important. She needed to do everything in her power to keep other children from having *her* nightmare of no home, no roots, no one to love them.

She poured her coffee and took the mug into her bedroom to continue preparing for the day. She might have had a lousy sleep, but she needed to be at the top of her game today. The facility was scheduled for its quarterly state inspection and she wanted to ensure that all her records were in order.

In the current economic climate, municipal, state and federal funding was being slashed left and right. She didn't need to give the inspectors any excuse to deduct a dime from her budget.

By six she was in her car and on her way to work. While she drove the fifteen minutes to her office, she ran through a mental list of everything that would be scrutinized today: case files, staff certifications, building-inspection clearances, the kitchen, financial data and a review of all the spaces to ensure that they were being used according to the information on file.

For the past two weeks, the entire staff had evaluated each of their assigned areas, reviewed charts and made sure that every corner of the house was spic and span. She was confident that, as always, Someplace Like Home would pass with flying colors, but she was never one to leave anything to chance.

Thankfully, she found a parking space on the right side of the street and wouldn't have to worry about moving her car during the day. Alternate side parking was one of the frustrations of New York life.

Mike, the overnight security guard, greeted her. "Good morning, Dr. Scott. You're earlier than usual."

"Morning, Mike. Busy day today. How is everything?" She shook off the chill of the outdoors.

"Quiet night."

"Quiet is good." She started for her office down the hallway.

"Uh, Dr. Scott…"

Verna stopped and turned back.

"I really hate to ask this," Mike began, his usual open expression now tight and drawn. "I was wondering… since you're in early, would it be all right if I clocked out? My wife called during the night. She's not feeling well and she thinks our daughter is coming down with something, too."

Verna walked back to where Mike sat and pinned him with a hard look. "You mean to tell me that you've been here all night and your wife and daughter are sick?"

Mike sputtered out a response that Verna didn't bother trying to decipher.

"Get up. Get your things and go home. Now." She pointed straight for the door. "And don't come back until they're better." She exhaled a rush of frustration. "What's our motto around here?" she asked as Mike scampered to collect his belongings. He dared to glance at her.

"Family first."

She gave a short nod of agreement. "Exactly. Now go. Take care of your family. I'm sure that Paul can cover your shift."

Mike shoved his arms in his jacket. "Thanks, Dr. Scott. Really."

Worry pulled at the corners of his eyes and Verna wished that she could loosen its hold. Mike was a good guy. A hard worker. He made sure everything and everyone in Home was safe and looked after, but now it was time for him to turn that same attention on the people who needed him the most.

Verna patted his shoulder and walked him to the front door. "My best to Kim and Lisa."

"Thank you." He put his wool ski hat on his bald head and stepped out into the chilly morning.

"Keep me posted," she called out after him as he hurried toward his car.

"I will."

Verna closed the outside door and locked it. She took a quick mental inventory as she walked to her office. Gail, the cook, should arrive any minute. Phyllis, the housemother, was already here and would go off duty at eight. Nichole and the rest of the staff would get in around nine.

She unlocked her office door and left it open, went straight to the cabinet and took out her laptop. The representative from the state would be here at eleven and she'd planned a short staff meeting at ten to go over any last-minute items and make sure they were all on the same page.

Just as she powered up her computer to review the staffing schedule her phone rang. Her stomach jumped. Phone calls at this time of the morning didn't bode well.

"Good morning. Someplace Like Home, Verna Scott speaking," she said, bracing herself.

"Oh…Ms.…Dr. Scott. I, uh, this is Ronald Morris. We met at the conference."

"Yes." She sat up straighter in the chair and gripped the phone a bit tighter. "How are you? Is something wrong?"

"No. Not at all. I'm an early riser. I knew if I didn't call now the day would get away from me again. I was expecting your voice mail."

The stiffness in her spine eased. She leaned back in her seat and laughed lightly. "Something else we have in common," she said, taking them back to their conversation in the parking lot. "Early risers."

"You're right."

"So…what can I do for you?"

"I know when we met I said I wanted to come for a visit. That's the reason for the call. I was wondering what day would be good."

"Today." She said it so quickly she surprised herself. "Later, of course," she qualified. "We have an inspection this morning and I'm sure you have to work." She was babbling for some unknown reason. *Zip it,* she warned herself.

"Today would be great. I get off at four. I could be there by, say, four-thirty. Would that work for you?"

"Perfect. You have the address?"

"Yep."

"So I'll see you at four-thirty."

"Looking forward to it."

She smiled. "Have a great day."

"You, too. And good luck with the inspection."

"Thanks."

Verna slowly hung up the phone, and for reasons she didn't dare examine, she realized that she felt incredibly good.

The day was packed with the staff meeting, schedule juggling, the two-hour inspection and then haggling with one of her vendors, yet Verna still found herself watching the clock and waiting for four-thirty.

As prepared as she was for Ronald's arrival, she felt nervous when one of the case managers came to her office to tell her that a Mr. Morris was waiting to see her in the family room.

"Thanks. I'll be right there."

Why was her heart racing and her thoughts suddenly fuzzy? She'd given hundreds of tours, and countless pitches extolling the virtues of Home. This was no different. She slipped on her suit jacket and went to meet Mr. Morris.

Ronald felt her presence before he saw her and turned toward the open door. She was prettier than he remembered, and he caught an instant of uncertainty in her light brown eyes and a hesitation in her step that surprised him in an oddly pleasant way. It showed a hint of vulnerability that wasn't present when they'd first met.

Her mint-green suit was professional yet feminine at the same time. The burst of color at her throat from the scarf she wore brought out the warmth of her skin.

"Mr. Morris." She extended her hand as she entered. "Thank you for coming."

"I try to keep my promises," he said, shaking her hand. "How did the inspection go?"

She smiled and he noticed a tiny dimple in her right cheek.

"Quite well. They're always looking under the beds for dust bunnies," she said, and he had a feeling she was only half joking. "But I run a tight ship. My staff knows what I expect and they know what to expect from me. We keep each other in check."

Ronald nodded as she spoke, listening and not

listening. He watched the way her full lips moved, the way her face became animated and her brows rose over her wide ebony-lashed eyes.

"So…we can get started, if you're ready."

"Uh, sure," he said, forcing himself to refocus.

"We'll start on the top floor and work our way down."

"How did you manage to get the neighborhood to agree to have the facility right in the middle of a residential block?" Ronald asked while they walked up the carpeted stairs. He admired the artwork that hung on the walls and recognized several pieces by John Biggers and Elizabeth Catlett.

"It wasn't easy at first. We met with the community board for months, as well as the block association. We had to smooth a lot of ruffled feathers. Too often residential facilities have totally disrupted a neighborhood. But we assured everyone involved about the type of program we were running and how we planned to maintain the integrity of the neighborhood. We also impressed upon them the importance of having a homelike environment for the kids. It took some time," she added, mounting the last flight of stairs. "But we got everyone on board and we haven't had any problems or complaints since we opened."

"I'm sure it's in large part due to the tight ship you run," he said.

She glanced over her shoulder and caught the playfulness in his eyes. "Thank you."

They reached the top floor.

"This is our residential floor. We have four bedrooms, two on either side of the hall, two bathrooms and a common space. They're mini apartments but they give our girls a sense of having something of their own."

Verna knocked on the door of 4A. Several moments later a young girl who looked to be about fifteen answered.

"Hi, Ms. Verna." She took a quick look at Ronald.

"April, this is Mr. Morris. He's a guidance counselor at Lexington High. I'm giving him the five-cent tour. Mind if we come in? You can show him around."

For a moment, Ronald felt as if he'd been hurled back in time. Maybe it was her eyes or the curve of her chin that reminded him of someone he'd known years ago. His heart inexplicably raced, but it was April's cheery voice that brought him back to reality. He blinked several times to clear his vision.

"Sure." The girl beamed and stood a little straighter. "Come in."

She stepped aside and Verna and Ronald walked in.

"This is our living room," April said.

The room was furnished with a small sofa and two matching chairs in a warm bronze color. Frilly white curtains hung at the windows, and a short wooden wall unit held a television and a compact stereo system.

"We spend a lot of time in here," April said, picking up a jacket from the couch and a discarded backpack from the floor. She draped it over her shoulder.

"Very nice. Who do you share the apartment with?" He couldn't stop staring at her, but he had to. He couldn't have her thinking the wrong thing about him.

"Carmen Long. She's pretty cool." She grinned at Verna.

"They've come a long way," Verna said. Her right brow rose in emphasis, causing April to blush.

"Yes, ma'am, we sure did." The teenager drew in a quick breath and pointed out the efficiency kitchen that opened onto the living room. Then she took them to her bedroom, which for a fifteen-year-old was amazingly neat.

"Looks like you ladies take good care of your apartment," he said, making conversation.

"We try. We like having something to call our own, ya know?"

"I totally understand."

"Carol and Yvonne have the other two bedrooms," Verna said. "The setup is similar on the other side of the hall. Thanks for the tour, April." Verna headed toward the door. "How was school today?" she asked over her shoulder.

"Pretty good. I aced my Spanish test."

Verna turned to look at her. "Congratulations. Excellent! I told you you could do it." She placed a gentle hand on the girl's shoulder. "You can accomplish anything you put your mind to. *You* determine your life path, not the other way around."

April shifted from one foot to the other. "Yes, Ms. Verna."

"Okay...so I will see you later. Keep up the good work."

"Good to meet you, April," Ronald said.

"You, too."

"Nice girl," he commented as they descended the stairs, still trying to shake off the shock of meeting April and the memories that seeing her stirred within him.

"She's been here about six months. When we got her she was beyond angry. She'd been through at least a dozen foster homes, a couple of group homes, kicked out of school. No family."

"Hmm. You'd never know it," he said, his tone thoughtful.

"We work hard at changing lives. April…so far…is one of our success stories."

They stopped on the third floor. "This is our library," she said, opening a sliding door. "Small but functional."

Books were broken down by subject and lined the walls on built-in shelves. There was a small couch, several chairs with tables in front and three computer workstations. A woven rug in brilliant colors of red, bright green and golds took up the entire center of the room. Two teenage boys sat at the computers.

"Alex and Shawn, this is Mr. Morris."

They turned from the computer screens and scrambled to their feet. To Ronald's surprise they approached him and extended their hands.

"Alex Cortez."

"Shawn Daniels."

"Pleasure to meet you both. What are you working on?" He nodded toward the computers.

"Homework," Alex said.

"Facebook," Shawn admitted with a sheepish grin.

"Homework all done, Shawn?" Verna asked.

"Yes, ma'am."

"You guys need a ride home this evening?"

They both nodded. "I'll get someone to drive you." She looked at her watch. "Be ready by six."

She turned back toward the door.

"That library looks pretty well stocked. Better than ours."

"We get a lot of donations for the library. The staff purchases books and I have it built into a budget. We're on an honor system. If any of the kids take a book out of the room, they sign for it on the sheet and check it off when they bring it back."

"What about the computers?"

"The computers were donated from the Gates Foundation and from Apple. So we have Macs and PCs throughout the building."

"Amazing," he said in admiration. "We need you to come and revamp our school."

Verna chuckled. "Believe me, it's a team effort. And a lot of favors."

She took him to the rec room, where he met more of the kids, then to the kitchen and common dining area and the offices.

The last stop was the backyard, which boasted a small vegetable garden waiting to be tilled.

"All the kids help with the planting and gardening. It's not only cost effective for us to grow our own vegetables, but it's incredibly therapeutic for the kids. There's something about working with the earth, planting and watching a tiny seed bud into something beautiful."

Ronald watched the rapturous expression on her face, felt her passion for what she did and heard the pride that lifted her voice.

"Like the kids," he said softly.

She focused on him and a slow smile moved across her mouth. "Yeah…" She nodded. "Like the kids. All anyone needs is someone to care."

Their gazes connected and a quiet understanding passed between them.

"Well…" Verna said on a breath. "That's the tour. We can go back to my office."

"Sure." He followed her inside, totally impressed with Someplace Like Home. And more impressed with Verna Scott.

CHAPTER
~ THREE ~

Verna opened the door to her office and they went inside. "So what do you think?" she asked, offering him a seat.

"You have a wonderful facility. The brochures don't do it justice." He sat down. "How can I help?"

Verna grinned. "I was hoping you would say that. Right now, as I mentioned at the conference, we could really use volunteers who are willing to basically serve as mentors to the kids. Come in a day or so a week, talk with them, maybe take them out sometimes. And your skills as a counselor would certainly help."

"Not a problem. My schedule is pretty tight during the week, but I can come in on weekends."

"That would be fine. I have to warn you, though, the house is pretty hectic on the weekends." She chuckled.

"Trust me, I'm used to hectic."

She pressed her hand to her forehead. "Where are my manners? Can I offer you something to drink or eat? Gail is fixing dinner."

"I don't want to impose. But some juice or water would be fine."

She popped up from her seat. "I'll be right back."

Ronald watched her leave and realized how good he felt. He glanced around the room and it screamed Verna Scott—classy, cozy and inviting. He got up and wandered over to the book-lined wall.

The volumes were mostly texts and reference books on child psychology, but a few novels were tucked on the shelves. He pulled one out. It was an autographed copy of *Glorious* by Bernice L. McFadden. He flipped it over and read the back. Then reached for another. *Uptown* by Donna Grant and Virginia Deberry, plus works by Baldwin, Morrison, Ann Petry, Gabriel García Márquez, Ru Freeman, as well as several autobiographies. Her literary tastes seemed to span the gamut. He was just returning a copy of Obama's memoir to the shelf when Verna came back into the room.

"Sorry." He jerked his head toward the shelves. "I'm a sucker for books. My biggest vice."

"Really?" she asked, wide-eyed. "Me, too. I love to read. Ever since I was a child." At the mention of her childhood, a shadow crossed her features. She tugged in a breath, walked over and set two glasses of juice on the table. "Hope you like mango. It's a house favorite." Her eyes looked everywhere but at him.

"It's fine." He studied her for a moment, sensing a change in her as if she'd been pulled in a different direction. "Everything okay?"

Her gaze jerked toward him. "Yes." She reached for her glass and took a swallow. "So, which weekend do you think you want to start?" she asked, getting back on solid ground.

"This coming weekend works for me. What time do you need me to be here?"

"How's noon?"

"Not a problem." He finished off his juice and returned the glass to the table. "I guess I better get going."

"I should, too."

"Do you live nearby?"

"About fifteen minutes away."

"Don't tell me you live in Bedford-Stuyvesant."

She angled her head. "And if I did," she hedged.

"Then we'd have one more thing in common."

She laughed out loud. "You're kidding."

"Nope. I live on Decatur and Patchen."

"And I'm on Macon and Tompkins."

"Neighbors," they said in unison.

"I'm surprised we haven't run into each other before now," Ronald said.

"This small world is still a big place. How long have you lived in the area?"

"Pretty much all my life," he told her. "I grew up in Bushwick. And moved to Bed-Stuy as a teen." Where he'd met Patrice and his life changed, he thought. " I left and moved to D.C. for college. Thought about staying there permanently. Got a job in counseling down there for about six years, but I missed home. Came back about five years ago and I've been here ever since."

Verna reached for her coat on the rack and Ronald hurried to her side to help her put it on.

Her pulse skipped. She could feel the warmth of his breath on her neck. For an instant she shut her eyes and enjoyed the moment.

"Hey, why don't we grab a bite of dinner away from work."

She turned and she was practically in his arms. "Dinner? Now?"

"Yes and yes. We could talk. You could tell me about some of the kids."

"I…okay. Sure. Why not."

"I know just the place." He extended his arm toward the door. "After you."

Verna totally forgot about doing her end of shift rounds or anything that had to do with work. All she could think about was the feel of Ronald's arm brushing against hers, the inviting scent of him and the way he looked at her. It might be all in her head. She could be imagining more than what was actually happening. But for now she was going to enjoy her little fantasy.

They stepped out into the twilight. Verna stopped.

"Did you drive?"

"Yes. You?"

"So did I. Where did you have in mind? I'll meet you."

"Night of the Cookers on Fulton."

Her expression brightened. "The seared-salmon salad is to die for."

"I take it you like the place," he teased.

She scrunched up her face. "Kinda."

"Come on—let's go."

"How many?" the hostess asked when they stepped in.

"Two," Ronald said.

"Right this way."

They followed her past the bar, which was filled for a Tuesday night. The tables at the front of the restaurant were taken as well. They turned the corner and the hostess seated them at a private table in the back, where a live jazz quartet was playing.

"This is a treat," Verna said, as Ronald helped her out of her coat and into her seat.

"Not a lot of people know that they have live music on Tuesdays. It's become a favorite haunt of mine."

"You eat out a lot?" she asked, but really wanted to know if he went alone or with someone.

"Probably more than I should. But when you live by yourself, it's just nice to get out, especially after a long day at work."

"Oh." She swallowed and focused on the band.

"What about you?"

She looked at him then glanced away. "I don't get out much." She shrugged her right shoulder. "Work... the house."

The waitress stopped at their table. "What can I get you?" she asked. "Something to drink?"

"I'll have an iced tea," Verna said.

"Make that two."

"Do you want to order now, or do you need more time?"

Ronald looked at Verna.

"I'll have the seared-salmon salad with tahini dressing."

"Make that two."

The waitress picked up the menus from the table. "I'll be right back with your drinks."

"That was easy," Ronald said with a grin.

Verna tilted her head to the side. "It was, wasn't it." She looked at him and wondered why she felt so incredibly comfortable around Ronald. It was as if she'd always known him.

"This is going to sound crazy, but I feel like…I've known you a long time." Ronald's brows drew closer together as if he was having a hard time believing what he'd just said. He smiled. "Crazy, right?"

"What's crazy," she said softly, "is that I was thinking the exact same thing."

He leaned forward. "You're kidding."

"Nope." Her laughter was soft and warm.

"Wow." He shook his head in amusement. "We seem to be racking up the things we have in common."

Verna shifted in her seat and looked away.

The waitress returned with their iced tea. "Your meals will be out momentarily."

"So, we're supposed to be talking about the kids," Ronald said, seeing the veil come down over Verna's eyes. He needed to back off. This was the second time he'd seen that trapped-rabbit look come over her. And both times it was after he touched on something personal. This was business, he reminded himself, and it was presumptuous of him to think otherwise.

CHAPTER
❧ FOUR ❧

"Thanks for suggesting dinner," Verna said. They stood in front of her building. "I can't remember the last time I was out on a weeknight. You really didn't have to follow me home."

"No worries. It was my pleasure. I enjoyed myself tonight."

She glanced away from him. "Well…I better get inside. Another long day tomorrow."

"Me, too."

They faced each other, and Verna was sure Ronald felt as awkward as she did.

"I'll see you this weekend?" he asked.

"Sure." She didn't work weekends, but if it meant seeing him, she'd make the sacrifice.

"Great. Well, good night."

"Night."

Ronald turned away and walked to his car.

Verna went up the steps to her front door. When she got to the top she glanced over her shoulder and saw Ronald looking up at her. Her heart thumped. He waved again and got in his Honda. She stuck her key in the door and for a moment she wished she'd asked him to come in for coffee…or tea or something.

The Honda peeled away from the curb, and the moment and Ronald were definitely gone.

"Morning," Nichole said, sidling up to Verna in the kitchen. She reached for her mug, dropped in a tea bag and poured in the hot water.

"Hey, how are you?"

"Now that we have the inspection behind us, I'm great." She leaned her narrow hip against the counter and peered at Verna. "You okay? You seem kind of… distracted."

Verna turned halfway toward Nichole. "Um, remember when I told you that I met someone at the conference who seemed interested in volunteering?"

Nichole nodded.

"Well, he came by yesterday. You were already gone."

"And?" Nichole took a sip of tea.

"We, uh, went to dinner last night."

Nichole's brows shot up and she grinned in delight. "Get out! Is he cute?"

"Very." Verna bit back a smile and couldn't meet her friend's steady gaze.

"Well, don't leave me in suspense. What happened?"

"Let's talk in my office," she said, looking around as sounds of the building coming to life filtered into the kitchen.

Nichole hooked her arm through Verna's and headed down the hall to her office.

"Tell, tell," Nichole said, settling down in a chair.

"Not much to tell. He wants to volunteer. Really nice guy." She fidgeted with her mug.

Nichole waited, but Verna didn't offer any more information. "I know you didn't bring me in here to tell me he's a nice guy."

Verna felt uncomfortable. "It's just…strange."

"Strange how? What does that mean?"

"From the time we met there was this…connection." She suddenly found it difficult to express herself.

"Why don't you tell me what it means to you," Nichole gently coaxed.

They'd known each other for years, Verna thought, but this was about as close as she had ever come to revealing anything really personal about herself.

She glanced toward the window. "What it is, is ridiculous. I mean, I don't know the man. Not really. He's great to look at, he's funny, intelligent, loves his job."

"Doesn't sound bad so far."

"I know," Verna said, her voice strained. "It's been a while since…well…since I've been involved with anyone." Even to her own ears, Verna sounded as if she was exaggerating the whole thing. She sat up straighter. "I'm being silly and totally getting ahead of myself. It was just dinner. Two colleagues."

Nichole leaned forward and covered Verna's hand.

"Sweetie, it's really okay to be attracted to a man. It proves you're human and not superhuman."

That made Verna laugh and the tightness in her stomach slowly eased.

"So tell me about him?"

Verna smiled. She told Nichole about meeting Ronald at the conference and how it had felt to see him again.

Her friend shrugged. "I don't see the problem. You're both adults. Take your time and see how it goes. From what you've told me it sounds like he's just as interested in you as you are in him. He's here on the weekend and you don't work weekends. If it's something worth pursuing, you'll both have to make an effort."

"True," Verna said. "The main thing is that we have a new volunteer. Heaven knows, we could use the help."

Verna had been mentally castigating herself for her babbling confession. That was so out of character. She'd always made it a point to keep her personal life away from the job. Not that she had much of a personal life. But she wasn't one to share her feelings, her hopes and fears with someone else. Her life had been filled with people who didn't stay. By the time she was ten she knew she could never depend on anyone to be there. She could not share her secrets or talk about her future because that would mean getting close to someone. Getting close always brought hurt. By the time she was twelve she'd grown tired of being hurt one time too many. So she had to find a way to protect herself. And she did. She stopped opening herself up to anyone. It was safer that way.

* * *

Ronald went to work the day after his dinner with
Verna feeling oddly renewed. Inspired. No challenge
was too big. He could handle whatever was thrown at
him. He slid into his seat behind his cluttered desk and
the simple organization of Verna's work space came to
mind. He glanced around at the stacks of folders. His
habit was to review folders, make notes and set them
on a pile on the desk. That stack had overflowed to the
chair, which he always had to clear if a student or teacher
dropped in. But that was going to change as of today.

He began sorting and organizing and two hours later
his office looked as if it belonged to someone else. He
laughed out loud at the transformation. He'd even found
the pocket calculator that he'd lost.

A knock on the door drew his attention.

"Hey, Cara."

"Wow." The assistant principal put her hands on her
hips and looked wide eyed at Ronald. "Did you hire a
cleaning service or what?" she teased.

"Very funny. And the answer is no."

"You do have a chair!" She crossed the small room
and sat down, bracing her arm on the clutter-free
desk.

"You're full of jokes today, I see."

"What brought all this on? Who are we going to tease
in staff meetings now?" She ran the tip of her manicured
finger across the desktop and it came away dust free.

"You're going to have to find someone else to pick on.
And to answer your first question, I…guess you could
say I had an epiphany."

"Really?" She looked skeptical. "Board of Health?"

"No."

"Department of Education sanction?"

"No."

"Mary, the cleaning lady? She threatened you, didn't she?" Cara said, leaning forward to press her point.

Ronald tossed his head back and laughed from deep in his gut. "No. None of the above. And I'm wounded you would think I needed threats or professional intervention."

"Okay, okay, I give up. Who is she? Because only a woman has the power to change a man."

Ronald couldn't help grinning.

"It is a woman!" She pointed a finger at him in triumph. "Well, it's about time. Who is she? Come on, tell me," she demanded, not giving him a chance to respond. Her voice rose to a hoarse whisper. "Is it someone from here?"

"Cara…" He got up and went to the file cabinet, leaning against it. "Must you know everything about my life?"

"Yes," she said with all seriousness. "That's what nosy best friends are for."

He chuckled and shook his head. He and Cara had met in grad school while they were both studying education and counseling. They became fast friends. Their classmates used to call them the odd couple. Cara was barely over five feet and Ronald topped six. They were always arguing over some point the professors made, but they were inseparable. And it was pure chance that they wound up at the same school, Ronald as a guidance counselor and Cara as an assistant principal.

"If you must know…yes, it is a woman."

"I knew it!"

"We met at that conference I went to a couple of weeks ago. She was the presenter."

She snapped her fingers, trying to conjure up the name. "Um, Scott. Dr. Scott. She runs that facility in Bedford-Stuyvesant for troubled teens."

"Right. Someplace Like Home."

Cara crossed her legs and settled back to listen.

Ronald talked about her inspiring presentation and their meeting afterward and how uncanny it was that they simply seemed to hit it off. "Like a vibe. Know what I mean?" he said even as he struggled to make sense of it himself.

"I know exactly what you mean. I married my vibe, remember. So then what happened?"

"I went to take a tour of the place and…well, I was hooked. It's phenomenal."

"And apparently so is she."

"It's something I can't put into words." He crossed the room and sat down. "To make a long story short, I volunteered to work at Home on the weekends."

Cara looked at him for a moment. "Now, is that because you're really passionate about the program or because it will give you a chance to see more of Dr. Scott?"

He exhaled slowly. "To be honest…a little of both."

"Wow. She must be special."

"I think so. But I really am looking forward to the

work. I met some of the kids, saw what goes on there, and it's something that I want to be a part of."

Cara leaned forward and placed her hand on his arm. "If there's one thing that I've always admired about you, Ron, it's your passion for helping kids. They're lucky to have you."

He grinned. "Thanks."

Cara pushed up from her seat. "Be careful you don't overdo it. We still need you here at one hundred percent."

"I know. I figure a couple of weekends a month. Just to help out."

"Hmm." Her murmur echoed the skepticism in her eyes. "We'll see how long that lasts."

She turned to leave, glancing back at him, then around at his transformed space. "Amazing," she murmured on her way out.

CHAPTER
❧— FIVE —❧

"What are your plans for the weekend? I'm having some friends over for an all-girls brunch tomorrow," Nichole said as they finished up for the day.

"Actually, I was going to come in tomorrow."

Nichole looked at her curiously. Verna never worked weekends, so this would only reinforce her friend's belief that this guy must be something special.

Verna ignored the real question in her eyes. "Ronald Morris is coming in tomorrow. It's his first day. I thought I should be here."

"Isn't Brad on duty tomorrow?"

She shoved a folder into her soft brown leather brief-case. "Yes, but I thought it was only right that I be here, too." She zipped the bag closed.

"Sure that's the only reason?"

"What other reason could there be?" Verna asked, trying to sound innocent.

"The fact that you want to see him again, for one."

"Oh, no," she insisted. "It's nothing like that."

"Sure it is. And it's fine. Just take your time, feel him out, see how it goes."

Verna exhaled slowly. "I feel like a kid," she suddenly admitted, her words laced with bewilderment. "I'm anxious one minute. Determined not to let it matter the next. Honestly, I can't wait for Saturday to get here just to see if all this stuff that's going on in my head is for real or something I imagined."

"All I have to say is, you're long overdue. And if it's meant to be something more than a congenial working relationship, then that's what will happen. Be yourself."

"Hmm, myself, that's what scares me." She took her coat from the rack and put it on. "Actually, it would be great if you were here tomorrow. Then I won't seem so obviously desperate to see him again."

"You may be a lot of things, Verna, but 'obviously desperate' isn't one of them." Nichole turned off the light and followed Verna out of the office.

"That's what it feels like," Verna admitted as they stepped outside.

"Why?"

"I don't know. It's all so random and sudden. Took me by surprise, I guess."

Nichole patted her shoulder. "That's the best kind," she said. "Just go with the flow." She walked to the curb. "What time is he coming?"

"Noon."

"I'll come in before the brunch. I'll be here at eleven-thirty...like I am every Saturday." She winked.

Verna smiled. "Thanks. I'll see you tomorrow."

Ronald circled the block about three times before he finally found a parking space. It would look pretty bad to show up late on his first day, he thought as he locked the car door behind him and started walking back toward the house.

He'd always loved this part of Brooklyn. There was a richness to its historic architecture, and the area had a culture and a rhythm all its own. Over the years the neighboring streets had been populated by Italians, Jews, African- and Caribbean-Americans. Many of the original groups had moved away, come back and been joined by Asians, Hispanics and Arabs, all building their own communities as part of the whole. Walking through the streets of Brooklyn was like taking a trip through a history book. And now with sky-high prices in Manhattan, young professionals were crossing the Hudson and making their own eclectic contributions to the mix. Boutiques and outdoor cafés were springing up, and the place had a vibrant energy.

This was how the world was supposed to be, he thought as he watched a group of teenagers of different ethnicities hanging out together, laughing at each other's jokes and simply being kids. Or the interracial couples that sat in the park with their children.

He smiled and turned onto the street where Home

stood. That was the way it *should* be. He opened the waist-high gate and walked up to the door to ring the bell.

Moments later a young man with curly blond hair and the bluest eyes he'd ever seen came to the door.

"Yes, may I help you?"

"Ronald Morris. I'm volunteering. Just starting today."

A light smile tugged at his mustached mouth. "Right. Dr. Scott said you'd be coming." He pulled the door wider. "She's in her office."

He locked the door behind Ronald. "I'm Paul. I work security, evenings and weekends mostly." He went behind the desk that was situated in the foyer and handed Ronald a clipboard. "If you could just sign in for me—and I'll need to see a copy of your driver's license."

"Sure." He wrote his name then dug his license out of his wallet.

Paul took a cursory glance and handed it back. "I'll let Dr. Scott know that you're here. You can wait in the family room if you want. Next door on the right."

"Thanks." He walked down the hall to the room, listening to the sounds of activity in the house—raucous laughter and shouts and the thump of footsteps coming down the stairs. The aroma of something decadently delicious floated under his nose, reminding him that he hadn't eaten.

Silly, because he always ate breakfast, yet for reasons that he couldn't wrap his head around, he hadn't been hungry earlier.

"Good morning!"

He turned to the door and saw Verna. A sensation of warmth radiated outward to his limbs, just the way it did when sitting in front of a fireplace after coming in from the cold.

They walked toward each other. Ronald extended his hand. "Good to see you. Had a tough time finding parking. Sorry I'm a little late."

Verna waved off his explanation with her free hand. "Don't worry about it. We're simply glad you're here. Come, let's get you settled. There are some people I need you to meet. The weekend staff who you'll be working with. Brad Lewis is our senior counselor."

"Lead the way."

They walked down the hall and turned into a room that had been converted into an office. Verna tapped on the door. "Brad." She poked her head in.

The counselor stood and came out from behind his desk, a smile and a hand outstretched to welcome Ronald.

"Brad Lewis, this is Ronald Morris."

Brad heartily shook Ronald's hand with both of his. "Good to meet you. Verna tried to bring me up to speed on your background and everything, but we'll talk." He swiped his glasses from the bridge of his wide nose and rested them on the top of his head, grinning. "I could sure use the help on the weekends. That's when all the kids are usually here."

Brad Lewis was in his early forties, Ronald guessed. There was a quiet maturity about his presence even before he spoke, and a youthfulness in his eyes.

"Not a problem. I'm here to help."

"Cool. Well, welcome. When you're ready we can sit down and go over some of the charts, I'll introduce you to the kids and we'll take it from there."

"Sounds like a plan," Ronald said.

"I'm going to take Ronald around to meet the rest of the weekend crew and then I'll turn him back over to you," Verna said.

"I'll be here. Speaking of which, I'm surprised to see you, Doc. Didn't know you did Saturdays."

Verna hoped Ronald didn't notice the mortified look on her face. "Um, just for today. I wanted to, uh, make sure that Mr. Morris got settled." How silly did that sound? Her face was on fire.

Brad's thick brows drew together for a moment. "Oh, sure. Of course." His eyes darted from Verna to Ronald.

Verna walked out, for a moment wishing that she could keep going.

"I get the sense that you don't work weekends," Ronald said.

She turned to look at him for a moment as they headed down the hall to her office. "I generally don't. I didn't think it would be right for me not to be here on your first day."

"I appreciate that."

Verna's heart thumped in response to the low throb of his voice. He seemed to be saying so much more than the words themselves. She opened her office door. Nichole was seated in one of the club chairs reading a magazine. She plopped it down on the table and stood.

"You must be Ronald Morris."

He crossed the room to shake her hand.

"Ronald, this is Nichole Graham. We worked at the Agency for Children's Services together and she helped me open this place."

Nichole grinned. She tucked a stray strand of blond hair behind her ear. "Trust me, Verna gets all the credit for this place. I was on the sidelines, wondering how she was going to pull it off."

Verna chuckled. "Don't mind her. She totally under-estimates herself, which of course she accuses me of doing. Nichole is more than the assistant director, and the bottom line is I couldn't function without her."

They shared a glance of mutual admiration and respect.

"I bet you say that to all the staff," Nichole joked.

"Yeah, I do, don't I?" She turned to Ronald. "But seriously, we're all one family here. You'll see that as time goes on."

"Absolutely," agreed Nichole. "That's why it works. Every adult is a surrogate parent to these kids. And we all work really hard at making them feel cared about, and safe, and so they know that no matter what happens, they can come here and we're going to find a way to work out the problem."

"I'm going to finish introductions," Verna said, uneasy at the gleeful speculation in her colleague's eyes. "I'll catch up with you later." Ronald followed her out.

Verna introduced him to Phyllis, the housemother, before she darted out for the day, and Gail, who did all the cooking, then formally introduced him to Paul.

"I'm going to turn you back over to Brad," she said once they'd completed the rounds. "He'll have some forms for you to fill out and then take you to meet the kids. Today is actually a great day for you to start. We do group on Saturday."

Ronald nodded and followed her down the hall.

"What's on your agenda for the day?" he asked.

"Nichole is having an all-girls brunch at her house and she convinced me to come."

"Sounds like fun—for girls that is." He chuckled. "What do you normally do on a Saturday night?"

"Catch up on notes, read, watch old movies."

They stopped in front of Brad's door.

"What are you doing later this evening, after brunch?"

If she'd been walking, she would have tripped on air. She blinked several times. "Um, this evening?"

"Yes, about eight?"

"Nothing special. Why?"

"I thought you might like to grab a little dinner, hear about my first day and listen to some music."

"Wow…well, sure. Sounds wonderful. Yes."

"Good. I think I remember the street, but I don't have your address." He pulled out his BlackBerry and added her information.

When he looked back at her with those bedroom eyes, Verna had an overwhelming desire to kiss him. It took her by such surprise that she stepped backward, breaking the spell between them.

It was as if they'd both been awakened from a trance, and had to adjust to reality once again.

"I'll see you at eight," Ronald said, regaining his balance.

Verna nodded. "Eight. Right. Have a great day, and thank you again." She turned away and hurried down the hall to her office before she did or said something utterly silly. When she stepped inside, Nichole greeted her with a great big grin.

"Okay, I totally see why your head is all scrambled. He is a cutie-pie, and nice and sexy. Wow. Jackpot!"

"He asked me out to dinner tonight," she said, sounding a bit breathless.

Nichole leaped up from her seat and rushed over to grab Verna's shoulders. "You did say yes, didn't you?"

Verna grinned. "Yes."

Nichole let out an exaggerated "Amen" and hooked her arm through Verna's. "I think we'll have champagne spritzers to celebrate at brunch."

Ronald sat in on the group session as an observer, watching the kids, seeing how they interacted with each other and how Brad responded. It was a good group. The kids were funny, sad, needy and brutally honest. They were all in, or had been in, foster care. Two of the girls were graduating and going to community college; three of the boys were in group homes and had been coming to Home since it opened. Home had an agreement with several local group homes and foster-care agencies that allowed the kids to spend time here and participate in activities. It had taken a lot of negotiation and legal hurdles, but Verna had made it happen.

Brad knew how to handle each of them, knew how much rope to give them and when to reel them back in. Ronald could tell that the teenagers not only liked Brad, but respected him.

"Before we break," Brad said, "I want to give Mr. Morris a chance to give you guys his impressions of the group."

All eyes turned in his direction, expecting something, and in his entire professional life he'd never felt so unprepared to be professional.

He drew in a breath and leaned forward.

"First, I want to say that I am totally impressed with each of you." His steady gaze moved from one to the next. "We all, including me, have baggage, a past, things that mess with us. I want to learn from you and I hope to be an ear and a guide when you need one." He cleared his throat. "I play a mean game of basketball, Jay-Z is one of my favorite rappers." That comment got him a few smiles and nods. "And I can take on the best of you at Nintendo." They chuckled.

"I grew up not too far from here, so I know that your environment doesn't define you," he continued, getting serious again. "So wherever you decide to go with your life is up to you. I graduated from Howard University and I firmly believe that education is the ticket to tomorrow. And I'm here to help anyone who wants to go to college." He slapped his knees together. "I guess that's it for now."

"Thanks," Brad said. He checked his watch. "That's all for today, crew. See you next Saturday."

They began filing out. Two of the boys stopped in front of him. "So what position do you play?" the taller of the two asked.

Ronald got up. "Power forward. You?"

"Guard."

He stuck out his hand. "What's your name?"

"Mark."

"Nice to meet you." He turned to the other young man. "And your name?"

"Felix."

Ronald nodded. "Maybe we can get together on the court one weekend."

"Yeah, maybe," Mark said. "Come on, man," he said to Felix, and they sauntered out.

"Hey, Mr. Morris."

"April. Good to see you again." That feeling of familiarity flowed through him again.

She beamed him a smile. "I'm thinking about college."

"Good. What grade are you in?"

"Sophomore."

"Now is the time to start figuring out where you want to go."

"Yeah." She lowered her head. "Just thinking about it. I know I'm not gonna be able to do it."

"Why not?"

"I gotta go." She brushed by him and walked out.

He was going to stop her just as Brad approached. "So what do you think?"

Ronald turned to Brad. "Great group of kids," he said, wanting to go after April and find out what she meant. He picked up his jacket from the back of the chair.

"Yeah, they just have to believe in themselves. But it's hard since no one else has for most of their lives. They think their future lies in the few square blocks where they live. It takes a lot of time to unravel what has been done to them." He drew in a breath. "But we make progress every day." He clapped Ronald on the back. "Didn't scare you off, did we?" he joked.

"Naw. I'm up for the challenge." They walked out of the session room. "Listen, do you do field trips with them?" he asked Brad as an idea came to him.

"Depends on how far. But we take them out. Sure. What are you thinking about?"

"I just remembered there's a college fair next Saturday at the Institute of Technology downtown. You think they might be interested?"

"Sure," Brad said. "I'll run it by Verna and get the names together during the week."

"Great," Ronald said. "I'll pull all the details together and give you a call on Monday when I get into the office."

They walked to the front door. "Glad to have you, man," Brad told him. "Seriously."

"Thanks. I'm looking forward to getting to know the kids."

Brad opened the front door. "Talk to you on Monday." They shook hands. "Will do."

* * *

On his drive home Ronald ran through the events of the day and felt really good about how things had turned out. The kids were an interesting mix and he was eager to get to know them better. They would certainly prove a bigger challenge than his kids at Lexington, but he was looking forward to it.

He smiled to himself. Verna Scott ran an amazing program, and he was just as eager to get to know her better.

CHAPTER
∽— SIX —∽

Verna was a nervous wreck as eight o'clock approached. She'd changed her outfit three different times, and not knowing where they were going didn't help. Finally she'd settled on a sleeveless, multicolored top with splashes of purple, gold and soft green that flowed from her shoulders into an A and swung around her hips. The slender slacks matched the gold in her top, and low-heeled nut-brown sling backs finished off her ensemble. She added chunky wooden bracelets and wore small gold hoops in her ears. As she stared at herself in the mirror she was pleased with the final result. It had been a while since she'd gotten dressed up and it felt good.

Not one to use much makeup, she went with the basics, a little mascara to lengthen her lashes and a light lip gloss with a tint of cinnamon. She'd brushed her short hair until it gleamed, and with nothing left to do, she paced and checked the time and paced some more. As much as she thought she was prepared for Ronald's arrival, she nearly leaped out of her brand-new shoes when the doorbell rang.

She checked herself one last time in the mirror and revisited Nichole's advice at brunch. "Just relax and let it flow." With a steadying breath, she went to open the door.

For an instant Ronald seemed at a loss for words.

"You look...fantastic," he stammered, as if he'd met his favorite celebrity.

Verna's heart was pounding so hard and fast that she felt light-headed. She ran shaky fingers through her hair. "Thank you...so do you."

He wore a full-length black cashmere coat over black slacks and a gray shirt that was open at the collar, casual but classy. His smooth brown complexion seemed lit from underneath and his dark eyes sparkled in the light.

Verna shook her head to get the neurons moving. "Please come in a minute." She stepped aside and let him pass. The heady, manly scent of him went straight to her head. Get it together, girl, she warned herself. She shut the door and followed him down the short foyer that opened onto the living room.

"I just need to get my coat and purse. Would you like something to drink?"

"No. I'm fine, thanks." He looked around. "Wow, nice place. You have great taste," he said, taking in the vaulted ceiling and bay windows draped in sheer bronze. The taupe-colored walls were dotted with art, and one contained built-in shelving filled from top to bottom with books and videos. The hardwood floors gleamed, the two glass tables held a vase of fresh flowers on one and magazines on the other, and an overstuffed chocolate-brown sectional looked plush and comfortable enough to spend a night on. The opposite wall contained a mounted plasma television. He turned to her. "It's totally you," he said with a smile.

"Totally me?"

"Yes, well put together, classy, elegant and inviting."

Her stomach did a three-sixty. "Thank you."

"You obviously put your heart into this place. I was looking at your library. Impressive. A lot of first editions."

Verna's expression radiated pride. "It's one of my passions," she admitted. "I haunt bookstores and flea markets."

"I thought I had an extensive collection, but yours puts mine to shame."

"There's more in the attic *and* the basement."

Ronald laughed. "Yes, you definitely have me beat."

The way he looked at her, Verna once again had the overwhelming desire to reach up and kiss him.

"I'll, uh, get my coat." She went to the hall closet, Ronald at her side.

"Here, let me." He took the coat and helped her, taking longer than he needed to.

Verna grew so hot she was sure she would combust, and it had nothing to do with the wool coat. She needed some air.

Finally they went out to the car, but sitting so close to him in the confined space only made her hotter.

"Mind if I open the window a little bit?" she asked.

"Sure. It is warm. Can't tell what to wear with this weather. One day it's spring, the next it's winter," he said, almost babbling.

"So tell me, how was your first day?" she asked, getting them both on solid territory.

He recounted his day, his meeting with the kids, and then told her about his idea for the college fair.

"That's a great idea." She angled herself in her seat and took in his solid profile. "I'll make sure they get permission slips."

He told her about his brief conversation with April, which sparked the idea. "I got the impression that she doesn't see college in her future."

"Unfortunately, most of the kids don't. April has had it rough. Living at Home is the first taste of stability in her life. I think going to the fair is just what she needs. They all need to see that there is possibility out there and that they are worthy. That's our biggest hurdle, getting them to believe that they have value."

Ronald snatched a glance at her, stirred by the rising passion in her voice. Her features were tight and pinched as if she was in pain. She was staring straight ahead, but he was pretty sure she wasn't looking at the Saturday-night traffic.

"Ever been to Frank's Lounge?" he asked, drawing her back from wherever she had been.

"No. But I'm sure I've passed it a million times. Is that where we're headed?"

"Yep, and I think you'll be in for a treat. It's truly one of the gems of Fort Greene."

"I'm going to hold you to that."

"You're on," he said and stole a look at her.

Ronald slowed the car and began searching for a parking space. Couples were filing in and the sounds of live jazz floated out of the door every time it opened. He found a spot around the corner and they walked back to the club. Ronald pulled open the door and Verna stepped inside.

Frank's Lounge oozed class with a relaxed feel. The customers were a mix of couples and singles, both young and old. Beneath the low lighting were round tables covered in red linen, booths for larger groups and a horseshoe-shaped bar already packed with patrons. Tap-your-foot music was coming from the small stage closer to the back.

A young hostess greeted them. "Seating, or would you prefer the bar?"

"Table. Anything close to the stage?" Ronald asked.

"On the side. Is that okay?"

"Fine."

She took two menus and led them around the tables to the back of the lounge. Before long they were totally wrapped up in the music, the atmosphere and each other.

Over white wine, grilled shrimp, saffron rice, tossed salad and soothing music, they did something that they both said they hadn't done with anyone in a very long time—talk about themselves and their private lives.

"Your first love," Verna said with a teasing smile.

Ronald blushed. He lifted his drink. "Patrice Holloway." He shook his head and smiled wistfully. "Patrice and I were together our last two years of high school. Inseparable. I was going to marry her. She refused. She told me she didn't want me to hate her later for ruining my life and tying me down." He lifted his wineglass and took a sip. "I always thought that was a crazy statement, but she wouldn't change her mind. So I went to Howard University on a full scholarship. She stayed in New York with her grandmother. Her mother checked out on her when she was a kid. I promised to come back as often as I could, but I didn't. I got involved in school and…" His voice drifted off. "We wrote each other the first couple of months and then her letters stopped. She didn't return any of my calls and then the number was disconnected. I came home for holiday break and went to see her, but they were gone." The memory brought back a familiar feeling of loss. "Someone else was living in their apartment. I talked to everyone and no one could tell me anything. Just gone."

"Did any of your friends know where she was?"

"Let's say we didn't travel in the same circles. We attended different schools, had different friends, lived in different neighborhoods. I met her in the supermarket." He chuckled. "I always wondered what happened to her."

Verna seemed uncertain of what to say. "Ronald... I..."

He held up his hand. "It's okay. It's been a lot of years." He picked up his drink then put it back down. "I guess that's why I got so involved with kids. Patrice had a tough life. No mother. Her grandmother wasn't in the best of health, from what I can remember. They were pretty poor. I guess in some way I want to do for other kids what I couldn't do for Patrice. Give them a chance." He looked away. "There's a part of me that hopes I'm going to find her somewhere. There are days that I see her in the face of every young woman I meet. I just hope that she's happy wherever she is."

They were silent for a while.

"I can't believe I've never been here before," Verna said, shifting the topic.

"I stumbled onto it a couple of years ago with a friend of mine."

The waitress returned and asked them if everything was all right. Ronald asked for a refill and Verna ordered another drink as well.

"So tell me Verna Scott's story."

She turned her water glass in a slow circle on the table. Deciding what she was willing to share? Ronald wondered. At last she raised her eyes to meet his.

"I'm a certified product of the system," she admitted.

He frowned, and then his brows rose as the meaning of her words came through. "Really? I would have never guessed. But it explains why you're so passionate about your work." He paused a moment, considering whether he should ask the questions that were running wild in his head. Verna beat him to it.

"I never knew my father. My mother had me at seventeen. I don't remember her." She glanced away. "She gave me away, or so I was always told. I went into the foster system when I was about two."

Her words were perfunctory, as if she was going down a grocery list, Ronald thought, but her eyes were distant. She had stopped turning the glass and now gripped it with both hands.

"You don't have to talk about it," he said gently.

Verna blinked, returning from that lonely place. She inhaled deeply. "I haven't really talked with anyone about my past, my growing up."

"Too painful?"

"Sometimes. But there were good times. Good homes. Good families." She gave a half smile. "That's what I wanted for other kids like me—the good. A few years ago I went on a training trip to Canada. One of the places we visited was Eva's Initiatives. A truly phenomenal place."

Ronald leaned forward to hear her over the music. "What kind of programs do they run?"

Verna told him about the Family Reconnect Program that helps runaways who want to reconnect with their families. "They're brought back together through meetings, counseling and support services. There are so many reasons for dysfunction in the family, for why kids leave or parents put them out. The program works with those children and families that want help in bridging the gap while providing a safe place for the kids."

"Sounds wonderful."

"They've been extremely successful. Eva's Initiatives was my inspiration for Home. I want as many young people as possible to have a chance—I want to bring some good into their lives."

"You're an example for all of them. You didn't let what happened to you *define* you. You took charge of your life."

Verna stared into the kind eyes of the man across from her.

How could she tell him that what happened to her *did* define her. She never became attached to anyone. She didn't dare. The fear of someone she cared about being taken away was more powerful than the aching loneliness that was as much a part of her as the hair on her head.

"I suppose you could say that." She released the glass. "It's what I try to instill in the kids."

Ronald nodded in agreement. "If we allow the baggage of our life to weigh us down, we'll always stay in the same place."

She grinned and shook a finger at him. "I like that. I'm going to have to use it."

"Be my guest, I did."

Verna's eyes widened in amusement. "Who shared it with you?"

"One of my professors in college. Got me through some tough times."

"You seem to have turned out okay. I guess you manage your baggage."

"Some days I feel as light as air, ready to leap tall buildings. Other days…"

Verna didn't get a chance to ask him about the "other days." The waitress had returned with their drinks and they put the heavy conversation aside and enjoyed the entertainment.

"I really had a great time tonight," Verna said when they pulled up in front of her door.

"So did I. I'm glad you came. I hope we can do it again sometime."

Verna's heart thumped. *He wanted to see her again.* "I'd like that."

His look of appreciation held her motionless and then his lips touched hers, so tenderly, so lightly that she could have imagined it. Her entire body warmed and her stomach fluttered like birds' wings. No. This was no daydream. This was for real.

Ronald leaned back. He traced her cheek with the tip of his finger, sending little shivers rippling through her. "What are you doing tomorrow?"

Verna blinked and told herself to respond. "Um, nothing special."

"Do you like basketball?"

She wrinkled her forehead. "Yes, why?"

"Ever been to a live game?"

"Only in the parks," she said, laughing.

"Well, I have two tickets to a Knicks game tomorrow

at Madison Square Garden. They play against Orlando. How about it?"

"Well...sure. Sounds like fun."

Ronald grinned. "I'll pick you up at two."

"I'll be ready."

He leaned down and kissed her cheek. "Rest well."

"You, too. And thanks again." She gently squeezed his fingers. "Good night," she whispered.

"Night," he said, and turned to walk back to his car.

As Verna snuggled down in bed that night, thinking about her lovely evening, she couldn't keep her mind from returning to what Ronald had told her about Patrice Holloway. Something he'd said had clicked in the back of her mind, but she wouldn't know for sure until she returned to her office.

CHAPTER
❧—SEVEN—❧

Unfortunately, the Knicks lost to Orlando, but that didn't dampen the incredible time that Verna had with Ronald. Being with him in the midst of hundreds of screaming fans, watching the live action of the players and his total immersion in the game—from jumping up and hurling advice, to complete euphoria when his team scored a point—made her see him in an entirely new light. He was the total package.

They filed out with the throng, arm in arm, laughing and rehashing the highlights of the afternoon.

"I had an absolute ball," Verna joked. "No pun intended."

Ronald slid his arm around her waist, and when she didn't pull away, he eased her a bit closer. "Told ya. Nothing like a live game."

She liked the feel of his warm body against hers.

She couldn't remember the last time she'd felt so completely comfortable with a man. As they walked out of the Garden, she glanced up at him. His expression was positively glowing. All traces of their serious conversation the night before were gone. Maybe going to basketball games was one of the things he did to lighten the baggage. He let himself enjoy life outside work, something she'd deprived herself of doing. Maybe it was finally time for a change.

When he dropped her off at home it was like awakening from a wonderful dream that you didn't want to end.

"Since you don't work weekends, I guess this is it," Ronald said as they sat in his car in front of her building.

Was it over already? She knew she shouldn't have allowed herself to believe that she could open the doors to her emotions.

"Unless you'd still like to see me again, after watching me act the fool all afternoon."

The speed of her thoughts came to a screeching halt. "What?"

"If I didn't totally convince you that I'm crazy, I hope you'll let me take you out again." He was angled halfway toward her.

Even in the dim light she could see the hope in his eyes. "I...I would love that."

Ronald exhaled a soft breath of relief. "Great. I'll call you. Or if you're in the mood, you can call me."

Verna nodded, too excited to speak.

He leaned forward, hesitated a moment, then gently kissed her.

Verna sighed against the firmness of his lips as he cupped his fingers behind her head to pull her closer. All too soon he eased back and she was shaken to the soles of her feet.

She took slow deep breaths as the softness of his smile caressed her face. At last she found her voice. "I should be going." She reached for the door handle and pulled the door open. As she glanced at him over her shoulder, she felt wonderful all over again. "Good night."

"Night."

Ronald lost count of how many times during the day he wanted to pick up the phone and call Verna, just to hear her voice and find out how her day was going, but he didn't want to seem overeager. If this was going to work, he'd have to take it slow. If Verna carried scars from her childhood, then he knew from experience that she was not going to jump into anything too quickly. Kids who had gone through foster care or group-home settings tended to shy away from the whole notion of emotional attachment. The anxiety of losing people you'd come to care about was too great. At the other end of the spectrum, the foster child became attached to everyone who showed the slightest bit of interest in them. His feeling was that Verna fell somewhere in between the two extremes.

* * *

The morning meeting had broken up and Nichole lingered behind as the other staff filed out.

"You look like someone lit a lightbulb inside you. You're glowing."

Verna's face heated. "Is it that obvious?"

"Yes, very." Nichole said. She sat down in a chair facing Verna. "So how was the weekend?"

"Wonderful," she said on a sigh of contentment. As much as she avoided opening herself up to others, she found it getting easier to do just the opposite. She needed to tell someone how good she felt, the new feelings that were stirring inside her. More important, she knew that beyond their working relationship, Nichole was her friend. Her girlfriend. She smiled inside, then launched into the details of her weekend.

"He really seems like a great guy, Verna." Nichole's approval was obvious.

"Yes," she said softly. "He is." She drew in a breath and stood. "This is new for me. I want to take it slow. But other times I feel like a freight train that needs to get to the next station fast."

Nichole grinned. "I know the feeling. Just follow your heart and the rest will fall into place." She stood. "I better get busy. We got a new referral. She's being brought over from Child Protective Services this afternoon."

"Right. Denise Fisher. Hey, Nikki…"

"Yes?"

"Thanks."

Nichole winked and walked out.

* * *

Verna had a stack of grant proposals to look through to see which ones Home could qualify for, but she couldn't keep her mind on her work. Not after what she'd discovered, or at least thought she had. Finally, she gave up and decided to do something physical. Starting in the basement, she made an inspection of the house, working her way up to the residential floor, stopping along the way to chat with the staff. As usual for a weekday, the house was quiet. That was the atmosphere she wanted for the young lady who would be coming. Whenever Home got a new referral, the staff tried to schedule it so that the teen came during the day when it was peaceful. That way the child wouldn't be overwhelmed and would have a chance to ease into the program.

From what Verna recalled from reading the file, Denise had been in foster care pretty much since birth. Her young mother had been in and out of jail. No known father. Child welfare took her when she was four. A neighbor found her in the yard eating out of the garbage. Heartbreaking. Growing up alone was a trauma that was almost too difficult to overcome. But that's why Home was in place. Verna's goal was to change that outcome for as many kids as she could.

Verna was returning to her office when the front doorbell rang. She went to answer and found a stout woman with a young girl at the door.

"Hazel Davis from Protective Services." She flashed her ID. "This is Denise Fisher."

Verna focused on Denise, who was popping gum and staring at her shoes.

"Hello, Denise."

She didn't respond. A look passed between Verna and the social worker. "Please come in." Once they were inside, Verna locked the door behind them. "My office is this way." She led them down the short hallway. "Have a seat. Can I get either of you anything? A snack, something to drink?"

"Nothing for me," Hazel said. She turned to Denise. "Would you like something, Denise?"

The girl continued to stare at her shoes.

Hazel handed Verna a thick manila envelope. "All the paperwork is in here."

Verna took the envelope and placed it on her table. Nichole generally did the intakes, but Denise's demeanor, the sadness that poured out of her body language, tugged at Verna's heart. Now was not the time to turn her over to yet another person.

"Why don't I give you a tour of Home," Verna said softly. "Then I'll show you your room. You'll be rooming with April. Her roommate moved into one of the single apartments."

Denise's dark brown eyes flickered toward Verna and she saw the tears welling there. Verna came and put her arm around the girl, signaling for Hazel to leave them for a few minutes. Hazel quietly left the room.

"I know this is hard. It's new and frightening. You've been tossed around all your life and there are days when you can't feel the ground beneath your feet." She clasped Denise's thin shoulders. "But all that is about to change."

Denise dared to look up. Tears now swam in her eyes.

"I promise." She took the girl's cold hand and led her into the kitchen, where she introduced her to Nichole and Brad and Gail. Then she took her on a tour of all the rooms, showed her pictures of the many kids who had come to Home and constantly returned to visit. They climbed the stairs to the top floor and Verna knocked on April's door even though she knew April was in school. She wanted to show Denise that respect of one's privacy was important. Using her key, she opened the door to the two-bedroom apartment.

Throughout the tour, the stiffness in Denise's body began to ease, but when she entered the apartment, Verna saw the first signs of hope filter into her expression.

"This is all yours—to share, of course. A utility kitchen, a bathroom and living room. Down the hall is your room." She led her to the closed door and opened it. Denise's mouth all but dropped open.

Tentatively she stepped inside and looked around in wonder. Her own bed, dresser, desk, closet and even a small television. She turned to Verna.

"This is really mine?"

Verna's heart nearly broke. "Yes, it's really yours. And we expect that you keep it neat and orderly. Your roommate will be home around four. You'll get to meet her then. We have dinner at six, but if you're hungry before then, Gail always has something cooking." She grinned. "Brad will bring up your bags and then you can get settled."

There was a knock on the door. Verna turned to Denise. "It's your apartment." She folded her arms as the girl walked past her to the door.

"I believe these are yours," Brad said, holding two suitcases and a backpack. "Where would you like me to put these, ma'am?"

"Uh...my room is back here."

"Lead the way." He put the bags in her room. "You'll like it here," he said. "Welcome Home." He gave a short nod to the ladies and walked out.

Verna turned to Denise. "I'll let you get settled. If you need anything, the intercom is in the kitchen. Press Office and it buzzes in the offices downstairs."

Denise nodded, still clearly awestruck by her surroundings.

"Nichole will meet with you a bit later and go over some things...expectations, rules of the house, find out if you need anything...anything at all. Okay?"

"Okay," she murmured.

Verna drew in a deep breath. "See you a bit later." She gently squeezed Denise's shoulder and left.

Denise stood in the center of her room, taking in the floral bedspread, the curtains in the window, her own desk and dresser. She flopped down on her bed and stared up at the ceiling. She didn't dare feel comfortable or too happy. Nothing lasts forever, she reminded herself. Especially for her.

CHAPTER
~ EIGHT ~

Ronald's day was finally over. Somehow he'd made it through without calling Verna, but that was about to change. He checked the time. Four o'clock. He picked up the phone and dialed her number. She answered on the third ring.

"Someplace Like Home, Verna Scott speaking."

"Well, good afternoon, Dr. Scott."

"And a good afternoon to you, Mr. Morris. How are you today?"

"Better now that I've heard your voice. How was your day?"

She told him about their new resident, giving him a little history.

He sighed heavily. "It never ceases to astonish me how much some kids go through."

"And their resiliency."

"I'm looking forward to meeting her. You said she's rooming with April?"

"Yes."

"What happened to April's roommate?"

"Carmen has moved up in the ranks. She was given her own room. It's the last transition step. She'll be eighteen in a few months and legally she can be on her own. This is just a way of preparing her."

"Makes sense. Hey, how about if I stop by after work? I'd like to meet Denise before I see her in a group session."

"That's fine. I think it's a great idea. I was going to suggest it, but I didn't want to impose on your time."

"Believe me, it's not an imposition. Besides, if I hurry, I can get to see you for a few minutes."

Ronald didn't imagine the soft intake of breath at the other end of the line. "See you when you get here," she said quietly.

Denise and April were in the family room when Ronald arrived.

"Hello, ladies."

"Hey, Mr. Morris," April greeted him. "This is my new roommate, Denise. That's Mr. Morris. He's pretty all right," she said with a half smile.

"Hi, Denise." He approached the teenager slowly. "I'm pretty new myself."

Her heavily lashed brown eyes flickered at him.

"I just started working here and I like it already," he said.

"It's okay, I guess."

"I'm sure April will show you the ropes. What grade are you in?"

"Ten."

"So that would make you about fifteen."

"I'll be sixteen next month." Her voice was a flat monotone.

"Get out," April said. "Me, too."

Ronald's chest tightened. He made himself smile at both girls. "We'll have to talk to Dr. Scott about a sweet-sixteen party."

"The parties here are the best," April offered. "We always find a reason to have a party."

Denise almost smiled.

Ronald chuckled. "So I've heard."

"I thought you only worked weekends, Mr. Morris," April said.

He glanced from one girl to the other. "I made a special trip to meet your new roomie."

He almost expected Denise to roll her eyes or shy away, but she simply stared at him. Ronald smiled. "See you ladies on the weekend."

"What did you think?" Verna asked when he returned to her office.

"She's scared and on guard."

Verna nodded in agreement. "With the right support systems, hopefully we can help her."

Ronald stole a glance toward her open door then dared to move closer to her. He lifted her chin with the tip of his finger so that they were eye to eye. "If anyone can help her, you can." He meant it. "I was thinking that I have a few evenings I can spare during the week," he said, stepping back. "I could come in…if you thought that was okay."

Verna barely hesitated. "That would be great."

He grinned. "I was hoping you'd say that. If it's good with you, I'll start tomorrow night."

"Sure—I mean, fine."

They stared at each other until they both began to laugh.

"I'll see you tomorrow," he finally said.

"Tomorrow."

"Have a good evening."

"You, too." He waved on his way out.

Ronald felt almost giddy inside. He knew he couldn't rush her, but he also wasn't about to waste time. There was definitely something going on between them.

Before long Ronald was a full-fledged member of the staff. Verna was amazed, and privately proud of the way he dealt with the kids, making time for each of them. There were many afternoons when she'd find him in the yard shooting hoops with some of the boys or in the family room with the girls, or peeking over Gail's shoulder to see what was on the menu. He got along with all the staff, who had come to rely on him for his on-point insight into the kids. And their relationship was growing slow and steady, like a heartbeat. They spent nearly every weekend evening together, talking, taking in a play or a movie or dinner in Manhattan. She'd never been so happy, yet there was that nagging old weight holding her back from totally giving in to her feelings.

His effect on April and Denise was nothing short of

amazing. The two had bloomed like roses that finally found some sunshine. April was seriously looking into college and preparing to be on her own when the time came. She actually wanted to go away to school, and Ronald was working with her to raise her marks and research the scholarships she might qualify for.

As for Denise, Verna actually saw her smile whenever Ronald was in the vicinity. The teenager always found a reason to talk with him alone or insisted only "Mr. Morris could help her." A part of her was thankful that Denise was coming out of her shell, adapting to her new home and engaging with the other kids. But the other part of her was worried about her growing attachment and dependency on Ronald.

One Wednesday evening when he arrived for his two hours, she asked him to come to her office.

"I wanted to talk to you about something."

"Sure." He sat down. "You look worried. Is everything all right?"

Verna sat behind one of her tables, keeping a professional distance between them. This was business.

"You've been with us almost three months—since early March—and I still wonder how we were able to get along without you."

He grinned. "Thanks. But I get the feeling this isn't about what a great job I'm doing."

"Actually…maybe you're doing your job too well."

His thick brows drew closer together. He leaned forward, resting his arms on his hard thighs. "Too well? What does that mean?"

"Denise has a crush on you, if you haven't noticed."

He jerked back in his seat. "Verna, I never gave her..."

She held up her hand to forestall an unnecessary explanation. "I know you haven't done anything to warrant it. It happens. I just need you to be aware and to keep that in mind when you're dealing with her. She may seem like she's getting it together, but she is still very fragile."

He sighed heavily and nodded his head. "I should have been paying more attention. I know better and I know how vulnerable these kids are. I'll make sure that I keep the boundaries in place."

"I know you will. I just wanted you to be aware."

He was thoughtful for a moment, and Verna had the feeling he had something to talk to her about and it had nothing to do with Denise.

Then, he said, "Um, when you and I first went to dinner, I told you about Patrice."

Verna nodded, feeling uneasy. They hadn't broached the subject since that night.

"I don't know how to explain it, but from the moment I set eyes on April...something was there...a connection that I can't explain. The shape of her face, the curve of her brow..." He bit his bottom lip, frowning, as if he was struggling to find the right words. "I wanted to read her case file."

Verna sat straighter in her seat. "Why?"

"I know this is going to sound crazy and I probably should have told you what I've been thinking." He swallowed. "I'm pretty sure she may be my daughter."

"What?" Heat burned the rim of her ears.

"I know. I told you it would sound crazy, but it's a gut feeling and all the pieces fit. The timing. When we talked, she told me a little about her early life. Did you know that her mother's name was Patrice Holloway?"

Verna knew all too well that was April's mother's name. After that first dinner with Ronald weeks earlier, she'd come to the office and reviewed April's file again. She'd flipped it open and skimmed the case history, her heart beating so rapidly that she could hardly breathe. It couldn't be. In a city of millions, what were the chances of father and daughter meeting here after all this time?

Meticulously, she'd read every line. According to the records, April's mother died in childbirth. The grandmother passed away when April was three, after adopting her and giving her the last name Davis. No other relatives and no father were ever mentioned. The family had lived in Brooklyn, in the same neighborhood that Ronald talked about.

It was crazy. But the more she'd read, refusing to allow her incredulity to blind her to what was in front of her, the more the impossible became possible. But she had no intention of sharing that information. What if it was all a bizarre coincidence? It would be utterly devastating to April. So for weeks, she'd lived with the possibility and the hope that Ronald wouldn't make the connection.

She looked directly at him, quickly reading the anxiety on his face.

"Okay, let's just say that she may be your daughter. You certainly can't come right out and tell her that.

There is a chance that you could be wrong and that would completely devastate her. All the progress she's made since she's been here would be destroyed."

"I know, I know," he said, the words dropping like stones in water. "What do we do?"

Verna looked off into the distance. "I don't know," she said, the secret she held gnawing at her. Silence hung between them. Finally, she pressed her hands down on the table. "For the time being, we aren't going to do anything. *You* aren't going to do anything. We will all just do our jobs."

Ronald jumped up from his seat. "Are you saying that you intend to do nothing?" His disbelief at her dispassionate response elevated his voice. "You know that I would never do anything to compromise any of these kids no matter what it meant to me. And I would never do anything that would hurt you or this program."

Verna swallowed over the tight knot in her throat. "I do know that."

Ronald stared at her, his eyes like two hot coals burning into her soul. "Is that all you have to say?"

Verna lifted her chin. "Yes."

He glared at her one last time and spun away, slamming the door behind him.

Verna fell back against the cushion of her seat and closed her eyes. She should have been honest. She should have told him what she suspected. It was unfair to both of them. Yet if anyone else understood the irrevocable damage that a wrong move could make, it was her.

Tears welled in her eyes. The image of that day, that letter she'd received more than a decade ago was as painful as if it were yesterday. She'd searched for her biological mother from the moment she came of age. All roads led to nowhere until she started working at the agency. She'd used her contacts and all her resources and finally connected with a service that located her mother in Stone Mountain, Georgia.

A meeting had been scheduled and Verna took a flight from New York. The fear, the exhilaration, the questions, the anxiety had her twisted in an emotional knot. But nothing could have prepared her for what happened.

When she arrived, she was greeted by a solemn-faced administrator—Ms. Carlyle—who gently escorted her to her office.

"Is she here?" Verna kept asking.

"Let's talk," Ms. Carlyle had said.

Shaking all over, Verna sat down, clamping her knees together to keep them from knocking.

Ms. Carlyle took a seat behind her desk and removed an envelope from her drawer, handing it with tight-lipped pain to Verna.

Verna,
I spent a lot of years trying to rebuild my life,
make something of myself. Giving you up
was hard. I want you to know that. But that
was the past. It's over and done. Hopefully,
you've had a decent life. You must be doing
all right if you had plane fare and money to
track me down. I know that kind of thing

*don't come cheap. But it's got to stop right
here, right now. My family doesn't know anything about you or the kind of life I once
lived, drugged out and on the street. I intend
to keep it that way.*

*I'm sorry but I can't have you in my life
ruining everything. I can't.*

*I want you to leave me alone. Don't come
looking for me or writing or calling. That's
just the way it has to be.*

Ann

The letter and its finality had nearly destroyed her
emotionally. She'd never told anyone about it, but kept
it as a reminder of where she'd been and how far she'd
come, and she'd determined that she would never let
another child experience what she had if it was within
her power.

Like Ronald, Verna had identified with April from
the moment she'd met her. April was a reflection of
herself. She had to protect her.

But Ronald isn't Ann, a warning voice whispered.

CHAPTER
∽ NINE ∽

Ronald spent a fitful night. Verna might not be sure, but he was. He was as certain as he knew his own name. When he first met April, the resemblance to Patrice had caught him off guard, but he attributed it to his imagination, wishful thinking. He'd dealt with hundreds of kids throughout his career, but he'd never felt that inexplicable connection until he met April. And the more time he spent with her, the stronger it grew. April was his daughter.

Verna spent the night staring up at the dark ceiling, the carousel of her life spinning around and around. She needed to get off. She needed to make a decision. But she couldn't.

For the next few days, Verna lived in a state of limbo. She felt as if she'd aged ten years. Her body ached, but more important her spirit hurt, and the last thing she expected was a voice message from Ronald.

"Good morning. It's Ronald. I'm sure you have a busy day, but we need to talk. Soon. I was hoping that we could meet downtown today for lunch or coffee. Let me hear from you. I'm in my office all day."

She squeezed her tired eyes shut. She couldn't face him today or any other day and continue to lie to him. She pushed up from her seat and walked across the room to the window. What was she going to do? Finally she picked up the phone and dialed Ronald at his office.

"Hello, it's Verna."

"I wasn't sure you would call."

She didn't respond.

"Are you free around twelve-thirty?" he finally asked.

"Yes, I can work that out," she said, her emotions hiding behind a wall of professionalism. "Did you have someplace in mind?"

"How about Peaches, on Lewis Avenue. Do you know the place?"

"I can find it."

"So I'll see you at twelve-thirty."

She cleared her throat. "Yes. See you then."

The time went by much too fast and Verna was soon pulling into a parking space in front of the neighborhood restaurant.

She stepped into the dimly lit interior and saw Ronald at a table facing the door. Her pulse raced. She forced herself to breathe as she walked toward him.

He stood as she approached and helped her into

her seat. "Thanks for coming," he said once she was settled.

The young waitress, clad in black with a white apron, appeared at their table. "What can I get for you?"

Verna looked up at her. "I'm not really hungry. Maybe some soup."

"Shrimp chowder is the special today."

"That's fine."

"And for you, sir?"

"Make that two."

"Coming right up."

Verna let her gaze wander around the space, unready to focus on Ronald.

"I don't know how much time you have, so I think I should get to the point of why I asked you here," he began. He linked his long fingers together on top of the table.

"Our last conversation really rocked me, Verna." He breathed deeply and slowly shook his head. "I can't even explain how I felt when I walked out of your office." He leaned forward, his eyes burning into hers. "You need to tell me what's going on. Why won't you at least check to see if I'm right? Have you read her file? Is there anything in there that can confirm my suspicion?"

The questions came at her like an automatic rifle, one shot after the other. She reached for her glass of water and took a long swallow. Slowly she put down the glass. "I told you my feelings. Hunches are not sufficient and there's nothing striking in her file to…warrant pursuing this further." She looked over his shoulder as she spoke.

He peered at her in utter disbelief. "Why are you lying to me?"

Verna stiffened. What had he found out? What did he really know? "I'm not. Why should I?"

"That's what I want to know. Why?"

"You've taken this much too far, Ronald. Trust me, I totally understand your confusion and your frustration, but I'm not lying to you. My first priority is the kids. It's my responsibility to protect them as much as humanly possible. And what you're proposing—"

He reached across the table and covered her clenched fist. "But what if I'm right?" he said on a heated, urgent whisper.

When he touched her and she listened to the hurt in his voice and saw it reflected in his eyes, she almost gave in. Almost. She looked at her watch and pushed back in her chair just as the waitress returned with the soup. Flustered, she apologized to the waitress and then to Ronald for having to leave.

She spun away and hurried out to her car. Every fiber of her being trembled. For several moments she sat in the car trying to pull herself together before taking off. She glanced at the damning folder on the passenger seat, the one she had planned to share with Ronald, but at the last minute, she'd changed her mind and left it in the car.

The sudden knocking on her passenger window caused her to gasp. Ronald was standing there. He mouthed for her to open the door, then glanced down at the folder on the seat with April Davis's name in big, black block letters. His gaze jerked back to Verna's. She had every intention of turning the key in the ignition and hitting the gas. But how long could she keep running from the inevitable? At some point he would have to read her case file on his own. As an on-staff counselor, all he needed was her okay. What she was doing was unorthodox and probably unethical. She shouldn't have removed the file from the office. If anyone ever found out, she could lose everything she'd worked for. But even if Ronald didn't feel he could trust her, Verna knew she could trust him.

She pressed the button on the armrest and lowered the window. She picked up the file and handed it to Ronald through the opening. "I'm sorry," she murmured before closing the window and driving away.

"Looks serious," Nichole said, stepping into Verna's office.

Verna sighed and motioned to a chair. "I need to talk to you."

"Sure." Nichole sat down. "What is it?"

Slowly, Verna told her of Ronald's belief about April and the information that she'd been able to obtain from the agency and from the foster homes where April had lived over the years. All the details had been filled it. The last piece of truth was only one step away.

Nichole rocked back in her seat. "Wow." For several moments she couldn't put her thoughts together. "I don't know what to say. Have you told Ronald what you've found out?"

"Not exactly." She looked away.

"What does that mean—'not exactly'?"

Verna drew in a long breath. "He now knows as much as I do." She told Nichole that she'd given Ronald the file and hoped that she would understand.

"How do you plan to handle this?" Nichole asked, not missing a beat.

Verna breathed a sigh of relief. "That's why I told you. I can't afford to mess this up. I've already breached protocol by removing the file from the office."

"We won't worry about that. But we have to tell April what we think. She has a right to know."

Verna looked away. "I have to find a way to break it to her. And see if she is willing to submit to a DNA test."

"I think both of us should be there to talk with her."

Verna sent her friend a smile of gratitude. "Thank you." She paused, then said, "April's experienced so much disappointment. We have to be careful. I just wish we had the irrefutable proof *before* we told her."

Thoughtfully, Nichole nodded. "So do I."

For the rest of the afternoon, Verna and Nichole discussed how they would approach April.

"If this all pans out, Ronald will become a full-time father," Nichole said as she and Verna sat together drinking the last of several cups of coffee. "Are you ready for that?"

"Ready for what?" she hedged.

"Being the lady friend of a man with a child."

"I haven't thought that far. I just want to get over this hurdle."

"How are things between you and Ronald?"

She took a moment before answering. "Things are…
were great. He's a wonderful man. Over these past few
months we've really gotten to know each other." She
swallowed. "I really care about him," she admitted, surprising herself. And once she'd said it out loud, it was
as if she were floating on a bed of happiness. She didn't
want to lose that feeling, not now, not after waiting for
so long. "I know he's hurt and angry at what I did. I lied
to him. Right to his face. And I wouldn't blame him if
he never spoke to me again. I should have been honest
from the beginning. I've probably ruined everything
and maybe he'll never trust me again."

Nichole stretched her hand across the table and
touched Verna's. "I've known you for a long time, Verna.
He's lucky to have you in his corner. You'll both work
it out no matter what happens."

Verna silently prayed her friend was right.

"You wanted to see me, Dr. Scott?" April stood in
the doorway of Verna's office. She spotted Nichole, and
her open expression turned wary. "Am I in trouble?"

"No, not at all. Please come in, April. Ms. Graham and
I both want to talk with you. Close the door, sweetie."

April's gaze jumped from one face to the other as if
she half expected to be cornered. She slowly sat, slouching down in the chair.

"April, we've come across some information…about
your father," Verna began.

The teenager wiggled up straighter. "What do you
mean?" She began shaking her foot back and forth.

"We've been going over all the records…" Nichole began.

Taking turns, Verna and Nichole told April as gently as possible that they may have found her father.

When they'd finished, April was rocking and tapping her foot and silent tears rolled down her cheeks. Her bottom lip trembled. She hadn't said a word the entire time and the room hummed with tense silence. She looked from one face to the other. "Who—who is he?"

Verna hesitated. "Sweetie, we think it's best not to say right now. Not until we know for sure."

"April…" Nichole reached out to touch her.

April snatched her hand away. "I hate him!" she screamed, jumping up from her seat. "I hate him! He left me. He never came for me." Her voice rose like a tidal wave and swept over them in fury. "He never looked for me. Never!"

Verna got up and pulled April into her arms. "I need you to listen to me." She hugged her tighter, feeling the tremor of the girl's sobs ripple up and down her thin body. "He may not have known what to do, sweetie." Verna kept on talking, soothing, comforting, finding the words that April needed to hear. She'd talk all night if she had to. She reached out and took both of April's hands in hers. "You must understand that we have to be sure. So you're both going to have to agree to a DNA test. But you have to keep in mind that there's a chance that he's not your dad."

Finally, after what seemed like an eternity, April's sobs quieted to little sniffles.

"Can I go now?" she managed to say, looking fragile and helpless.

"I think we should talk some more, April, and process this information," Verna said. "I know it's a lot to digest."

"I don't have anything else to say." She stared at the floor.

"Okay." Verna squeezed her shoulder. "Go on to your room. I'll be up to check on you before I leave."

Without a word, April walked out.

Verna and Nichole shared a look.

"This is exactly what I was afraid of," Verna said.

CHAPTER
❧ TEN ❧

Patrice Howell gave birth to a baby girl, April, in Kings County Hospital. Patrice died in childbirth and the child was given to the maternal grandmother, Phyllis Davis, who adopted April and gave her Davis as her last name. When the grandmother became too ill to care for her, April was placed in foster care. The grandmother passed away shortly after and there were no known relatives or arrangements made by Phyllis Davis.

That would explain the difference in the last names, Ronald thought as he put all the papers and notes into the folder.

He'd lost track of how many times he'd read April's case file, yet he knew in his heart that April was his daughter. His daughter with Patrice. Patrice was gone.

He still struggled with that painful truth. All this time and he never knew. He felt as if his insides were breaking into a million pieces. The joy was there, along with another emotion just as strong. Anger at Verna. How could she have deceived him like that? What kind of woman was she to keep this kind of information from him?

To think that he'd fallen for someone who could be so callous unnerved him. He cared about Verna, deeply, and he thought she felt the same way. The times they'd spent together were the happiest he could remember. He looked forward to their nightly phone calls, their weekend excursions. The woman he'd come to love was not the same Verna Scott who was keeping his daughter from him.

He was hardly conscious of driving to Verna's building until he looked up and saw he was standing in front of her door. He rang the bell.

Verna opened the door, and instead of apprehension at seeing him, she conveyed a sense of relief.

"Come in," she said softly.

More than an hour later, amidst tears and apologies, Ronald finally understood why Verna had not been honest with him. She'd shared her own past with him, then showed him the letter from her mother that she'd kept all these years. The roots of her hurt went so deep, and she'd sought to destroy the hold it had over her life by helping other young people, even at the expense of her own happiness. He understood that overwhelming need to make things right for others. Hadn't he spent his life doing the same thing?

"Look at me," he said gently from his seat opposite her.

With great hesitation Verna complied.

"What you did for April took courage. It took love. A love that can only be understood and given by someone who has gone through what you did." He moved from his chair to sit next to her on the couch. "But, Verna, just like you tell your kids, don't let your circumstances define you. It's your mother's loss, baby. Her loss. You are an incredible human being." He put his arm around her and pulled her close. She rested her head on his shoulder. "You need to know that, you need to believe it."

She nodded and sniffed, her voice shaky with emotion. "I'm sorry that I lied to you."

Ronald sat back and lifted her chin, forcing her to look at him. "How about if we make a deal? From here on out, if we're going to make this thing work between us…no more secrets. Just the truth, even if it hurts."

The shadow of a smile touched her lips. "Deal."

"I say we seal it with a kiss." He raised his fingers to caress the soft skin of her face.

"So do I."

April refused to come out of her room, except to go to school, and she wouldn't talk to anyone, none of the counselors, not even her friends, not even Ronald. Which, Ronald told Verna, was a bittersweet blessing. If she came to him and confessed what was on her mind, he wasn't sure if he could hold back from telling her what was on his.

Verna was concerned and she'd conveyed her concerns to him and Nichole. Ronald wanted to talk to April himself, but Verna strongly believed that the teenager needed to come to terms with her feelings. And with a little time she would come around. They would keep an eye on her and continue to try to break down the barriers that she'd erected around herself. But the tension was making everyone crazy.

About a week later, Verna was in her office working on some files when there was an almost indiscernible knock on her door.

"Yes? Come in."

The door slowly opened.

"April." Verna closed the folder and stood. "Please, come in."

The girl stepped tentatively into the room, her focus on her feet. "I want to take the test," she said, lifting her head to look into Verna's eyes.

Verna was jubilant. "We'll make that happen. I'll call the clinic tomorrow and set up a test date. We can have the results back in a couple of days at the most."

April inhaled a shuddered breath. Verna walked over to her. "I want you to understand that no matter what happens, I will always be here for you, and you will always, always have Home." She hugged the teenager tight and prayed for a joyous outcome.

The next few days while they waited for the DNA results were torture. Ronald could barely keep his mind on his work and April was short and snappy with everyone, flying off the handle at the slightest thing. Verna prayed that this would turn out right for everyone involved.

Ronald and Verna spent whatever spare time they had together, talking about the possibilities, their growing feelings for each other, how having a daughter could change Ronald's life dramatically.

"I'm ready," he'd said as Verna relaxed against him on his brown leather couch. "More than ready."

"Good morning, Dr. Scott. There's a FedEx package for you." The security guard handed it to her on her way to her office.

"Thanks," she murmured. She looked at the return address. It was from the lab. Her hands shook ever so slightly and the pressure began to build in her stomach. She went to her office and shut the door.

Trancelike, she walked to her chair and sat down. She stared at the innocuous envelope, unsure of what to do. Did she have the right to open it or should she leave that up to Ronald?

Knowing the answer, she picked up the phone and dialed his office.

"Lexington High, Mr. Morris speaking."

"Ron, it's Verna." She paused. "The package from the lab is here." She heard his sharp intake of breath.

"Did you open it? What does it say?"

"No. No, I didn't. I thought that you should." Her throat was so dry and tight she could barely swallow.

"I'll be there as soon as I can. I'll ask Cara to get someone to cover for me."

"All right."

"And, Verna…"

"Yes?"

"Thank you."

It was barely an hour later and Ronald was standing at her office door. She stood and came to him. Not caring who saw, she put her arms around him and they clung to each other. She listened to the rapid beat of his heart and raised her mouth to meet his.

His hand caressed her cheek and cupped her face as he looked down into her eyes.

"No matter what happens," she whispered, "I'm here for you."

He smiled. "I've always known that."

Verna took his hand and they walked to her table. The envelope dared him to pick it up.

Ronald glanced at Verna for a last glimmer of encouragement, then snatched up the envelope and tore open the seal. His hands shook as he read the report, and then read it again.

He turned to Verna, tears in his eyes, struggling for composure.

"She's…mine. She's my daughter."

Verna leaped into his arms and they smothered each other in tears, kisses and laughter.

Ronald arranged to take the rest of the day off. He wanted to be there when April got in from school. Verna was at the stairs when April arrived and asked to speak with her in her office.

"We got the results back today, sweetie."

April's eyes widened. Her throat moved, but she didn't speak.

"Your father is here. Do you want to meet him? Are you ready for that?"

She blinked in alarm. "He's here?" Her backpack thudded to the floor. She looked around the room with frightened eyes. "What should I do?"

"It's completely up to you, April. If you're not ready, you don't have to meet him."

April bit down on the nail of her forefinger. It seemed forever before she finally spoke.

"Okay."

Verna released a soft breath. She took April to the family room and went in search of Ronald, who was out back with the boys shooting hoops. The instant he saw Verna he quickly excused himself.

"She's in the family room," Verna said. "But why don't you take her for a walk—for privacy."

"Right, right," he agreed, nodding his head and realizing how nervous he'd suddenly become.

Verna walked with him to the entrance of the family room, squeezed his shoulder and left.

Ronald drew in a breath and walked toward April, who was huddled in the chair. Looking at her, he totally understood Verna's apprehension about the impact this would have on the teen.

He shoved his hands into his pockets and stepped closer. "Hi," he said softly.

She looked up at him, frowned in confusion, then

hesitantly glanced past him to the door, waiting for her father to walk in.

"I'm glad that you wanted to see me. I thought maybe we could go for a walk and talk a little bit."

"What?" She frowned again.

"I'm your dad, April." He held his breath.

She uncurled herself from the chair, stared malevolently at him for a moment, then tore past him and ran upstairs. Verna came out of her office and met Ronald in the hall.

"What happened?"

"I told her and she ran out."

Verna pressed her palm to her forehead and briefly squeezed her eyes shut. "Let me go up and talk to her."

"I should go with you."

She stopped him with a hand against his chest. "No. You wait here. Please," she added to soften her tone.

Ronald paced until he'd memorized every thread in the carpet. Verna had been up there for nearly an hour. What could they possibly be... A movement in the doorway halted his steps. Verna stood with her arm around April's shoulders. The girl's head was lowered, but he could tell she'd been crying. He looked at Verna, who mouthed, "It's okay."

"April," he said softly.

She didn't budge.

"Why don't you two go for a walk," Verna suggested, and gently urged April forward.

Ronald and his daughter stepped out into the warm spring evening and began to slowly stroll down the street. The trees were coming out in bloom, the once-bare limbs now clothed in lush green finery.

"I'm happy you decided to talk to me," Ronald said.

April glanced at him for a moment. "I was mad."

"Tell me why."

She was silent so long that Ronald thought he'd have to pose the question differently. But at last she spoke.

"Why didn't you ever come for me?"

Ronald's heart felt as if it had turned over in his chest. "Sweetheart, I didn't know…"

April stopped walking and came around to stand in front of him. "Tell me what happened."

Verna carved a new path between her door and the window. They'd been gone for more than two hours. Her mind ran wild. Just when she thought she couldn't take another minute, Ronald tapped on her door with April in tow. Both of them were beaming, the remnants of joyous tears still glimmering in their eyes.

"We had a good talk," Ronald said. "I promised April that no matter what, I'll be there for her."

"Everybody okay?" Verna gently asked, looking from one to the other.

They nodded.

"Better than okay," Ronald said, "but we have a long way to go, a lot of years to make up for."

April looked up at her father.

Verna felt as if her heart would explode with happiness.

"I made a decision, though," April said. She crossed the room and sat down.

"What decision?" Verna asked.

"I'm going to stay here until school lets out in June."

"It will give me some time to find a bigger place," Ronald said, "with two bedrooms."

April nodded. "And it will give me some more time with Denise. We've gotten really close and I don't want her to feel as if she's being abandoned, ya know."

Verna was so touched she could barely speak.

"April, I want to talk to Verna for a moment. Okay?"

The teenager gazed at Ronald as if she thought he might vanish.

"I'll come and get you in a minute. I promise."

She gave her father a long hug before she sauntered out of the room, taking short glances over her shoulder as if to make certain this wasn't all some wonderful dream.

Ronald closed the door.

Verna looked expectantly at him. "What's going on?"

He crossed the short space between them, took her hands and eased her down into a chair then sat opposite her.

"From the moment I met you, I knew my life was going to change and it did, day by day. The more time I spent with you, the deeper I fell in love with you. What you do here, at Home, is nothing short of a miracle, and what greater miracle could there be than me being reunited with my daughter." He squeezed her hand, lowered his head for a moment, then looked directly into her eyes. "You're an amazing woman and I want to spend the rest of my life helping you make miracles."

Verna could hardly believe what she was hearing. Ronald loved her.

"I know it's going to be a bumpy ride, but we'll figure out all the details as we go along."

The words that tumbled from her lips had never been so strong and sure. "There's nothing I would rather do than come along for the ride."

Ronald encircled her in his arms and kissed away all the hurt, the fears, the loneliness, and Verna knew that she had finally found the love and the family that she'd been searching for.

* * * * *

Dear Reader,

When I was asked to participate in Harlequin's *More Than Words* anthology, I was both thrilled and honored to be part of such an important initiative that recognizes those unsung heroes who make the world a better place. My excitement doubled when I was given the assignment of bringing to the page Eva's Initiatives and the Family Reconnect Program. The work that Nancy Abrams does with the Family Reconnect Program is nothing short of miraculous, and her effort is dear to my heart, having myself for many years overseen a residential facility for homeless teen mothers. In speaking with Nancy, her commitment and passion about working with teens and families in crisis and being the bridge that they could safely cross to "reconnect" was obvious—this was my inspiration for "Someplace Like Home."

I do hope that I did Nancy justice and that you enjoyed the journey that Verna and Ronald took to find each other and the family that they have both longed for.

Happy reading,

VICTORIA PETTIBONE AND SASHA EDEN

❧— WET's Risk Takers Series —❧

C lose your eyes when talking to Victoria Pettibone and Sasha Eden and you will be hard pressed to tell the two women apart. Little wonder. The founders of the acclaimed nonprofit WET Productions have been friends since they were teens. Today they're just as likely to share a twenty-year-old inside joke as a cup of coffee in the New York City office they split.

That closeness has worked for them. When WET (Women's Expressive Theatre) Productions isn't developing or producing theater or films that challenge female stereotypes, Victoria and Sasha run its Risk Takers Series for teenage girls. The free citywide media-literacy and leadership program uses film as a launching pad for discussion, teaching girls invaluable communication tools in a trusting environment, enabling them to distinguish empowering risks from damaging ones.

The program is designed to bolster girls' self-esteem,

providing them with leadership tools and valuable information on their health and well-being, ultimately helping
them take empowered steps to make their dreams come
true. An important component of the program is the
participation of guest artists from each film screened,
who provide inspiration to the girls in afternoon Q&As.
Past guests have included Frances McDormand, Kerry
Washington, Keri Russell, Mary-Louise Parker, Ally
Sheedy, Olympia Dukakis, Lili Taylor, among many
others.

Helping teen girls redefine themselves by finding their inner strength is a primary mandate of Risk
Takers. The program runs one Saturday a month for six
months. Over one hundred and fifty girls from more
than eighty schools throughout the city walk through
the doors at 9:00 a.m. and screen a film about a woman
or a girl being brave. Whether they're settling in with
The Breakfast Club (Ally Sheedy visited that day) or
North Country (Frances McDormand fielded questions),
the girls are encouraged to think critically about topics
ranging from domestic abuse to suicide, teen pregnancy
to overwhelming peer pressure.

Following the screening, they break into small groups
of eight or twelve led by adult mentors with a background in teaching, guidance and psychology for teens.
Feeling safe and protected, the girls have an opportunity
to open up about their own lives and explore negative
feelings and problems that seem insurmountable and
often dampen their self-esteem. "Changing the way
teen girls see themselves is paramount," says Sasha,
but just as important, "girls need to learn healthy ways

to communicate and address their fears and how to support one another. I know a lot of teenage girls who look in the mirror and say, 'I'm ugly,' and the others will say, 'No, I'm ugly.' Unfortunately that's more common than someone saying, 'Look how beautiful you are,' or 'But you're a genius.'"

Making a change

Victoria and Sasha's own teen friendship blossomed precisely because they didn't fall into this trap of self-hatred and competition. To this day the women openly and lovingly praise each other's best points. They're consummate cheerleaders who model what healthy female friendships should be. Girls can't help being inspired by them.

"Vicki was the bravest person I ever met," says Sasha about her first impressions of her friend, who got her pilot license as a teen. "She was sophisticated, funny and sweet and didn't try to be cool. She just was cool."

Victoria is just as likely to offer praise, claiming that Sasha has always been confident and charismatic. "She was a light when she walked into the room," Victoria says now.

The two women grew up across the street from one another in Manhattan and acted in plays and joined singing groups together. They lost track of each other during college, but reunited afterward while both were working in the entertainment industry. Through their work experiences, they quickly recognized the lack of complex female characters in the media, and the two women decided to make changes for the better.

"Rather than sitting around and complaining about things," says Victoria, "we've always been people who say, 'Okay, let's create what we want to see. Something positive.'"

In 2004, the two launched Risk Takers to get girls to openly question and challenge the messages the media offered and to feel empowered by the truth of their own strengths. Above all, the girls are taught how to take healthy risks rather than damaging risks.

"We recognize that all the best things that have happened to us have been because we took empowered, healthy risks," says Victoria. "And we realize how few young women are taught that."

The women are still taking risks every time they pick up the phone to cold call a celebrity and convince her to come speak to an auditorium full of teens. Happily, what once felt daunting is now just part of a day's work.

And it doesn't hurt that word has traveled in the film industry. Today many well-known actors, screenwriters, directors and producers think nothing of hopping on a plane to New York. In an effort to break down the myth of celebrity, most of the women arrive in jeans or sweats and are ready to dish on what empowered risks they've taken in their own lives.

The girls feel so validated by the experience, says Victoria, and the women are thrilled to be part of such an honest conversation about their work.

"It's incredibly life changing as a young girl to ask Mary-Louise Parker a question and have her say,

'Wow, that's a great question.' Teenagers want to be heard and need to be validated for using their voices constructively."

Never alone again

The messages stick. Victoria and Sasha routinely hear success stories from the girls, parents and teachers. Girls who go through the program say they no longer feel isolated and alone with their self-doubt. They feel stronger than ever and have the confidence to forge change in their lives—whether it is by breaking away from a bullying clique, saying no to drugs or applying for a college scholarship, the girls credit Risk Takers as the program that has made them take empowered risks to make their lives healthier and their dreams come true. One alumna has gone on to run her own film festival at school. Another teen, who was having serious problems in school and couldn't forge friendships, now has made a ton of friends from the program.

Alexandra Campos, an alumna who attended as a shy, high school freshman, says Risk Takers taught her the power of her own voice even years later when she was in college.

"Within my first month at school I was exposed to intense racism and confronted with viewpoints that were contrary to my own," she says today. "But I had resources, understanding and communication tools from Risk Takers. I had my voice and I knew how to use it."

Despite the successes, fund-raising is still an issue

for WET's Risk Takers Series. Victoria admits much of her time is spent writing grant applications and drumming up all the volunteers they need to make the program a go. But every time Victoria and Sasha sit in a darkened theater with the teens or hear about their personal-breakthrough moments, they know the hours of planning have been worth it.

"We tell the girls, 'Here is your chance to be that person you know you are inside. Here's a place where you will learn how to be true to yourself,'" says Sasha. "When you decide to take empowered risks to be your true self, amazing things can happen—your dreams become your reality."

JILL SHALVIS

WHAT THE HEART WANTS

CHAPTER
~ ONE ~

All Ellie Cahn wanted was to get home to the hot
bubble bath that had her name written all over it.
And maybe she also wanted a more reliable car,
since she was currently kneeling on the side of the road
changing her tire—her second flat this month.

Okay, and while she was making wishes, she'd also
like a housekeeper, and hey, why not a vacay in the
Turks and Caicos while she was at it.

But she was nothing if not a realistic woman. Vacations, like housekeepers and AAA cards, didn't grow on
trees. Neither did money. Her meager teacher's salary
didn't go far, plus it was further drained by funding
Powerful and In Charge—PIC—her nonprofit program
for teenage girls. That she was still in business at all in
this economy was a miracle.

One worry at a time. She stared at the set of pliers

she'd managed to run over and let out a long breath. Only her. When her cell phone rang, she answered without taking her eyes off the very flat tire. "Hello?"

"Honey, I'm glad I caught you," her grandma said in her eighty-year-old quavery voice that belied the fact that her mind was still sharp as a tack. "I found you a man."

Oh, boy. "I'm a little too busy for a man right now. Maybe another time."

"Bah. Being so busy with those teenage girls is exactly why you need one now. A man would give you something for yourself. He could balance out your life."

Been there, tried that. "I don't have time for that kind of trouble," she said, rather than rehash her last few spectacular men failures.

"Used to be you had *too* much time for that kind of trouble," Grandma said. "But these days you're taking the opposite path, and, honey, that isn't healthy either. Now, I happen to know that Nilly's daughter's boy is single again. His divorce just became final and he's looking for someone. He's got a real good job down at the lumberyard selling nails and—"

"No," Ellie said firmly. "No more blind dates. You promised."

From inside Ellie's car, a head poked out. Kia Rodriguez. Kia didn't say a word. She didn't have to. Her expression was dialed to *Bored* in the way only a seventeen-year-old could manage.

"Grandma," Ellie said, eyeing Kia, "I really have to go. I'll call you later, okay?"

"You off to save another teen?"

Ellie didn't save them, she simply did her best to provide a safe environment for them to learn self-respect and confidence. Or tried to anyway. She wasn't always successful, but she did her best and gave it her all.

"Remember," Grandma said. "Tough love, honey. It's tough love that saved *your* sorry-but-very-cute hiney."

Ellie figured she was probably the only one in the world who had a grandma who used the word *hiney*. "I remember." She wasn't likely to forget. Once upon a time, tough love *had* saved her, there was no doubt. Her grandma's tough love. The woman drove Ellie crazy, but there was no denying that her heart was in the right place. "Don't forget to take your cholesterol meds, okay? And stop trying to find me a man. Love you, bye." She ended the phone call and looked at Kia. "My grandma."

Kia just looked at her in that universally teenage bland stare that said Don't Care.

"She's a little crazy," Ellie explained.

"Does she really try to hook you up?"

"No. Well, maybe. The last time I let her set me up on a blind date, he took me trash hauling. In my best heels."

What might have been a very small smile twitched at the corners of the girl's mouth. This equated to great humor in Kia's world. "Maybe you should take your own class," she told Ellie. "You know, the one with the 'no guy's going to respect you unless you respect yourself' spiel."

"Ah, so you *were* listening." Ellie kicked her very

dead tire. "You should know, I'm not sure how long this'll take. I can change it, but I'm not the best."

"Whatever."

The girl's favorite word. Her hair was long, thanks to ratty extensions. She wore so much mascara and liner on her eyes that Ellie was surprised she could even hold them open. Her clothes were black on black, and fit like a second skin.

"Can't you call someone?"

Ellie fought with the car jack. "Like who?"

"I don't know. AAA. A guy."

Corners had been cut. AAA had been one of them. As for a guy...well, corners had been cut there as well.

"Bobby's supposed to pick me up at home in fifteen minutes." Kia checked the time on her cell phone. "I need to get ready, and he hates it when I hold him up."

Ellie's stomach dropped. "Bobby?"

Kia shrugged.

Bobby was a year ahead of Kia. He'd left high school and gone to work in construction. To say he was not the sharpest tool in the shed was an understatement, but that wasn't the problem. Bobby had a mean streak a mile long and a temper to go with it. He'd been kicked off the football team for it, and couldn't seem to hold a job.

"You're back with him?" Ellie asked lightly, not allowing any judgment in her voice. As she knew all too well, teenagers had a nasty habit of doing the opposite of what was good for them. She certainly had.

Another shrug from Kia.

"When we last talked," Ellie said, "you mentioned you were going to take a break from boys."

"I took a break. Break's over."

Just last month at PIC, Ellie had run a workshop about respecting your own body and making sure others respected it as well. Kia had admitted she'd let boys take advantage of her sexually. Made sense given that she'd been caught having sex at the high school four different times.

With four different boys.

She'd also been caught shoplifting lip gloss and suspended from school for fighting. She was one mistake away from ruining her life.

And twenty minutes ago, Ellie had caught her hitching a ride home from the PIC office. Ellie had nearly had heart failure. The office was really a leased warehouse that wasn't in the worst part of town, but definitely not the best either. Ellie's greatest wish was to move to a better location she'd already found but couldn't afford. Not happening, at least not this year. But Kia could easily have been mistaken for someone much older than seventeen, and in this area gotten herself into a situation she had no idea how to get out of.

Ellie had made her get in the car, then executed a U-turn to go to the other side of town to take the teenager home.

Except a pair of pliers had derailed the plan.

"Ms. Cahn?" Kia said.

"Yes?"

"Do you really not have a guy to call for help?" She was texting as she talked, her fingers moving so fast they were nothing but a blur. "Guys are really good at the tire-changing thing."

Ellie shook her head. "I told you, I can do this." Probably. "Maybe we should have a workshop on this at PIC's next session so you girls can learn, too."

Kia sighed. "Great."

"Knowing how to do things yourself is important."

"Uh-huh. But having a boyfriend to do it is better."

Ellie's last boyfriend had been smart, cute and gainfully employed as a dentist. He'd been great, except he'd neglected to mention something important—his wife. Before that, she'd dated an architect, but he'd traveled a lot and worked all the time. So did she, either teaching at the high school or at PIC. It didn't leave a lot in the tank for extras, like men. "I don't have time for a boyfriend right now," she said for the second time that day.

"That's what girls say when they can't get one." Kia looked her over. "Maybe it's the way you dress."

Ellie raised a brow as Kia took in her jeans and sweater. "What's wrong with how I dress?"

"It's... Conservative," Kia said politely.

Ellie laughed. "We're in Connecticut in the spring. It's cold outside. I dressed to stay warm."

"You could still wear a tighter sweater and do something with your hair. You're pretty, you know. Considering you're..."

"What?" Ellie asked, amused. "Old?"

"Well, yeah."

She was thirty-two. Not quite ready for the old folks' home. "You sound like my grandma."

"Does she think your jeans need to be tighter and lower, too?"

Ellie's jeans were plenty snug *and* hip-hugging, but it was true that they weren't spray painted on or revealing her underwear. "Tighter and lower are uncomfortable."

Kia shrugged, like maybe wedgies were the price one paid to have a hot guy.

Ellie gave up reasoning with her and struggled with the tire iron. Probably she'd done the car jack wrong, and she got down on her belly to check. In the mud. From above her, she could hear the keys of Kia's phone clicking as the teenager continued to text at the speed of light.

"You know," Ellie said, crawling out from beneath the car and brushing off her hands, "if you put half the energy into your grades as you do communicating by texting, you'd probably get into any college you want."

Kia lifted a shoulder. "No money for college, and I'm not texting."

"And yet your thumbs are moving."

"I'm writing something else."

"Like?"

"Like a stupid diary, okay? My counselor makes me." She sighed dramatically, as if it was a fate worse than death. "I have to write down my *feelings* or I'll fail English."

"So what are you feeling?"

"Right now? Bored to tears. Seriously, I don't see why I can't just hitch a ride."

"Kia, you're going to hitch over my dead body. I'll be

done soon." Hopefully. She was working hard on getting the lugs off the tire, which was much more difficult than she remembered. She swiped her forehead on her sleeve. "And there are plenty of college scholarships out there for the taking."

Kia took her gaze off her phone and eyeballed Ellie. She appeared to fight a smirk, but lost the battle.

"What?" Ellie bent low and inspected her face in the reflection of her hubcap. Two streaks of grease ran across her forehead in the shape of an L.

For loser.

She glared at Kia, who was still biting back amusement. "You could help, you know."

"I don't want to have an L on my forehead."

Ellie tried to wipe it off but, according to her reflection, she'd only succeeded in making it worse. "What if sometime after you get your driver's license, you get a flat tire?"

"Then I'll call my hot boyfriend." Kia let her smile loose. "See? I'm telling you, they're handy to have. You should try to get yourself one. You know, before it's too late."

"It's not too late!"

"Thirty-two," Kia repeated as if she was saying *eighty*-two. "You have any cats?"

"Two."

"Oh, yeah. Then it's too late for you."

"Because I have cats?"

"Hello," Kia said. "Having multiple cats is, like, the *crazy lady* signature."

Ellie wondered what Kia would say if she knew that

once upon a time, Ellie had been just as wild and uncontrollable as she was, if not more so. With a nonexistent father and a mother who'd spent a lot of time behind bars, raising Ellie had fallen to her grandma, who'd taken one look at an attitude-ridden Ellie and tossed her into a program called WET Risk Takers. Once a month for six months, her grandma would drive Ellie from Connecticut to New York City, where, through the power of film and strong female role models, Ellie had learned to respect herself, had learned that she alone held the power to carve her own destiny instead of following in her mother's bad footsteps.

Now, years later, she used the program that had once saved her life as the model to run her own. Like WET, Ellie utilized films with positive female role models, bringing in female writers and producers and directors when she could to give fun workshops for the girls, engaging them, showing them how important their education was, and what they could do with it.

Like the original WET program, Ellie had diversified, bringing in other strong female role models such as chefs, teachers, life coaches, anyone and everyone she could get to make positive impressions and be a good influence, and teach the girls to change and better their lives. She was always looking for new people and new ways to enrich the program, driven by a need to make sure no one slipped through the cracks. As she nearly had.

As she was deathly afraid Kia would.

"Ms. Cahn?"

Ellie had just gotten one of the lug nuts off and was

struggling with the second, her knees sinking in the mud. Damn soggy weather. "Hold...on."

"Okay, but—"

The lug nut gave unexpectedly, and Ellie fell backward onto her butt. Mud splashed up into her face. *"Crap."*

"Um, Ms. Cahn—"

Ellie blew a strand of hair from her eyes. Or she tried, but the mud on her face had it sticking to her skin like glue. "Kia, unless you want to get your pristine behind out of that car and help me, then—"

"Guy alert!" Kia whispered loudly.

Ellie once again tried to blow the hair from her face and failed. *"What?"*

"You know, cute guy at one, two, *THREE o'clock!"*

Ellie turned to her right and caught sight of a pair of long denim-clad legs.

"Ladies," came a low, husky male voice. "Looks like you have a problem."

CHAPTER
∽ TWO ∽

E llie looked up.
And up.
The long denim-clad legs bent at the knees until the man that went with them was crouched at her side, at least six feet of hard sinew and sheer strength. He wore a slightly oversize button-down, untucked over black jeans, a cool pair of boots, mirrored sunglasses and a carriage that suggested you might not want to mess with him.

Since she'd known him before his military training had hardened his expression, the shiver that raced up her spine wasn't fear.

Elbows on his thighs, he pulled off his sunglasses and revealed cool slate-gray eyes that warmed even as she watched, and she knew he recognized her too, despite all the grease and mud she had smeared all over her.

"Ellie Cahn," he said, a barely there smile crossing his lips.

She hadn't seen him for a long, long time. Not since she'd run as wild and uncontrolled as Kia, in fact. "Jack Buchanan," she said, extremely aware of Kia behind her practically falling out of the car to catch every word.

Jack's smile came into full bloom then, and something in her belly fluttered as just like that, the years fell away. "How long has it been?" she asked.

"Too long."

His voice alone had memories slamming into her. Fellow rebels through high school, they'd spent untold hours in detention, blaming everyone but themselves, and even more hours running wild from their demons—Ellie from her screwed-up home life, Jack from a family he couldn't please. The two of them had chased fun and trouble together for four years.

Until it hadn't been fun.

Until she'd grown up, the hard way.

But looking into Jack's face brought back only the good times. The best of times.

"So you two, like, know each other," Kia said.

"Used to." Jack's eyes smiled. "In high school."

But Kia didn't much care about that. "Do you know how to change a tire?"

"Kia," Ellie said. "Jack's not going to fix the tire. I told you I—"

But Jack dropped to his knees beside her and reached for the tire iron, his shirt stretching across the muscles of his back as he worked, effortlessly removing the stubborn lug nuts, then the flat tire, replacing it in less than four minutes.

"Your spare's not great," he said, inspecting the tread. Getting lithely to his feet, he pulled Ellie up to hers as well, his hand big and warm and callused on hers. "Make sure you replace the spare today."

"And get an AAA card," Kia muttered.

Jack's gaze never left Ellie's, and his thumb swept lazily over her knuckles. "It really has been a long time."

"Yes." She realized she was staring and shook her head. "Something like fourteen years, right? Since graduation. It's odd to think about it, since I work at the high school now, teaching."

He smiled. "I bet you're good at it. So what are you doing in this part of town?"

Ellie gestured to the building down the street. "I also run PIC—it helps out teen girls. We just finished a workshop."

Jack turned his head and took in the hardworking, slightly defeated neighborhood, and the warehouse that wasn't quite on its last legs but maybe getting close. "Bet you're good at that, too."

"How about you?" she asked. "You're out of the military?"

"Yes. And running self-defense studios with my brother. We have one downtown. No Limits Training Club."

She felt discombobulated, talking so lightly with someone who'd once been such an important part of her life. He was all long, tough ranginess, right up close and in her space. He'd shoved his sunglasses to the top of his head, making his military short dark hair stick straight up. He was tanned, and the build of his big, sinewy body said he worked it hard. Even the mud now clinging to his knees looked good on him.

Kia sighed and made a big show of looking at the time on her cell phone. "So we can go now, right?"

"Right," Jack said, tugging on Ellie's hand, bringing her in even closer. "It's really good to see you," he murmured, and hugged her.

Ellie opened her mouth to say "same goes," but Kia spoke first. "Ask him if he likes cats."

"Enough out of you," Ellie muttered. Extremely aware of Jack's gaze on her, she turned back to him. His eyes were flashing an emotion she couldn't quite put her finger on, but it felt both alluring and dangerous. "Well," she said. "Thanks for your help."

He nodded, and from somewhere in his pocket, his cell phone began vibrating. He ignored it to stroke a finger over Ellie's temple, pushing loose strands of hair from her face, tucking then behind her ear. "It should have been more."

She knew he was referring to another time and place, when he *hadn't* been there to help her when she'd needed him most. A time she'd nearly managed to forget, but he clearly hadn't, and the memory threw her a little bit. "Jack—"

His smile no longer meeting his eyes, he turned away. "Don't forget—get a new spare."

And with that, he got into a black Jeep and was gone.

"Yeah," Kia said. "It's definitely the cats."

Ellie slid behind the wheel. "It wasn't the cats."

"Yeah, it was. They're a total deal breaker. Probably you shouldn't mention them."

Ellie slid her a look. "*You* mentioned them."

Kia grinned.

Grinned.

"Okay, let me get this straight," Ellie said, unable to help laughing. "You finally smile, and it's at my expense?"

"I'm laughing *with* you."

Ellie shook her head and eased out into traffic. "You do know that getting a date with a guy isn't the be-all and end-all."

"No. Actually, a date with a *hot* guy is the be-all and end-all."

"Such a kidder today."

"Who says I'm kidding?"

Ellie spent the next week teaching math to kids who didn't want to learn it, while thinking a lot about her own high school past.

And Jack.

It'd been good to see him. Really good. It had brought back a lot of memories, all also good. The few that weren't so great were a vibrant reminder of why she ran PIC.

She had twenty-two girls in the current program. This week they watched a new independent film. The screenwriter, award-winning Sally Aberman, came and gave a talk about the plot's focus—healthy relationships versus abusive relationships; what to do if you were in one, or were trying to help someone get out of one.

Afterward, Sally and Ellie led a workshop where everyone role-played an unhealthy relationship. The idea was to teach the girls how to react in the most positive way for them.

And how to get out of a bad situation. One of the girls, Maddie, a sweet, small, dark-haired, dark-skinned, dark-eyed girl with a dark life, raised her hand. "How do you even know if you're in an unhealthy relationship?"

"Good question," Ellie said. "You can tell by asking yourself if that relationship makes you feel sad, angry, scared or worried. Or if that relationship makes you hurt."

"Like if he's abusive?" asked another teen. Celia. She was tall, skinny, her blond hair pulled back so tight that she was all eyes. Bright blue eyes. "Cuz my sister lets her boyfriend beat on her. She says he doesn't mean to."

"Do you believe that?" Sally asked.

"No."

"Good," Sally said. "Because it's all about trust. And if someone hurts you, they break your trust. You can't, and shouldn't, be with someone without a basis of trust."

Ellie liked that explanation. It put the issue into simple terms a teen could understand and easily explain. She noticed that the girls, most of whom spent their waking hours on Facebook or bored to tears, were actually listening.

Except for the one teen she wanted—needed—to listen.

Kia. She wasn't close to the other girls. She kept everyone at arm's length. And she was texting. Ellie moved to the back of the room and came up next to her, while Sally continued to speak.

"You know the rules about being on the phone during a session," Ellie said quietly.

"I'm not *on* the phone."

Ellie put her hand over Kia's cell. "Remember our talk about respect?"

"I'm respecting, I'm just not necessarily believing."

"This is a workshop I planned specifically for you," Ellie told her softly.

Kia went still for a telling beat, then went back to popping her gum and not paying attention.

"Kia."

"I'm not in an abusive relationship."

A lie. "You can trust me," Ellie said. "You can talk to me."

"Okay."

Ellie looked at Kia's expression of utter indifference and sighed. "Put the phone away," she said, and moved back to the front of the room.

The next week at PIC, Ellie brought in an author who'd written her own teenage biography. The girls were encouraged to write their own stories. Most gave it at least a halfhearted attempt, but Kia refused. In fact, she walked out.

After everyone else had left, Ellie found her in

the bathroom, crying as if her heart was breaking. "Oh, Kia."

"I have something in my eye." She turned away and swiped angrily at her face. "That's all. It's out now."

Ellen handed her tissues and met Kia's gaze in the mirror.

"It's stupid."

"Try me," Ellie said.

"It's just that I have no story to tell." Angrily Kia swiped at her tears. "None. I'm a…nobody."

"Are you kidding? You have a great story. You're turning your life around—"

"From what? My mother didn't mean to have me—did you know that? I'm nothing but trouble, and a terrible inconvenience. I'm a statistic, a…*broken condom.* Writing down my life would be a waste of paper."

Ellie's heart squeezed hard at the words. Once upon a time, she'd felt exactly the same way.

"You don't understand," Kia accused.

"Because I was never seventeen?" Ellie asked wryly, and Kia rolled her eyes. "When I was your age, my mom was in prison."

Even the toughened Kia looked shocked at this one. "For what?"

"Possession and intent to sell. You'd think that would scare me straight, but it didn't. I partied, I skipped school."

"You?"

"Well, I didn't start out wearing boring jeans and sweaters and owning two cats."

Kia cracked a very small smile.

"I did everything I could to follow the same destructive path as my mother."

"So what happened?"

"My grandma happened. I know she's little, but trust me, she's one determined old woman. And she's sneakier than me. She put me in a program called WET Risk Takers."

Kia sighed. "Here it comes. Cue the music, right?"

Ellie smiled, not insulted. "Not exactly. There's no easy happily ever after in real life."

Kia was quiet a minute, absorbing this. "I still don't want to write my story."

Ellie nodded. "I get that, but—"

"And I don't want to know how in time I'll feel different."

Ellie leaned against the counter next to her. "Okay. But I wasn't going to say that."

"Were you going to say that I should rise above it? Cuz that's a load of crap too. I don't want any empty platitudes."

"Wasn't going to say any of that," Ellie said. "Although *platitude* is a pretty good word. You could go to college with that vocabulary."

"Don't start."

They were silent for a full three minutes before Kia blew out a breath, hands on hips. "Fine. What were you going to say?"

"That you could use your journal to tell your story, the one you're doing for school." Ellie had done this all those years when she'd been in WET, and perhaps it was time to bring it to her program.

"Right. *The Musings of Pissed Off and Seventeen.* Fascinating."

"I'm sure it is."

Kia stared at her, then shook her head. "No."

"You don't want to share yourself."

"Well, duh. Did you?"

"No," Ellie admitted. "I never did. But maybe that's the problem."

"No, the fact that you have two cats is your problem."

"Forget the cats! If I write a journal too, will you try?"

"*You'll* keep a journal," Kia said, heavy on the disbelief.

"If that would make you happy."

"What will we write about specifically?" Kia wanted to know.

"Well…" Ellie thought about it. "Maybe about how you need to learn to rein it in a little bit."

Kia looked at her suspiciously. "And you?"

"And I have to do the opposite."

"Meaning?"

"Meaning I need to learn to put myself out there a little bit more. Not as a teacher, not professionally, but personally."

Kia nodded. "So…we write down our feelings, with no judging?"

"If you stop making fun of my cats."

Kia gave a half laugh. "Maybe. If you write about that guy, the one who made you blush."

"What guy?"

"You know, what's-his-name. Tire guy. Jack."

"He didn't make me blush," Ellie said.

"Well, it was hard to see beneath the dirt, but when he hugged you, you got all red. You don't get red when you teach math."

Not what she wanted to hear. "He's just an old friend, Kia."

"Uh-huh. A 'friend'." Kia put air quotes around the word.

From the street an engine revved, and both Ellie and Kia looked out the small bathroom window to see a huge, tricked-out truck parking.

Bobby.

"You're going to see him today?" Ellie asked.

"He apologized," Kia said.

"For hitting you?"

Kia's expression closed off. "He's my ride. I gotta go."

"Okay, but if I suspect he's hurt you again, I'm going to report him."

"He won't." Kia moved to the door.

"Wait. Why don't you let me drive you?"

"He's already here. And my mom said I could go with him. She gave you permission."

Yeah. Except moms didn't always do the right thing. Sometimes the moms were juvenile themselves, with a penchant for the wrong men and the wrong side of the law.

But Kia walked out of the bathroom and a minute later appeared outside. She climbed up into the monster truck and planted a kiss on the guy she liked even though he was bad for her.

Very bad.

Ellie could remember doing the same thing on a certain fated night long ago. She only hoped that if Bobby was stupid enough to lay a hand on Kia again, the teen would be strong enough to kick him somewhere extremely painful. "Be careful," Ellie said as the truck rumbled off with a show of speed, knowing she was talking to both Kia and the girl she herself had once been.

And also knowing no one was listening.

CHAPTER
∼ THREE ∼

Dear Diary,
I still hate you. But I promised Ms. Cahn, so
I'll try to hate you just a little bit less than I
did yesterday.
   Kia

Dear Diary,
So. Hi. My name is Ellie Cahn, and as it turns
out, I haven't put myself out there enough.
For a former wild child, how shameful is
that? I'm hiding behind my work because
it's safe.

   When did that happen? When did I become
afraid to live my life?

And what exactly am I supposed to do about it? I'll let you know soon as I figure it out. Wish me luck.
Ellie

The next week's PIC workshop was titled: Making Good Choices. Ellie and her guest speaker, former TV child Katie Stephens, spent half the day giving the girls the tools they needed in order to do just that—make good choices.

It hadn't started out smoothly. None of the teens were prepared to admit that they'd either seen people they care about making bad choices or done so themselves.

Then Katie Stephens sat on the floor with them and told them a story. *Her* story. In fine detail she described how she'd gone from being the happy-go-lucky middle child of a blue-collar family to one of the highest-paid child TV stars of all time to an unemployed, uneducated, homeless twenty-year-old. Her mistakes started at age fifteen, when she'd become emancipated from her parents, fired them as managers in order to get out from beneath their authority, then gone through handlers as fast as she'd gone through the booze and pot. By the time she'd hit nineteen, she was flat broke, and had no one who cared about her because she'd pushed them all away.

Her testimony had opened the floodgates, and by the end of the session, almost all the girls were sharing stories, and even laughing and having a good time.

Except for Kia.

Kia hadn't made any bad decisions, or so she claimed.

Celia and Maddie had snorted their disagreement, but Kia had held firm.

She was good, no regrets, nothing to fix.

Afterward, Ellie had walked out with the girls, almost everyone still smiling and talking—until they all came to a sudden surprised halt on the sidewalk by Ellie's car.

Mind your own business, Teach had been spray painted across her back window. With an *Or Else* beneath it.

A collective gasp rose from the girls.

"Who would do that?" Zoe whispered. Zoe was one of the younger girls, and had been sent to PIC because her mother suspected depression and didn't know what else to do with her. She shifted closer to Ellie and reached for her hand.

Ellie gently squeezed it. "It's just a prank," she said firmly, calmly, even though on the inside she was seething at whoever had changed the happy atmosphere to a fearful one.

And she had a feeling she knew exactly who'd done it. She carefully didn't look at Kia, but she felt sure the culprit was Bobby. She'd bet her last buck on it.

As for Kia, she'd gone positively green.

"You okay?" Ellie asked her.

"I broke up with him," she said softly, staring at the graffiti-smeared window. "After I realized...you know."

"That it was an unhealthy relationship?"

Kia nodded. "I think he blames you."

No doubt, but at least he hadn't gone after Kia.

"I'm so sorry, Ms. Cahn," she whispered miserably.

The other girls moved closer and huddled around her. She might be a handful, but she was *their* handful.

"Not your fault," Ellie said, hugging Kia before calling the police to make a report. When the girls were gone, she scraped the paint off the window the best she could, which wasn't all that great. Some of it was still visible, but it couldn't be helped, not until she got a chance to get a stronger soap.

She didn't sleep a wink that night, and woke up wishing she could wrap her fingers around Bobby's overbuilt neck.

But she couldn't give him more credit than he was due. It wasn't entirely Bobby's fault that she hadn't slept.

Ellie had never been much of a solid sleeper. Once upon a time, that had been due to nightmares. Now it was more anxiety related. Had she shut off the heater? Had she paid the water bill? The list was never-ending, and at two in the morning, things that didn't matter in the big scheme of things suddenly took on huge importance.

But adding a self-defense program to her PIC program... That *was* important in the big scheme of things, and something she'd been wanting to do for some time now. She'd just never had the means. If she could give that to the teens, the confidence they gained might help them realize they didn't have to be victims.

Which was how she found herself on the sidewalk in front of No Limits Training Club.

Jack's place.

She'd looked him up. That had been the easy part. But she stood there for a good five minutes, talking herself first into, and then out of, going inside. The hard part. Because it was one thing to run into a long-lost friend on the side of the road, another entirely to actively seek him out.

You need this, she reminded herself. *The girls need this.*

And that was absolutely true. The girls did need this.

But there was also another reason for standing here, one she didn't really like to put into words.

Simply put, she *wanted* to see Jack again. As for what else she might want, she didn't dare let her mind go there. All those years ago he'd been very important to her. Truth was, he'd been her closest ally, her best friend.

And yet when he'd left town, he'd left her behind as easily as he had all his troubles. Maybe she could have understood if he'd kept in touch.

But he hadn't.

She'd gotten over many, many things in her life, but that—losing one of the few people who mattered to her—had been one of the hardest, and all these years later she still wanted to understand why he'd done it.

Not that she was going to ask him. Nope. She had way more pride than that. This was about the girls. Period. And maybe if she kept telling herself that, she'd believe it.

She glanced at the sign again: No Limits Training Club.

No Limits. Did that apply to old best friends? She hoped so. "He'll say yes," she told herself.

"Yes."

She nearly leaped out of her skin at the low, husky voice in her ear. Whirling around, she came face-to-face with the man himself, looking lean and tough and badass in washed-out jeans—no mud on the knees today—and a long-sleeve black collared shirt.

And those mirrored sunglasses.

His brows rose above the lenses. "Another flat?"

"No." She let out a little laugh. "Though I wanted to thank you for helping me out."

"You already did."

Right. "Well, I wanted to do it again."

His mouth quirked into an almost-there smile. "Then, you're welcome. Again."

She hesitated. "Okay, and maybe that's not the only reason I'm here."

He just looked at her, tall and dark and very still, his face giving nothing away. He'd always been hard to read, but the military had fine-tuned and honed the skill. She let out a breath, her thoughts all tangled up now that she was face-to-face with him again. Because here was the problem—even on the best of days, asking for help wasn't easy for her, and this wasn't the best of days. Plus, it was Jack, who'd once been a part of her life. The *best* part.

Until he'd walked away without a backward glance.

"We didn't keep in touch," she said.

He registered no change in expression at the abrupt subject change, and she tried not to smack herself for letting her mouth run off with her brain.

"No," he said quietly. "We didn't."

"Actually," she said. "*You* didn't. That's what I really meant to say. *You* left. *You* didn't keep in touch."

"I went into the army, El."

El. His long-ago nickname for her, one she hadn't heard in years. It melted her a little bit, dammit. "I know, but even in the military, they have these new-fangled things called computers and email."

He let out a long breath that said maybe she was being a pain in the keister. Well, she might as well stick with what she was good at.

"I'm not great at communicating," he finally said.

No kidding. "If that was an apology, it needs work."

"I went into Special Forces."

She nodded. She'd known, and had worried about him. A lot.

"I was out of touch with everyone," he said. "Not just you. Family, friends…"

And he'd probably been so far off the grid that he hadn't wanted to keep in touch. She understood that too. "But then you came home. I don't know when. I wish I did."

He looked at her for a beat, not a muscle so much as twitching. She admired the whole stillness thing. It was a good skill. He was like a big predatory cat, dangerous and lethal. Beautiful. She wished she could pull that off herself. It might help her in the classroom. But she'd never done *still* well.

Or at all.

"How's your grandma?" he asked.

"Nice subject change."

"It worked for you a minute ago." He gave her a look that could still make her smile.

Damn he was good. She could lay the cause of most of her teenage wildness at the feet of that innate charm of his. Just one look into those bad-boy eyes and she'd have done anything he asked. "Grandma is alive and kicking and demanding great-grandchildren."

His face softened. "No one's swept you off your feet then?"

"I don't need to be swept off my feet. I want a partner, not a knight in shining armor." She paused. "How about you?"

"What about me?"

She had to shake her head and laugh. "I see getting you to talk about yourself is still like pulling teeth."

He flashed said teeth in a playful smile. If they kept up this playful banter, she was going to get sucked into his vortex. She had no doubt.

"So you don't want to tell me anything about yourself," she said. "That's okay. Maybe you have too many women to count."

His smile was pure testosterone-ridden maleness.

"Men," she said in mock disgust. "You're all the same."

"Now, there we're going to have to agree to disagree."

"Yeah? How long have you been back in town?"

"Two years."

"And why did it take us two years to run into each other?"

His smile faded, replaced by that cool, blank face.

"Wow," she said. "That's good, Jack. They teach you how to do that in Special Forces?"

"I didn't want to stir up bad memories for you."

She stared at him as she processed this. Bad memories? They'd had nothing but great memories until—

Until.

The night of their senior farewell, at a party in the hills afterward, packed with their entire graduating class. He'd left early with a girl that wasn't her and she'd let hurt feelings rule her brain.

Bad mistake. One she'd paid for dearly. "So you what?" she murmured. "You stayed away from me out of some sort of guilt?"

He didn't answer. He didn't have to, and she let out a low breath. "Seriously? Because that's the stupidest thing I've ever heard."

"It's true."

"Well." She tried to understand but found she couldn't. "I suppose if you're going to carry guilt around for, what, fourteen years, then I might as well use it."

His military training made it all but impossible to read him, but she was certain she saw a little light come into those gun-slate eyes of his. Affection for certain, and also warmth. The comfort of old memories.

She'd use that, too.

Hell, when it came to the teens, she'd do whatever she had to. "I could use a little favor."

CHAPTER
❧— FOUR —❧

Standing on the sidewalk in front of his building, Jack watched Ellie fidget, and despite the fact that he had a lot going on this afternoon, and not a lot to smile about while he was at it, he felt his mouth curve up anyway.

She'd always been able to make him smile, which was different in itself.

He wasn't a guy who smiled a lot. He'd been a rotten kid and an even worse teenager. He was the last of six kids born to two blue-collar, hardworking parents. He'd had little to no supervision, leaving him far too much time to find trouble.

And he'd found it, repeatedly.

After growing up fast and rough—all his own doing—he'd gone straight into the army, and then on to Special Forces.

Oddly enough, he'd thrived there, even if he had seen and done too much for his thirty-two years. Now that he was back in Connecticut where he'd started and not in mortal danger on a daily basis, little got to him, and certainly less disturbed him.

Except Ellie.

She disturbed him plenty. She put a ripple in his calm, a visceral, physical ripple that was more like a punch to the solar plexus. Not because of the attraction, though there was that. No, this was much more. Deeper.

Much deeper.

There'd been a time in his life when she'd been his only grounding force. She'd been a friend, someone to confide in, someone to watch his back.

Not sleep with though.

No, for all they'd meant to each other, they'd never been intimate. His teenage self had thought she was hot, but she'd been his friend. Yes, she'd skipped school, sneaked out of her grandmother's house, drunk under-age…but he'd known the truth about her, the truth she'd hidden from everyone. On the inside she'd been nothing but a lost girl, a *good* girl simply playing at toeing the line.

Unlike him.

He hadn't been playing at anything, and Ellie had been far too nice for the likes of him in that phase of his life. No way would he have touched her, no matter how much he'd wanted to do just that.

When she'd gotten hurt because of him…it'd nearly killed him.

And now she needed his help. Whatever it was, he would do it. "You going to tell me about this little favor?" he asked.

"Yes." She fidgeted some more. "But to be honest, it's not little so much as..."

"Big?" he guessed.

She grimaced. "Yes."

His eyes cut to her car, specifically to her back window, where something had clearly been painted on, and not quite successfully scrubbed off. "More car problems?"

"No, that's nothing. Don't worry about it."

Which meant the opposite, of course. "What did it say before you smeared it around?"

"It said, 'Have a nice day.'"

He gave her a long look. She'd never been able to lie to him. No one had.

"Okay," she said, caving. "So it wasn't exactly a greeting. It's not important, or related to the favor."

"What did it say, Ellie?"

She blew out a sigh and mumbled something beneath her breath.

"Didn't quite catch that, El."

"You're not going to like it."

"I already know that."

"Fine. It said, 'Mind your own business, Teach. Or else.'"

He felt himself tense. "New boyfriend?"

"No, this particular charmer belongs to Kia, the girl who was with me when I got the flat tire. Or he did belong to her until she dumped him. At my encouragement." Ellie looked at her window. "He's not happy with me."

"His name?"

She turned back to him, eyes sharp. "I fight my own battles these days, Jack."

"Did you at least make a police report?"

"Yes."

Her hair was loose and in her face again. Her eyes were flashing stubbornness and pride. She'd always been sure of herself, and that attraction and heat he'd once felt for her surged again. "Let's hear this favor you need from me."

She nibbled on her lower lip.

"I'm going to say yes, Ellie, so just spit it out."

"That's a lot of power," she said. "An open yes like that."

Yeah. If she only knew…

"What if I abuse it?" Her tone was playful.

Contagious. "Go for it," he said. "Try me."

"I can't decide if that's just overconfidence or stupidity," she said, studying him, hands on hips. "Giving me carte blanche like that."

"I can handle you."

She laughed, the sound joyful and easy, but suddenly he got the unsettling feeling that maybe she was right. Maybe for the first time in his life, he truly *was* in over his head. "Let's take this inside." Grabbing her hand, he opened the front door to the building, nudging her in ahead of him.

The foyer of No Limits was wide and open, lined with sleek black shelving where people shed their outerwear and shoes before heading into any of the four studios. To the left was the reception desk, behind which stood Kel, Jack's brother and business partner.

Kel wore a white tae kwon do teacher's uniform—a pullover-style jacket, loose pants and black belt. He'd just finished teaching a class, and his students, ten women varying in age from early twenties to fifties, were sagged on the benches, pulling their shoes back on, all flushed and shiny with exertion.

Kel hadn't broken a sweat. Body relaxed, a smile lurking behind his solemn eyes, he nodded at Jack, who introduced him to Ellie. Kel had been four years ahead of them in school, and though he had never met Ellie, he'd heard plenty about her. He alone knew what Ellie had meant to Jack and raised a brow.

Jack ignored him.

"You only teach women?" Ellie asked, glancing at the bench.

Kel gave Jack another long look. "No," he said. "Though it started out that way."

"Come on," Jack said to Ellie. "I'll show you around." Still ignoring his brother's dark, knowing gaze, he led Ellie up the stairs to his office. "We've recently expanded."

She went straight to the window on the far wall of his office, which looked down on the four studios below. There were two classes currently going on and she watched for a minute. "Nice place. You teach too?"

"Yes." It was his cause, and a big part of it was in fact because of her. Hence Kel's amusement.

Not that she knew that. Not that she ever would. He

moved up behind her to look over her shoulder, but ended up instead absorbing the sensation of having her so close. There was a longing inside him, and it wasn't the usual physical attraction he might feel for a woman.

Well, there was that. But again, it was more.

Far more. With Ellie, his heart was involved and always had been. Whether he liked it or not.

It had been a very long time since he'd been this close to her, other than when he'd hugged her that day he'd changed her tire. He'd hugged her that long-ago night, too. Hugged her just before he left her at that party in the hills and gone off with some girl he'd hardly known. Nicole something. Ellie had rolled her eyes at him and waved him off, intending to go home with her friend.

Instead, her friend had gotten wasted and left without Ellie, stranding her out there. She'd left with two guys from her class who'd promised her a ride home, only they'd tried for much more than that. She'd gotten away, but she'd been hurt, and Jack had never, ever forgiven himself.

Forget keeping his hands to himself. He slipped them out of his pockets and pulled her in against him.

Turning to face him, she wrapped her arms around his waist and hugged him back. Her hair teased his nostrils when he pressed in close for—hell, he didn't know for sure—comfort? Whatever he was doing, he had no business doing it.

"What are we doing?" she whispered into his chest.

"Hugging you hello," he lied.

"We did that last week."

"Hmm." She was warm and soft, and so small and vulnerable it made his throat tighten. He didn't want to let go.

"Are we going to hug every time we see each other?" She pressed her face into his throat as if maybe she couldn't help herself either.

"Is there a hug quota for old friends?" he asked, stroking a hand down her hair.

She pulled back just enough to meet his gaze. "Friends?"

"We were friends once."

"Yes, and you sure as hell never used to hug me like I was a piece of china that could break if not handled gently."

"I'm not doing that." But he was. Busted, he stepped back and forced a smile. "So let's get to this mysterious favor. You want to take a class?"

"No, but I know someone who does. Several some-ones." She paused and looked guilty. "Okay, *lots* of someones. I told you I've been running this specialized program for troubled teen girls."

"Teaching them what—how to sneak out of their grandma's house without detection?" he teased. "How to forge a signature on a late slip? No, wait—I know. How to procure alcohol."

She shoved his chest with a good-natured laugh. "Hey, I grew up."

"I know," he said, grabbing her hand. "And I know about PIC. I saw the write-up on you from the paper last year. You take a group of girls on for six months and teach them things like self-respect and confidence through film and other avenues, right?"

She nodded thoughtfully, and if he wasn't mistaken, he saw a flash of hurt in those green eyes as well. No doubt she was wondering why, if he'd known where she was all this time, he'd never looked her up.

He'd looked her up.

Plenty.

"If you know about my program," she said, "you probably realize that I'm dealing with the most troubled of girls. Most of them are smack in the middle of unhealthy relationships with their parents, their siblings, their so-called friends. Boyfriends..." She grimaced. "They see so much, they're exposed to so much. And the danger to some of them seems to be escalating."

He nodded. He worked with kids too. She wasn't telling him anything he didn't know. "How can I help?" he asked.

"I was hoping you'd be interested in teaching the girls self-defense. I realize that the six-month thing is a huge commitment, but we could make it work with whatever time you have to give, and—"

"Yes."

"I'd try to get you a fair stipend, but the truth is, PIC is nonprofit and barely making ends meet right now—" She broke off and paused. "What?"

"I said yes. No stipend necessary. I'll volunteer the time."

"Really?"

He arched a brow. "You thought I'd say no?"

"Well, I thought at the very least I'd have to work a lot harder to convince you."

He leaned back against his desk and studied her. She wasn't wearing a ring, but he already knew she wasn't married. She'd dated a dentist for six months last year, but had broken it off. Before that, she'd gone out with an architect.

Safe.

She'd dated safe.

When had she become a person who played safe? Since he was deathly afraid that that very long-ago summer night had caused the change, he purposely let out a protracted, calming breath. "You're right, convince me. I'll volunteer my time, and in return you'll..."

She gave him a careful, wary look. Smart girl. "I'll what?"

"Go out with me."

She blinked. "Out, as in...on a date? Like dinner or something?"

"Whatever you want."

She nibbled on the inside of her cheek and considered that. Considered him. "What if what I want is complicated?"

"How complicated can it be, Ellie?"

Her face flamed red and he found himself smiling. "I'd love to know the thought that put that look on your face. Should I guess?"

"No! I'm tired. And punchy. And you hugged me, and now all I can think about is—" She gave him a little shove. "Oh, never mind! This is about the girls. *No* NC-17 stuff."

"You're right," he agreed, happy to know her mind had gone the NC-17 route at all. "Maybe later."

"Jack!"

He was liking this conversation more and more. "Let's start out with dinner," he murmured, and ran a finger over her jaw, fascinated by the way her eyes seemed to darken when he touched her.

"Will you show me some moves first?"

Well aware she meant on the mats in one of the studios and not in his bedroom, he waggled a brow, teasing her. "Okay, but you should know, I don't do NC-17 stuff before dinner."

She closed her eyes. "You're not going to let me forget this, are you?"

"Not anytime soon, no."

Dear Diary,
Standing up for myself, getting out of a bad relationship, making the right choice—not a single one of those things worked out so well. So…any other bright ideas? No?
   Bite me.
   Kia

Dear Diary,
So if journals are for emotional growth, here's mine. I'm figuring things out, starting to see that my life got boring and staid right about the time I stopped really living it.
   Not good.

I'm changing that. Going for things. Starting now.

I realize the irony here, that I'm trying to keep the teens to a safe life and I want to leave my safe life behind.

But I'm also excited. I stepped outside the box and looked up Jack to help me with the girls. And it had hardly anything at all to do with the fact that I've missed him so very much.

Okay, it had a lot to do with that. Shh, don't tell him.

Ellie

In five minutes they were in one of the empty studios, shoes off, facing each other. "So," Ellie said, and gave Jack a come-on gesture.

She looked adorable and hot at the same time, and he wanted nothing more than to play, but being on the mats was a serious business. "There are rules," he said.

"Yeah, yeah. Bring it, Jack."

"El, I'm a black belt seven times over. I can't bring it, I'd hurt you."

"Show me the flip thingie," she said.

"What?"

"You know, where you flip someone over your shoulder to the ground, like you see in the movies. I've always wanted to learn to do that."

"That's an advanced move and—"

She made the sound of a chicken.

Okay, she was so going down. He smiled at her, letting the gesture come all the way through his eyes as he offered her his hand. Smiling back, softening for him, she automatically put her hand in his. With a yank, he tucked into her and flipped her over his shoulder. But instead of letting her go flying through the air to the mat as he would have with anyone else, he kept his hands on her and eased her gently down to the floor.

From flat on her back, she looked up at him. "You pulled your punch."

"Didn't want to hurt you."

She winced a little and his heart about stopped as he leaned over her. "Ellie. Did I hurt you—?"

Which was all he got out before she hooked a leg around one of his and tugged.

And dropped his sorry butt right on top of her.

CHAPTER
❦— FIVE —❧

Ellie barely felt Jack's weight before he caught himself and rolled them so that she was on top.

"Where did you learn that move?" he asked.

"TV." She lowered her face close to his. "You went easy on me, Jack."

His hands tightened on her, but he didn't say anything.

"Told you before," she said. "I'm not fragile."

He started to speak, but the studio door opened and his brother poked his head in.

"New type of defense?" Kel asked, amused. "Because I like it."

Ellie pushed upright and smiled triumphantly. "I pinned him."

Kel grinned. "Not many can say that." He shut the door.

Ellie looked down at Jack. In their misspent youth he'd been highly skilled at getting girls to fall at his feet. Apparently he'd lost none of that particular talent, because she *was* falling.

Hard.

He stared up at her, and as if he could see her feelings in her face, he very softly murmured her name. She might have been mortified, but he didn't give her the time for that. He rolled to his feet and pulled her with him.

He didn't bring up the moment that night at dinner, for which she was grateful. Instead, they talked about... well, everything else. She learned that his parents had retired to Palm Beach. His siblings had all left the area too, except for Kel.

"There's five grandkids," Jack told her with a baffled shake of his head. "More than enough to take the pressure off me and Kel."

"So you have no interest in the marriage-and-kids route?" she asked.

He shrugged, and her stomach did something funny. Either the food wasn't agreeing with her, or...

Or she was the tiniest bit disappointed.

"When I was in the army," he said, "my life wasn't my own. There was no successful way to have a committed relationship. I saw no reason to bring a family into that."

"But you're out now. And your life is your own." She paused, uncertain. "Isn't it?"

"I guess maybe I'm just not used to that fact yet."

"Maybe you just haven't met The One to make it worth it."

His gaze locked on hers for a long beat, during which she held her breath and waited for a response.

"Maybe," he finally said, so quietly she wasn't sure if she heard the words or read his lips. Whichever, they warmed her in a way she hadn't realized she needed warming.

The next day, Ellie sat alone in the PIC offices, staring at the envelope she'd just opened while going through the mail. Or more correctly, she was staring at a check with a lot of zeros on it.

An anonymous donation, which had come from a lawyer of a business labeled only BNL, Inc.

Enough money to move PIC to a safer location and sign a new lease. She was boggled, overwhelmed and touched beyond belief. And for the first time in a long time—too long—she took a deep breath without the punch of anxiety, and wished she could hug her mysterious benefactor.

Two nights later Jack was back in his studio with Ellie. They were planning out the self-defense curriculum for the girls at PIC. The rest of his employees and students had left for the day, leaving just the two of them in the building.

For thirty minutes he'd shown her the beginner moves he would teach the girls in their workshop. Ellie was working in her snug yoga pants and a tank top that didn't quite meet the waistband of the pants, both clinging to her damp skin.

Jack was trying not to notice.

They'd taken a break because her cell phone kept going off, and with each call she received, he better understood how much she took on herself to run PIC on top of her full-time teaching job. There were workshops to plan, speakers to arrange for, and then the responsibility for the girls themselves.

She finally ended her call and apologized for the umpteenth time, coming back to the mat.

"It's okay," he said. "You're swamped."

"Always."

"If I heard right, you just booked what sounded like a brain surgeon and a race-car driver for upcoming workshops."

"Yeah." She smiled. "Good stuff, right?"

He thought *she* was good stuff. "Come here, El."

"I don't know…" Her eyes sparkled with good humor as she stood facing him, hands on hips. "The last time, I ended up on my back."

That sat between them for a beat, and then she wisely changed the subject.

"Thanks for doing this," she said softly. "I love that the girls are going to learn this stuff. From you."

Nothing about Ellie Cahn was like any other woman he knew. She said what she meant, no hidden meaning. It was incredibly refreshing.

Not to mention just a little terrifying. He'd spent his entire life avoiding women who would want things from him.

Not that Ellie would ever ask for anything for herself...

But he wouldn't hurt her. Ever. So why he gave a little tug on her arms, making sure she was off balance enough to fall against him, was anyone's guess.

But when she smacked into him, he hugged her close. "You trying to save the world one kid at a time, El?"

"Maybe." Pulling back, she met his gaze. "When we were that age, I was on a fast track to nowhere. And then my only anchor left town."

Him. The knowledge was a hot poker in his chest. "I had to go," he said. "There was nothing for me here. I was a punk-ass kid with a chip on my shoulder looking for trouble. And I'd have found it too."

"I know." She entangled their fingers and brought them to her chest, right over her heart. "I needed to make something of myself, too. WET Risk Takers saved my life. They taught me some self-respect, and how to take care of myself. How to stop walking the line of danger and stupidity, because I was worth something and deserved more. I knew if I could maybe do the same for even one girl, then I had to try."

He stared at her and felt the catch deep within him. Heat, definitely. But affection too, and something more, much more than either. "You're amazing, Ellie, you know that?"

She shook her head, a quiet smile on her face. "You gave your life to protect this country for what, ten years? *You're* the amazing one." The light in her eyes shifted, going from fun and games to that same something that was happening inside him.

It had happened the instant he'd first seen her again, on the side of the road trying to change her tire, muddy from head to toe.

It had happened again when she'd first sought out his help here at his studio.

And again every time he so much as looked at her.

"Do you want to go get something to eat?" she asked, her smile fading when he paused. "And by your hesitation, I'm guessing you're trying to figure out how to say no and back out gracefully. It's okay, Jack. I understand."

"No, you don't," he said. "And yes, I want to get something to eat."

"Are you going to tell me what I don't understand?"

"No."

She considered him for a beat, then stood and stretched. Offered him her hand.

Actually, she was offering more than a hand and they both knew it. He wasn't an easygoing, lighthearted, laid-back sort of guy. He'd seen a lot. Hell, he'd done a lot. He battled the dark memories with hard work.

And the occasional relationship.

Okay, maybe more than occasional. But no one ever snagged his interest for long. Little did. The studios were successful, and doing great, but if someone had only last week asked him if he was happy and satisfied, he'd have to say he wasn't quite there.

And now, with Ellie, he was even more confused because emotions had been added to the mix.

It made him uncomfortable. *Vulnerable.*

But suddenly she was right in front of him, touching

his face. "Jack," she whispered, looking into his eyes. Slowly she smiled, then kissed him, and by the time she pulled back, neither of them was breathing steadily.

"So," she murmured. "We have the workshop down, I think. It'd be great if the girls could dress appropriately for your class, as they would here at your studio. I was wondering how much uniforms are, and what kind you'd want."

"I'll provide uniforms."

"No, Jack. I can't ask you to do that—"

"You didn't ask. You wouldn't."

She looked bemused. "What does that mean?"

"That you'd find it more preferable to choke on your pride than ask anyone for help."

When she opened her mouth to protest, he arched a brow, daring her to say otherwise.

"It's called independence," she finally said.

"Or pigheadedness," he corrected. "Consider the uniforms a done deal, Ellie."

"I don't know what to say."

"How about 'thank you'."

She smiled. "Thank you."

"And maybe, 'I'm forever in your debt, Jack.'"

With a laugh, she shifted close again. She slid a hand along his arm until he automatically stepped into her, going for the embrace, registering a split second too late her wicked intent as she hooked a leg behind his calf and dropped him.

Not a complete fool, he took her down with him, and—

"Hello? Ellie, is that you?" came a tinny voice.

WHAT THE HEART WANTS

Ellie lifted her head off the floor in confusion at the voice echoing in the studio around them. "Grandma?"

Jack blinked. *Grandma?*

"Dear?" came the older woman's disembodied voice. "I think you pocket-dialed me again."

Ellie pulled her phone from her pocket and winced. "Yep, that was me. I'm sorry."

"You sound breathless, dear. What are you doing?"

Ellie's gaze flew to Jack. He started to speak, but she put a hand over his mouth. "I'm exercising," Ellie said to her grandma, then grimaced at the lie.

Jack grinned.

"Well, don't overdo it," her grandma said. "You might get hurt."

Jack ended the call for Ellie and tossed the phone aside.

"Am I going to get hurt, Jack?"

He looked into her eyes for a long moment, then rose and pulled her up to her feet. "No," he said firmly, and took a big step back from her to ensure it.

For the rest of the week, Ellie kept herself too busy to acknowledge the ball of sadness in her chest. She told herself that it was midterms, and she had kids panicking, not to mention papers to grade and PIC to deal with. She was taking applications for kids for the next session, and planning new workshops and...

And.

It wasn't school.

It wasn't PIC.

It was the look on Jack's face when she'd been in his studio.

Determination.

To not hurt her.

He was backing off so that he wouldn't, couldn't, hurt her.

Which was fine. She understood. She really did. And telling herself that, she simply stepped on the hamster wheel and kept going.

Fortunately, there hadn't been any more unpleasant messages left on her car. Even better, she'd procured a lease on a building in a safer area and was making plans to move PIC for the next session.

Unfortunately, Kia had come to school with some suspicious bruising on her arm, which she'd claimed had happened at basketball practice.

Ellie hoped that was true.

At the end of the week, one day before Jack was to give his first self-defense workshop at PIC, he appeared in the doorway of Ellie's classroom about fifteen minutes after the last kid had left.

"Hey," she said from behind her desk, doing her best to remain cool and calm. Not easy when he was the best thing she'd seen all week. "You need help with preparation for tomorrow?"

"No."

She waited, but he said nothing more.

"Is this a social visit?" she asked.

Instead of answering, he pushed off the doorjamb and came close, leaning a hip on the edge of her desk as he studied her. "I have a question."

Uh-oh.

"Are we avoiding each other for any particular reason?"

She met his inscrutable gaze and decided to go with the only thing she had—honesty. "I don't know about you, but I got the impression you were walking away from a personal relationship with me, and I didn't want to face it. Denial is my friend."

He didn't smile. "I'm not walking away."

"Regret then. You're regretting...me."

His eyes were reproachful. "Don't put words in my mouth, El."

"Then give me your words."

He pulled her out of her chair and into him. His arms came around her, warm and strong and familiar, and in spite of herself, she melted against him. "Maybe I got... unnerved," he said.

"Maybe? Or definitely?"

He let out a breath and pressed his forehead to hers. "Definitely. But I'm working on it."

"Yeah. How's that going?"

An almost smile quirked the corners of his mouth. "I'll keep you updated. I can be...a little slow on the uptake."

"Yes. It's a genetic flaw in the male design."

His huff of laughter said he agreed. "I was hoping for patience from you."

"I have buckets of patience."

His mouth twitched. "Want to exercise some of it while we go to dinner?"

"Now?"

"Yeah. Now."

As if she could resist.

They drove to the shore. Since it was early spring and freezing, they were the only crazy people there. Jack took her to a small seafood café on the water, and afterward they walked along the pier. Side by side they watched the last of the day fade away.

Then Jack shifted to face her and looked deep into her eyes. She liked that, she'd discovered. Far more than she should, given that he was a huge risk to her emotional well-being, not to mention her heart, which wanted to roll over and reveal its tender underside to him. "You're going to face twenty teenage girls tomorrow," she said. "Nervous?"

He laughed softly.

"Right." She shook her head at herself. "I guess compared to the things you've faced, it's going to be a walk in the park."

He pressed his mouth to her jaw and said nothing.

"You probably saw things," she said. "In Special Forces."

He kissed the spot beneath her ear and she shivered. "You're trying to distract me."

"No, *you're* distracting me." He shifted to the corner of her mouth.

"Where were you stationed?"

And then the other corner… "In places hotter and sandier than you can imagine."

She ignored the fact that her knees were wobbly. "Did you ever get hurt?"

"Yes."

Her heart ached. "A lot?"

"More than I wanted to."

Her eyes met his. "Did you ever think you were going to die?"

He sighed and lifted his head. "Yes."

"What happened?"

"I didn't." He cupped her face. "Any more questions that you need answered right now?"

She could feel his body against hers, strong and warm. "No," she whispered. "Not right now."

"Good." And his mouth covered hers.

CHAPTER
❧ SIX ❧

Dear Diary,
Ms. Cahn is always telling me that I'm stron-
ger than I think. That I can walk away. That
I can say no.

That I have the power.

If that was really true, I'd have longer hair
and better eyelashes. I'd have better grades.
I'd have friends who liked me for me and not
for the fact that they think my boyfriend is
cool and want to date his friends.

I'd have a mom who was home more. And
a dad who hadn't moved on to his second
family, forgetting me.

And a boyfriend who never expected me
to do things I didn't want to do. You know?

Oh, why am I even asking you? You're a text file.
Kia

Dear Diary,
Putting myself out there is a thrill I'd forgotten about. I feel happy, exhilarated.
Alive.
Probably I'm heading for a world of hurt but I'm going to have to worry about that later. Because now is working for me for the first time in a long time.
Keep wishing me good luck. I think it's helping.
Ellie

The next day, Jack was at PIC, surrounded by a group of teenage girls wearing martial arts uniforms provided by No Limits. He'd been introduced to each of them by Ellie, who stood at the back of the large room, leaning against the wall.

Watching him.

"Do you know why I'm here?" he asked the girls.

"Yes," said a dark-haired, petite girl with the biggest brown eyes he'd ever seen. "You're going to teach us how to protect ourselves."

"My mom says violence is *never* the answer." This from a blonde.

Kia, standing next to her, made a teenage sound of disagreement. "It's *always* the answer."

Jack looked at her, not missing the defiant misery in her eyes. "Martial arts isn't about violence." He focused on all of them. "Or about gaining the winning edge in a fight."

"But I thought that's exactly what it is for," Kia said, sounding as if she needed to believe it, as if she had a few fights of her own coming up. "To win fights."

"It's true that the disciplines were conceived in the context of hand-to-hand combat," Jack said. "But most masters have zero tolerance for using their skills aggressively."

"What should they be used for?" one of the girls asked.

"Exercise for one, or a way to strengthen your body and soul."

Kia looked hugely disappointed. "Strengthen a soul? How do you strengthen a soul while kicking butt?"

Jack resisted looking at the woman at the back of the classroom, the woman who strengthened his soul by just being. "Through balance," he said. "Through flexibility, coordination, stamina and posture. For instance, you're slouching. Do you know what that tells me?"

Kia lifted her chin. "That I'm bored?"

"That you're not very sure of yourself. Which leaves you open and vulnerable, and all because of perception. Perception is everything."

Kia immediately straightened her shoulders and he nodded. "That's good. Show inner strength. Even if you have to fake it. Fake it long enough and it becomes habit, and more importantly, real." He looked around the room as every girl in it straightened their shoulders.

"You all look stronger already. Now let's train to avoid conflict."

Kia didn't say anything to that, and Jack knew he had to show, not tell. Gesturing them to the mat, he began with a few basic white belt jujitsu moves. An hour later, they'd learned how to escape from a wrist grab, a front stranglehold, and how to fall.

"I want to learn how to drop someone," one of the girls said. "My brother. He's obnoxious and mean, and shoves me around all the time. If I could drop him just once, he'd leave me alone, I know it."

Jack gave Ellie a 'come here' gesture.

"Uh-oh," she said, but she was smiling when she stepped close, her body language warm and open.

And he couldn't help but smile back. "Throw a punch," he told her.

Game, she did just that, which he stopped with a basic inside forearm block, stepping in with his left foot to the left of hers. Twisting on the ball of his foot, he slid his arm behind her, holding her bicep as he rotated his upper body, sweeping her leg back, and out from beneath her. But instead of letting her fall, he lowered her gently to the ground.

Everyone clapped and applauded, and in the next minute, they were all eagerly trying it out on each other.

Much later, when the session was over and it was just himself and Ellie left alone at PIC, she smiled at him. "They liked you."

"They like the sense of power I gave them."

"That too." She walked up to him, her hips swaying

gently, a soft smile on her face. "I sure like the power you give me." She kissed his jaw and blew all his brain cells with nothing more than the feel of her lips on him. "I like having you in my life, Jack."

His heart skipped a beat. It'd been a long time since he'd let someone in. Longer still since he'd wanted to. He knew very well he'd started this, but it didn't stop the doubts. Or the knowledge that eventually he'd hurt her if they kept at this. "Ellie—"

"Shh, Jack," she said softly, which completely and utterly belied the distinctly *un*gentle way she used his own move against him, dropping him to the ground.

For the third time since they'd found each other again. Maybe he should just stay down for the count. He hit the mat and stared up at her. "You're getting good."

She laughed. Hands on her knees, she bent over him. "Need to be more aware of your surroundings, soldier."

"True." Then he kicked her feet out from beneath her and caught her as she fell, rolling her flat to the mat and pinning her there beneath him. "Likewise."

Not looking particularly disturbed, she grinned up at him.

Take your hands off her, he told himself. *She's looking for more than you ever planned to give her.* It was all over her. "Ellie," he said, voice raw, and rolled her off him.

Ellie watched as Jack rose literally to his feet in one economical, graceful movement, pulling her up as well. "I have to go, El."

"Scared you off, did I?"

"I have other classes to teach this afternoon."

Not exactly an answer, but she nodded, even managed a smile when he leaned in to kiss her goodbye. He looked at her in a way that stole her breath. The way he touched her, kissed her, how he'd stepped in to work at PIC…it all spoke of how much he cared.

And yet…and yet when they had a moment, whenever there'd been the threat of getting too close, of possibly giving too much of themselves too fast, he backed off.

Shaking her head, she went to her office to catch up on paperwork. Much later, she'd gotten little done other than staring out the window. Oh, and she'd twirled her hair around her finger. And connected her paper clips into a long string. Nice multitasking. She moved on from that to thinking about Jack.

She was going to get hurt.

That was pretty much a given. Just like all those years ago, he allowed himself into her life—up to a point. He'd give her the shirt off his back and probably the last dollar in his pocket if he thought she needed it, but he'd withhold his heart.

She more than anyone understood the need for self-protection, but at least she wasn't afraid to go for what she wanted. And she had no idea how someone as strong and tough and brave as Jack could be, either. She'd like to ask him outright, just say "what are we doing here?" but she wouldn't.

Couldn't.

She refused to show him how much it would hurt to watch him walk away again.

Leaving PIC, she drove on autopilot toward home, but the oddest thing happened. Her car took her to No Limits.

She found Jack in the middle studio, wearing black-on-black martial arts gear, going hand to hand with another man. The hits came solid and steady, each man's face fierce with intense concentration. Less than a moment in, it became clear to her that Jack was far better and stronger, and when he dropped the other man to the mat, he offered him a hand.

The guy shook his head and stayed down. "Uncle," he gasped.

Jack swiped a forearm over his brow. Though his skin gleamed with sweat, his breathing was steady and even. "That was much better, Mike."

"And yet here I lie."

A small smile crossed Jack's mouth, and again he offered a hand, pulling Mike upright, clapping him on the shoulder. "See you next week."

Mike straightened with an exaggerated groan and headed toward the locker rooms.

Jack turned to Ellie then. "Hey."

"Hey."

"Not that it's not good to see you," he said, "but what are you doing here?"

"I had a question for you." She watched the wariness come into his eyes and wondered what he was afraid of. Did he really think she'd ask him for something he didn't want to give?

"Call on line two for you," Kel shouted to Jack through the opened studio door.

"Saved by the bell," she murmured.

"No." Jack grabbed her hand when she would have walked away. "Your question."

"You have a call."

"Question first."

"Don't worry about it. It was just something along the lines of, Are you about to run like a little girl because this is getting too real? That sort of thing."

A ghost of a smile curved his mouth. "Like a little girl?"

"Jack!" Kel called again. *"Phone."*

They walked out of the studio to the front desk, Jack not letting go of Ellie's hand, sending yet another mixed message.

Tuning out his phone conversation, she let her gaze wander around. There were awards on the walls and pictures of both students and teachers. The reception counter was neat and clutter free, except for a sign-in sheet and a stack of outgoing mail, and—

And her eyes snagged and held on to the return label stuck to the top envelope.

BNL, Inc.

Her stomach constricted, and suddenly there wasn't quite enough air in the room.

"Ellie?"

Jack had hung up the phone and pulled her around to face him. "What's the matter?"

Fighting to match his calm, she said. "BNL, Inc." She pointed to the envelope. "I was just standing here trying to figure out how I know that name."

Because it was the name of PIC's mystery benefactor, the one who'd sent her the huge anonymous donation.

Jack's face was carefully blank, but he nodded. "It stands for Buchanan's No Limits, the name we're incorporated under. Kel and I have several other studios in other cities."

She stared at him for a long beat. She had no idea what she'd expected, but it hadn't been this easy confession. "You're BNL."

"Yes."

"You gave me money because…" She struggled a moment with that, couldn't think past what was happening between them—or more accurately, what *wasn't* happening between them. "Because you thought I couldn't make it."

"No. No, that's not it at all. You were stressed and I wanted to help."

"You did. So very much. But this way, all stealthlike, makes it feel like you didn't believe in me—"

"Jack," a little boy called from the door of one of the studios. "Come look at me kick."

"Give me a second, Jeremy," he said without taking his gaze off Ellie. "Look, you needed help and I had the means. The end."

Ellie let out a breath and nodded. "And I'm very grateful for that."

He studied her carefully. "So…are you okay? Are we okay?"

"When were you going to tell me?" It took two seconds of searching his gaze to know. "You weren't going to tell me."

"Jack!"

He nodded at the little boy. "One more minute, Jeremy. I'll be right there, I promise." He shifted closer to Ellie. "I didn't tell you because I didn't want you to feel indebted. And I didn't want it to change anything between us."

"And what's between us exactly? Or is it all about you thinking you have to take care of me because I've never done a good enough job on my own?"

"Ellie." He closed his eyes. "Don't do this."

"Guilt," she said tightly. "You've helped me out of guilt because of a silly mistake you think you made as a kid."

"I wasn't a kid. And you paid for that mistake. *My* mistake. You paid dearly."

"I paid for my own stupidity. You weren't responsible for me that night, Jack. I was. And I survived. I took a really horrific experience and turned my life around. So did you. You should be proud. You should celebrate life every single minute. You should…" *Want me.* That's what she'd nearly said, but she had more pride than that. She closed her eyes, shook her head and then opened her eyes again. "You have to go," she said quietly. "And so do I."

"Ellie—"

She stepped out into the warm afternoon sun, and felt cold all the way to the bone.

CHAPTER
∽ SEVEN ∽

Dear Diary,
So as it turns out, I let a stupid guy take my
self-esteem. I let a guy be more important
to me than…me. Good thing I'm done with
being stupid.

I have the power. And while I'm learning
to rein it in, I'm discovering something else. I
don't want other girls to make my mistakes.
I asked Ms. Cahn and she said that at the
next session at PIC, I can lead a discussion
on how to ditch bad boys. Can't wait to show
the girls some good moves.

Thanks for listening, diary. Sorry I said I
hated you.

Kia

* * *

Dear Diary,

Okay, so I did get hurt. I put my heart on the line and it got a little trampled. My fault, really. I knew Jack wasn't open or receptive to what I wanted, but I can admit I'd hoped... Oh, well, that's what life is for, right? It's okay.

Or at least, I'm working on it being okay. Probably that's going to be a while. A long while.

Ellie

"No, Grandma," Ellie said into her cell phone, resisting the urge to thunk her head down to her kitchen table. "I don't want to join one of those internet-dating services."

"I'd love to see you get a man who appreciates you for the wonderful woman you are. Just don't tell them that you work with teenagers—that'll scare any man off. At least the smart ones."

Ellie sighed. "You're right. I want a man who understands what I do. And I'm not going to find that on the internet."

"Honey, what you do is amazing, a real service to the community. But let's face it, you need more in your life. Someday you'll get it, you'll see that you can't save them all, but you *can* save yourself."

"By finding a man?"

"By being happy."

She'd been working on that. Too bad it had blown up in her face. Her doorbell went off. "Grandma, someone's here. I have to go." She looked through the peephole and her heart leaped into her throat.

Jack.

She drew a deep breath to find her cool and calm, but she had none left in the tank so she opened the door.

Distance. That was key here. He'd helped her. He was fond enough of her to be there for her, big-time. And not just her, but the people she cared most about—the girls.

But he didn't want what she wanted, what she'd secretly always wanted from him.

His heart.

"I thought maybe we'd have dinner," he said in greeting, eyes hidden behind reflective sunglasses.

Reaching up, she pulled off the sunglasses and looked into his eyes. "Why?"

"Because I'm hungry."

"Jack."

He stared at her for a long moment, swore, then backed her inside, shut the door and pulled her into his arms.

"What—"

"I *am* proud of you, El." He tightened his grip on her. "So goddamn proud of all you've done and the woman you've become. I hate that you didn't know that."

She opened her mouth, but he covered it with his fingers. "I think about you 24/7. If I'm not thinking about you, I'm dreaming about you."

"Which scared you," she said.

"It *surprised* me."

"Yes, well, you can join my club." She gave him a push. "Now tell me why you played guardian angel without saying a word."

"Angel?" His mouth curved. "I was pretty sure you were thinking I was an ass."

"No. An ass is a guy who neglects to tell you about his wife."

"The dentist. Want me to hurt him for you?"

"Okay, I'm not going to even ask how you know about the dentist," she said.

He kissed her softly. And then not so softly, and she forgot about the dentist.

"I helped you out because you're important to me," he said. "I didn't want to be intrusive, but I wanted you to be okay. And safe."

"Oh, Jack." She cupped his face. "I've always been okay. But I could be better."

"How?"

Look at him, all big and tough and willing to slay her dragons. "You helped me," she whispered. "You helped the girls. That means so much to me."

"But…?"

"But there's something else I want from you."

"Name it."

"You."

He closed his eyes and dropped his forehead to hers. "El."

"You going to tell me you don't feel the same? That you haven't always felt the same?"

He drew in a deep breath. "But you remember who

I was back then—a complete punk, always looking for trouble and finding it. I was never going to bring you down with me."

"Jack, I was as wild and messed up as you were. You have to stop thinking of me as…as some good girl you needed to protect from yourself."

He just looked at her.

"You were not a punk," she said softly. "You were a troubled kid, just like me. Then you went into the army, which made you all dark and badass."

His brow shot up, and that sensual warm mouth quirked.

"Yes," she said. "Dark and badass. The military gave you direction and discipline, and now you're a business owner who sneakily rescues old friends when they need a helping hand. Which actually means you're also a big old softie, too."

He dropped his head to her shoulder. "Is there a point in there somewhere?"

"I know what I want," she said again, wrapping her arms around him. The way he squeezed her back told her everything she needed to know. "And I'm willing to wait for you to want it, too." After a quick hug, she backed away from him, grabbed her keys and walked to the door. "You coming?"

He just stood there, looking a little baffled, poor baby. "Coming?"

"Food," she said very gently. "You're hungry, remember?"

They ended up at a little Mexican place on the outskirts of town, eating and talking, and even laughing.

They had a good time, and in his eyes Ellie could see what she'd wanted to see. She wasn't alone in this. Yes, she was falling for him, and hard.

But so was he.

So when he walked her back up to her door several hours later, she dragged him inside with her.

Because if they couldn't yet say it out loud, they could at least show it.

When Ellie woke up the next morning, Jack was gone. Not allowing herself to give in to the disappointment, she got up and headed into the kitchen, and caught sight of herself in the hall mirror. She was wearing an undeniable glow.

Not to mention a goofy, ridiculously dreamy smile.

And nothing, not even the realization as she stood in front of her empty kitchen cabinets knowing she didn't have any caffeine in the place, could make it go away.

She was contemplating her breakfast options—severely limited since she hadn't gotten to the store—when her cell rang. She glanced at the ID and frowned. "Kia?" She was surprised to hear from the teenager on a Sunday, much less at six-thirty in the morning. "You okay?"

"N–no."

The sole word was choked out and followed by a sob. "I…I need a ride."

"No problem," Ellie said, her stomach plunging as she grabbed her keys and stuffed her feet into her running shoes. "Where are you?"

* * *

It took Ellie ten long minutes to cross town and get to the address Kia had given her. The buildings on this side of town were close together, neglected and dilapidated.

Forgotten.

She parked, and with her phone in hand, she ran up the walk to a small duplex. She was not happy to see Bobby's truck in the driveway, because that meant they were on his home turf. With a knot of fear in her gut for Kia, Ellie knocked on the door.

It swung open, revealing a dark cavernous room she couldn't see into.

Not good… "Kia?"

All she heard was a soft whimper. Worry drove her forward as she walked through the dark, running a hand along the wall looking for a light switch to combat the fact that the curtains were drawn. *Kia.*

A light came on farther inside the place, illuminating a kitchen. Kia appeared in the doorway, giving Ellie a frantic "come here" gesture.

Ellie rushed toward her through the still-dark living room, her relief short-lived when she tripped over something on the carpet and went sprawling.

Kia gasped and ran forward, helping her to her feet. "Hurry! Move away from him before he wakes up!"

Him?

Ignoring her now-burning hands and knees, Ellie let herself get dragged into kitchen. "Tell me I didn't just trip over a body," she hissed.

"Bobby."

Oh, God. "Is he—?"

"No. Just sleeping." Kia nibbled her lip. "Sort of."

"Are you okay?"

"Yes." And then Kia smiled grimly. "He didn't want to hear no, so I dropped him."

Ellie stared at her. "You what?"

"Yeah, just like Jack showed us at PIC, remember? I dropped him to the floor. Except he hit his head on the corner of the coffee table going down." Her face fell. 'Which is my fault, right?"

"No," Ellie said firmly, grabbing Kia's hand to tug her close. "Did he hurt you?"

"No. And he's still breathing, I checked. I just got scared that he'd wake up and be even madder. I wanted to leave, but he drove me here, so I—" She broke off with a startled scream at something behind Ellie, but before Ellie could react, a hand wrapped around her ankle and tugged.

For the second time, she hit the linoleum floor hard, then rolled and blinked up into Bobby's menacing, pissed-off face.

Uh-oh.

"You," Bobby said, pinning her beneath him, frowning as if he had a headache. No wonder, given the bruise blooming across his forehead and temple.

"Let me go," she said with a remarkable calm that she didn't feel.

"I don't think so."

"The police are coming," she lied.

"Good. I did nothing wrong. That bitch attacked me."

"It's illegal to sleep with a minor, did you know

that?" Ellie was proud of her cool, even voice as she struggled like mad to wriggle free. "You're eighteen, she's seventeen. That's statutory rape."

"Not if she wanted it, it's not." Bobby dipped his head, looking Ellie over lewdly. "You want it, too?"

"No." And she jammed her knee up between his legs.

His eyes widened. He let out a squeak and slowly fell off her to his side, curling into a fetal position.

Ellie reached for her phone, but she must have dropped it at some point between tripping over Bobby and being taken down by him. "Call 911," she gasped to Kia, rolling over, getting to her knees. "Hurry."

"But I hit him."

"Self-defense. *Call!*" Ellie staggered to her feet and looked up in time to see someone step inside the front door. It couldn't be the police or medics, not yet. Her biggest fear now was facing Bobby's friends—which wasn't going to end well for her or Kia.

The tall, looming shadow stepped through the living room, and she realized there was only one man that big who could move so silently, with the grace of a cat.

Jack.

He had a dangerous, edgy air to him as he came into the kitchen, the light falling over the taut, tense features of his face as his gaze landed on her with relief and concern.

"I'm okay," she told him.

He didn't speak until he'd made sure for himself, looking over every inch of her before hauling her up against him. "What happened?"

She gave him the short version. Behind them, Bobby stirred and groaned. Jack let go of Ellie and turned to Bobby. "Get up."

Bobby held on to his crotch and shook his head.

Jack shook his too, as if he couldn't quite believe Bobby was going to let go of his bully status with such a whimper. Then he hauled Bobby to his feet, pinning him against the wall so they were nose to nose.

Bobby closed his eyes.

Jack gave him a little shake until he opened them again. Jack didn't raise his voice or give any indication of being furious, but the air crackled.

Bobby swallowed hard. "I didn't mean to mess with your chick."

"Don't talk. Listen. You're not going to touch Kia ever again. You're not going to talk to her, see her or think of her. Same for Ms. Cahn. In fact, you're not going to be within twenty feet of either of them. Do I need to tell you why?"

Bobby shook his head vehemently. He didn't have to be told why.

"You sure?" Jack asked in that terrifyingly quiet voice.

Bobby nodded like a bobblehead.

"Jack," Ellie said, setting a hand on his bicep, which might as well have been solid rock.

Jack let Bobby go.

Bobby slid back to the floor and curled into a ball, still holding on to his family jewels, which Ellie hoped were in his throat.

Five minutes later, the police arrived.

Followed by an ambulance.

In the organized chaos, Ellie turned to Jack. "How did you know where I was?"

"I went to make you breakfast but you were low on supplies. I went to the store."

She stared at him, then winced guiltily. "I thought you'd left."

"When I pulled back onto your street, you were peeling out of your driveway like a bat out of hell."

"I thought you'd left," she said again. "And then Kia called me needing help."

"And you went running." He wrapped his arms tight around her. "Trying to take care of the world."

"I was afraid for her."

"And I was afraid for you." He buried his face in her hair and inhaled deeply.

He'd held her plenty of times now. In fun. In heat. In simple affection. Each and every time she'd sought the comfort in his embrace. But this…this was different.

Because this time *he* was taking comfort from *her*. "I'm okay," she said again softly, tightening her arms around him.

"I know." But he didn't let go. His scent was familiar, as was the feel of his strength and warmth surrounding her, and she sighed and pressed her face to his throat.

"Ellie."

Lifting her head, she looked into his face.

"I did leave."

She went still. "What?"

"When I woke up, you were all warm and soft and…" His mouth brushed her temple. "Perfect," he said quietly.

"And I felt…" He let out a breath. "Everything. I felt everything."

"So you…ran?"

"Yeah." He grimaced. "I'm really hoping you can get past that part."

"You *ran*," she repeated, trying to absorb that.

"But not far," he said. "I only got to the corner before I realized I was an idiot. Then I saw the bakery, and went in to get you breakfast."

"A goodbye breakfast."

"No. By then I'd realized something."

"What, that you were acting like a little girl again?"

"A little bit." He kissed her, soft and coaxing, and then not so soft. "You hit me hard, El. I didn't know what to do about you."

"And you think you figured it out?" She already knew the answer. It'd been in his kiss.

He ran a hand down her arm until his fingers entwined in hers. "In the military I survived off brute strength. It's what I use in my job, too. But with you…" He shook his head. "Strength doesn't seem to impress you all that much."

"No. Neither does you writing a secret check instead of telling me how you feel. I told you, Jack. I don't need a guardian angel."

"And I had no idea that I did."

He was still holding her. She had her hands on his chest, and could feel his heart beating strong and sure beneath her fingers.

"You opened me up," he said. "You reminded me to

live." And while her heart fell out onto the floor at his feet, he added, "I love you. I think I always have."

She felt her throat go tight. "I love you too, Jack. So very much."

His smile came slow and sure, and stopped her heart. "I thought it'd be so hard to say," he murmured. "But it turns out it's not hard at all." He cupped her face. "I plan on feeling this way about you forever, El. Does that work for you?"

"More than you'll ever know."

❧ EPILOGUE ❧

One year later

Dear Diary,
Sorry it's been a while, but you'll be happy to
know that I'm finding lots of great ways to
release my pent-up feelings that won't get me
in trouble. Who knew all it would take was
thinking about Bobby's face when I practiced
my kicking at No Limits gym?

I graduated high school last week, and
with a 3.0, which means Ms. Cahn has to
buy me ice cream every week for a year. She
promised.

Oh, and I think you'll be happy to know
I'm going to a junior college in the fall, and
I'm thinking of studying to become a social

*worker. Who knows, maybe someday I'll be
helping teenagers the way PIC helped me.*

*Speaking of PIC, I work there. Cool, right? I
just answer phones and make files and stuff,
but Ms. Cahn says I can be in charge of social
media. So I get to make PIC a Facebook page
and give it a Twitter account and stuff. Better
than flipping burgers, right?*

*Oh, and the biggee…Ms. Cahn's getting
married! To Jack. Duh. And I get to be a
bridesmaid and everything. It means wearing a pale purple dress, but the shoes are
rockin'. And I helped her make the music list
for the deejay so the reception will be really
cool.*

*I'm not really dating. But there's this really
cute guy who works at the rec center. He
smiled at me today. He might be worth a
second look.*

*Because I am. Worth a second look. I know
that now.*

Kia

Dear Diary,
*Hey there, it's me, Ellie. I know, I know, you
probably thought I forgot how to use a pen
and paper. Yes, it's been a while since we
last talked, but as it turns out, Jack's a really
good listener, too.*

I've been pretty busy with teaching, and also at PIC. The new location is working out, and I have a staff now, so we're able to get more teens through the program.

Oh, and I think you'll get a kick out of knowing that I've decided to follow Grandma's advice and get a man in my life.

Jack, of course.

He's smart and fun and sexy, and I want to spend the rest of my life with him. We're getting married on Saturday.

So...I guess I'm writing to tell you good-bye. Don't be sad. It means I'm moving on to happier things. And if it makes you feel any better, at the next PIC session, I'll be having thirty-five girls start writing to you every week.

Best of luck with that.

Love, Ellie

* * * * *

Dear Reader,

When I was asked to write a short story for this collection, I was thrilled and honored. Not only do I love the other authors writing in this *More Than Words* volume, but I also love the cause—WET (Women's Expressive Theater).

My story centers on a heroine who, in addition to being a teacher, is running a program for teenage girls. The young women in her life are near and dear to her heart—something I can relate to as well. I have three teenage girls of my own, and another we've adopted into our hearts and home.

Yes, this means that I have four of these sullen, attitude-ridden, odd and unusual creatures in my house. The amount of estrogen alone is enough to take down an entire civilization. But as my story shows us, love and acceptance is truly the only path.

And a sense of humor doesn't hurt either!

I loved writing this novella, and I hope you love it, as well.

Happy reading,

Jill Shalvis

PREVIEW OF
PAMELA MORSI'S
— DAFFODILS IN SPRING —

CHAPTER
~ ONE ~

C alla stepped off the bus on Canasta Street and
made a quick stop at the Korean grocery before
walking the three blocks to her home. Typically
this time of year she made the walk all bundled up and
with her head down against the wind. But this fall was
gorgeous in Chicago and the city was, for a brief time
at least, a place of bright sunshine and vivid autumn
colors. Only the slightest nip in the air foretold of the
cold winter to come.

She'd lived on Canasta Street for sixteen years. She
and her husband, Mark, had moved into their house
when their son was still just a toddler. Now, Nathan was
in his last year of high school and had just completed his
early-action application to attend Northwestern, his first
choice for college, next year. Calla smiled to herself. She

couldn't help but be proud. She just wished that Mark had lived to see it.

As she approached her block, all the tiredness of the long workday seemed to lift. There was something about a home surrounded by neighbors and friends that just buoyed a person. Every step she took along the well-worn sidewalk was as familiar to her as the back of her hand.

From his porch, old Mr. Whitten waved to her. Next door to him, the Carnaby children, along with their cousins, friends and assorted other stragglers, were noisy and exuberant as they played in their front yard. Two houses past them, Mrs. Gamble sat on her steps, her daughter, Eunice, at her side.

"You're home early," the older woman called out.

Calla just smiled. She was home at exactly the same time she was home every day.

"Did you buy something at the store?" Mrs. Gamble asked.

"Just milk," Calla answered. "And a half-dozen apples. You know Mr. Ohng's produce is hard to resist."

"Come and sit a spell with us," the older woman said. "We haven't had a good visit with you in ages."

"Oh, I'd better get home and see what Nathan is up to."

"He's sure up to nothing at home," Eunice said with just a hint of superiority in her voice. "He's across the street in 2B with Gerty's wild grandniece."

Calla kept her expression deliberately blank. Eunice undoubtedly wanted to get a rise from her, but she wasn't about to give the woman the satisfaction.

"Oh, come up and sit," Mrs. Gamble pleaded. "That way you can see him when he leaves."

Calla wouldn't have walked across the street to talk with Eunice. But Mrs. Gamble was a genuinely sweet older lady who was trapped all day with the bitter un-happiness of her daughter.

So she opened the gate on the Gambles' chain-link fence and made her way to the porch. Setting her little bag of groceries beside her, Calla tucked the hem of her skirt behind her knees and seated herself on the fourth step, just slightly below Mrs. Gamble and directly across from Eunice.

"How was your job today?" Mrs. Gamble asked.

Calla shrugged. "Fine," she answered. She knew the woman was eager for details. Calla had been a nurse in Dr. Walker's ear, nose and throat practice for over a decade. Mrs. Gamble loved stories about diseases. Es-pecially ones where the patient had to overcome great odds to recover.

There'd been no such dramatic cases today. With the coming of fall, the office had been full of allergy sufferers fighting off sinus infections. Calla was not sure how entertaining the stories would be when all the characters were blowing into tissues.

"It's been pretty routine at the office the last few days," Calla told her.

"Well, there's nothing routine about the goings-on around here," Eunice piped in. "That girl has got her hooks in Nathan and no good is going to come of it."

Calla couldn't stop herself from casting a nervous glance in the direction of the apartment building across the street. Gerty Cleveland had lived there for twenty years, at least. She was about Mrs. Gamble's age and had a large family scattered across the city. Less than a month ago, Jazleen—or Jazzy, as Nathan called her—had come to live with her. Calla didn't know the whole story, but there were plenty of rumors swirling about.

The girl's mother was on drugs. Or maybe she was in jail. Jazleen herself had been in trouble. Or maybe she just was trouble. Gerty was Jazleen's last chance. Or maybe she was the only chance the teenager had ever had.

Calla had heard what everyone was saying. But what resounded with her louder than all the neighborhood whispering were the words of her son, Nathan.

"She's okay, Mom," he assured her. "She's a good person."

Calla trusted her son, but she worried, too. Young men could often be blinded by a pretty face or a good figure. Jazleen was no great beauty, but she had sweet features and the requisite number of teenage curves.

"Once you get to know her," Nathan said, "you'll like her."

That was slow going so far. Jazleen had been in their house many times. She was mostly silent and slightly sullen. Those were hardly traits to win the heart.

"I don't think we should jump to conclusions about the girl," Calla told Eunice. "Nathan says she's nice."

Eunice sucked her teeth. "Yes, well, I'm sure that's what the boy would tell his mother."

Calla was very tempted to remind Eunice that since she obviously didn't know one thing about mothers and sons, it might be best if she just kept her opinions to herself.

She was saved from making any comment by the now-familiar tap of shiny shoes coming down the sidewalk.

"It's him!" Eunice breathed, barely above a whisper.

Calla didn't need to ask who she meant. Every woman on Canasta Street, single, divorced, married or widowed, like Calla herself, knew the only man who would attract such attention.

Deliberately Calla kept her gaze on Mrs. Gamble. She flatly refused to turn and look, though she could see the man perfectly in her imagination. Landry Sinclair had moved into the house next door to her just weeks ago. He was polite and friendly, but so far no one had really gotten to know him. What Calla and the other women did know was that he was tall and trim, with a strong jaw, a handsome smile and thick, arched brows. He went to work every morning and returned every evening dressed in impeccably tailored suits. And, so far, there had been no visitors at his place. No wife or girlfriend, not even a one-night stand. He seemed unattached, which provoked much speculation.

"That is the finest-looking man I've ever seen in my life," Eunice stated in a hushed whisper. "And I think he's just about my age. Don't you think he's probably my age?"

Calla nodded. "More or less," she agreed. Though she thought the years certainly held up better on him than on Eunice.

"Have you noticed his accent?" the other woman asked.

Of course Calla had noticed. She noticed everything about him.

"I think he's from the South," Eunice said.

"No, he's not from the South," Calla replied, shaking her head. "I have relatives from South Carolina and Georgia. He doesn't talk like the South at all."

"Well, he's not from here," Eunice insisted.

Calla shrugged agreement. The man clearly was not a local. But he was almost as mysterious as he was good-looking. He wasn't secretive. He answered any question he was asked. But the men on the street seemed satisfied to exchange pleasantries and opinions on sports teams. The women were all too curious, but didn't trust themselves to stick to casual questions. So the basic information of where he was from and where he worked remained unknown, as well as the most critical fact to some—whether there was a woman someplace waiting for him.

"Good afternoon, Mr. Sinclair!" Mrs. Gamble called out as he passed by the gate.

Calla turned to look at him then, as if she'd been unaware of his approach. The man was dressed attractively in a single-breasted brown suit with narrow beige pinstripes. He looked businesslike, successful. She smiled in a way she hoped would appear to be polite disinterest.

"Good afternoon, Mrs. Gamble, ladies." He doffed

his fedora, revealing dark hair that was just beginning to thin on the top. "It's a beautiful afternoon to sit out and enjoy the weather."

"It surely is," Mrs. Gamble agreed. "Why don't you come and join us."

Calla heard Eunice draw a sharp, shocked breath. She couldn't tell if Landry Sinclair had heard it or not.

"I wish that I could," he answered, smiling broadly. "I sure wish I could."

He did not give a reason why he couldn't, but for an instant Calla's glance met his. His eyes were deep brown with a sparkle that was as much intelligence as humor. Calla found him completely irresistible.

Which was precisely the reason she had never spoken to him.

That was the last thing in the world she needed, to get all goofy and love struck over some man. She'd had her man. They'd had a good marriage and raised a wonderful son. Romance for her was over and done now. She was a grown-up, sensible woman, not some silly teenager.

It was after six when Nathan got home.

"It's about time you showed up," Calla said. "Dinner's almost ready."

"Yeah, I smelled your cooking all the way across the street and came running," her son teased.

He hurried to the bathroom to wash up as she set the table. Two plates, two forks, two knives, two spoons.

It had been just the two of them now for almost five years. But two was an excellent number. She and Nathan were a team, and they shared the same goal. Getting him through high school and into a good college. That goal had often seemed so far off that Calla had thought it would never happen. Now their dream was nearing realization. And it was as if all those years of reaching for it had gone by in a flash.

Nathan hurried to the table and took a seat. "Give me a pork chop before I bite into the table leg," he threatened.

Calla chuckled lightly as she seated herself and passed him the platter of meat. Everyone said that Nathan was just like her. But when she looked at him, she saw so much of her late husband. Nathan was lean and lanky. He had a bubbly humor that charmed everyone he met. But he also had a streak of kindheartedness that was as wide as Lake Michigan. Calla was absolutely certain he hadn't gotten *that* from her. And she worried where it might lead him.

"I guess you've been over at Mrs. Cleveland's place," Calla said with deliberate casualness. "Visiting her niece. That's very nice, of course, but you mustn't neglect your other friends."

Nathan eyed his mother with open amusement. "My other *friends* understand completely why I want to spend time with Jazleen."

Her son was grinning. Calla didn't like that much.

"She's pretty lonely," he continued. "It's bad enough

to be going through a lot of stuff, but then to spend all your time alone—that just makes it worse."

"Isn't she making friends at school?"

Nathan hesitated slightly. "She's sort of blown off school."

"What do you mean by that?"

"She pretty much ignored it the last couple of years, and when she showed up this year to enroll, they transferred her to the alternative high school. That ticked her off. She said if she couldn't take classes with me, then there was no point going."

Calla raised an eyebrow. "That doesn't make any sense at all."

Nathan shrugged. "She was so far behind, she wasn't going to be able to keep up in my classes anyway," he said. "But it is kind of worthless to sit around all day watching TV, just waiting for me to get home."

Calla agreed with that. She was not happy, however, that the girl was planning her life, living her life, around Nathan.

"What does Mrs. Cleveland say about her dropping out of school?"

"I don't think she knows, Mom."

"What do you mean? She must know."

Nathan shook his head. "Her job is way across town. She leaves to catch her train before seven in the morning and she doesn't get home until after five. She and Jazzy hardly say two words to each other. I seriously doubt they've talked this out together."

Calla's dinner was suddenly tasteless. "You know I'll have to tell her."

Her son nodded. "Yeah, I know. Jazzy really needs... she really needs something, someone...I don't know. Mom, she's clever and smart and doesn't have a lazy bone in her body. But she's just...you know...drifting without any direction."

Calla nodded. There were a lot of young people like that.

"I try to talk to her about college and the future and all the things that I'm working for," Nathan said. "I might as well be telling fairy tales. She doesn't see how any of it could ever apply to her."

"Well, it probably won't," Calla said. "If she can't stick it out in high school, then she'll never get a chance at college."

"But she could stick it out, Mom," Nathan said. "I know she could."

Calla wasn't so sure.

Saturday morning dawned sunny with a bright blue sky. Seated at the breakfast table in her robe, Calla lingered over her coffee. It was just laziness, she assured herself, and had nothing to do with the view outside her window. Her kitchen looked directly into Landry Sinclair's backyard, and the man himself was out there, clad in faded jeans and a sweatshirt that clung damply to his muscular torso. His sweat was well earned as he attacked the ground with a shovel and hoe. He looked very different without his tailored suits. She'd always thought of him as tidy and professional. Not the kind of man to get his hands dirty.

He was certainly getting dirty this morning. And

he looked really good doing it. Calla watched him as he worked, allowing herself the secret pleasure of lusting after a man who wasn't hers. She thought she'd left all that nonsense in the past. But somehow, from the moment Landry Sinclair moved into the neighborhood, she'd felt differently.

And she didn't like it one bit. Every woman on the block had already staked a claim for him. Calla hated to follow along with the crowd. And she despised the kind of mooning over men that a lot of women her age engaged in. It was one thing to be boy crazy at fourteen. It was downright undignified to be that way at forty.

Still, she could hardly take her eyes away from the vision of Landry Sinclair sweating over a garden hoe.

A knock sounded at the front door. She glanced at the clock. It was barely nine. She couldn't imagine who would be visiting so early. She went to peer through the peephole. The familiar figure standing on the porch was visible only in profile. Her long, thin legs and round backside were encased in tight jeans. Her skimpy jacket showed off her curves, but wouldn't provide any protection if the weather turned colder. And her long dark hair was a flawless mix of braids and curls.

Her expression, however, even from the side, appeared wary and secretive.

Calla opened the door.

"Good morning, Jazleen."

The girl's suspicion toughened into something that looked like hostility.

"Where's Nathan?" she demanded with no other greeting.

"He's sleeping," Calla answered. "It's Saturday morning. That's what he does on Saturday mornings."

"We're going...someplace," Jazleen hedged. "He's supposed to be ready."

"He probably overslept. Come in and I'll wake him up."

"I'm okay on the porch," Jazleen said, her chin slightly in the air.

"Come in," Calla insisted, knowing the girl's hesitation to enter the house was because of her. Jazleen had been inside with Nathan many times.

Hesitantly she followed Calla. "I'll go wake him," Jazleen said.

"No!" Calla answered firmly. "You wait here, pour yourself a cup of coffee. I'll wake my son."

As she went up the stairs, Calla glanced back toward the girl. She stood in the doorway of the kitchen, her arms wrapped around her as if she was cold or protecting herself.

At the top of the stairs, Calla turned right and knocked on her son's door.

"Nathan? Nathan!"

An unintelligible rumbling was the only reply. Calla opened the door and peered into the shadows for an instant before crossing the darkened room and pulling up the shades. A wide shaft of sunlight revealed her son completely cocooned in a tangle of blankets.

He groaned.

"Better get up," Calla told him. "You've got company downstairs."

"Huh?" he asked without bothering to poke his head out from under the covers.

"Jazleen is here," she said. "Apparently you were going someplace together this morning."

Nathan moaned again and rolled over, flipping back the blankets to reveal his face and T-shirt-clad torso.

"Oh, yeah," he said. "I told her I would take her to Oak Street Beach. I couldn't believe she'd lived here all her life and never been."

Calla nodded.

With a sigh of determination, Nathan rolled out of bed. "Let me get a quick shower," he told his mother. "Tell her I'll be downstairs in fifteen minutes."

Calla left him to get ready and returned to the kitchen. Jazleen was still standing in the middle of the floor.

"Nathan says fifteen minutes," Calla told her. "Would you like a cup of coffee?"

"No," Jazleen answered too quickly.

"Are you sure?" Calla asked. "I'm going to have another cup."

Jazleen hesitated. "I don't mind," she said finally.

It wasn't exactly "yes, please," but Calla decided it was the best excuse for manners that the girl could muster.

"Sit down," she told her as she set the cup on the table. "There's milk and sugar."

Jazleen reluctantly seated herself. Calla took the chair opposite her. The girl continued to eye her warily. The silence lengthened between them. Calla was racking her brains for a neutral subject and was just about to comment on the weather when Jazleen spoke.

"That man next door has got a shovel," she said. "I think he's burying something."

Calla glanced in the direction of the window. She couldn't see Landry Sinclair at this angle, but she could still perfectly recall the sight of the man.

"He's digging a garden," Calla said.

Jazleen's brow furrowed and she snorted in disbelief. "This time of year? Not likely. He's burying something."

So much for neutral conversation, Calla thought.

"Nathan said you two are headed for an outing to Oak Street Beach."

Jazleen didn't answer. She eyed Calla suspiciously and then sipped her coffee as if that gave her permission not to comment. Her eyes were widely set and a rich dark brown. She was wearing a bit too much makeup, but a cleft in her chin made her look vulnerable.

"We used to go to Oak Street Beach a lot when Nathan was a little boy," Calla told her. "Lots of fresh air and room to run around. On a crisp fall day it's absolutely the best. He would sit and just look at the boats on the water."

She paused, but again Jazleen said nothing.

"I'm sure that's what he wants to share with you," Calla continued. "Even if it does mean giving up a sleepy Saturday morning."

Calla was frustrated when the girl made no attempt to keep up her side of the conversation. She decided maybe questions and answers would be easier.

"Nathan says you watch a lot of TV?"

"Some."

"Have you seen anything good lately?"

She shook her head.

"I like those dancing shows," Calla told her. "But more often I prefer reading."

Jazleen sipped her coffee.

"Do you like to read?"

The girl shrugged.

"When I was your age, that was what I loved best."

Jazleen raised a brow. It wasn't exactly an eye roll, but Calla was fairly sure it had the same meaning.

"Do you know how to read?" Calla asked.

"Of course I do!" Jazleen snapped. "I'm not stupid."

"I didn't think that you were," Calla said. "But a lot of very smart people don't read, or don't read very well."

"I can read fine, thank you."

"Okay, good." Calla hesitated. "Nathan said you've dropped out of school."

"Maybe. I haven't decided."

"What does your great-aunt think about it?"

"I'd guess she'd think that it's none of her business," Jazleen declared. "And it's sure none of yours."

The young girl's expression was angry. Calla was not feeling very friendly herself.

"If you're seeing my son, then I make it my business," she answered.

"What? You trying to turn him into some mama's boy?"

"Every male on this earth is a mama's boy," Calla said. "He may love her or he may hate her, but there is nobody else in the world who can talk to a man the way his mama does."

Jazleen's jaw set tightly with anger.

"Nathan and I are very close," Calla told the girl quietly. "If you stay tight with him, you're going to have to deal with me. So maybe you should think about getting used to it."

After the teenagers left, Calla didn't even attempt to get back to lazy-day musing. Saturdays were busy days with chores she put off all week, but she couldn't help thinking about Nathan and Jazleen. So it wasn't surprising that just after lunchtime, she headed across the street to have a chat with Gerty Cleveland.

The woman took her time getting to the door. The tiny apartment was crowded with furniture, but it was neat as a pin except for the area around the recliner that sported TV trays on either side loaded with food, drink, tissues, assorted junk and the remote control. As soon as Calla walked inside, Gerty returned to the chair and popped it into the raised position.

"I try to keep my feet up every minute that I'm home," she explained to Calla. "As it is, I'll be lucky to get five more years of work out of them."

It seemed to Calla it was probably already time for Gerty to stop working. Steel-gray hair covered her head, her hands shook and she didn't hear all that well.

"I wanted to talk to you about Jazleen,"

"Say what?"

"I wanted to talk to you about Jazleen," she repeated a bit louder.

"Jazleen? She's a sweet girl," Gerty said. "I was real reluctant to take her. Her mama's no good. And my sister, her own grandma, gone to Jesus twenty years ago. She was living with my daughter, Val, for a month or two. But there was some kind of trouble with Val's man. So there was no one else and here she is. But she keeps the place tidied up, and when I get home from work, she's always got some kind of dinner for me. That's been nice, real nice."

"Did you know she's thinking of dropping out of school?"

"No, I didn't pay no attention to that. Guess if she's not going to school, she should get a job. That's what I did. I left school and got myself a job."

"Things were different back then," Calla told her. "Nowadays it's tough to find a job if you don't finish high school."

The old woman nodded absently. "That's likely true."

"You shouldn't let her drop out," Calla said.

"I hope she won't," Gerty said. "But truth to tell, as long as she don't get into no trouble, I'm tempted to just let her be."

Calla shook her head to disagree, but her neighbor forestalled her.

"You don't know the life that girl has lived," Gerty said. "She's had troubles like you and me have never seen. That doesn't happen to people and leave them unmarked. If she can find some happiness on her own, then I'm all for letting her have it."

Calla continued talking with Gerty for a half hour or more, but it was clear that the old woman had no plans for Jazleen's future and was only vaguely interested in the young woman's present.

"But you must be worried."

"The girl will be all right," Gerty assured her. "She'll find her way. I don't have the time or the energy to make sure she does this, that or the other. She's nearly grown, so she's on her own. Besides, she has that boy of yours to make do for her."

"What?"

"It was real smart of her to latch onto him," Gerty said. "He's got a lot of gumption and he's not afraid of hard work. He'll be like his daddy, a good family man. Jazleen is lucky in that."

"Nathan is off to college next year," Calla explained.

The older woman eyed her skeptically. "That's what you're hoping," she said. "But he seems mighty sweet on her."

Calla shook her head. "No, it's just a passing thing. It's not serious between them."

Gerty Cleveland didn't believe a word of that.

Calla left the woman's apartment and went straight to the supermarket to do her weekly shopping. The day had gotten significantly colder, but she found the chilly wind invigorated her.

It was too bad about Jazleen, she thought to herself. The girl might be stuck-up and rude, but she was still a girl. And someone Nathan seemed to think was special. But if she was pinning her hopes on snagging Calla's son, she was doomed to be disappointed. Jazleen would end up like a thousand other girls. Working at a menial job as she struggled to raise kids she could hardly support.

Calla decided it would be her goal to make sure that none of those kids were on the way before she could get Nathan safely off to college.

By the time she'd made it home from the store and put the groceries away, she was tired. The house was cozy and warm. She settled herself on the couch with a book but hadn't read more than a half-dozen pages when her eyelids began to get heavy. She set her book open upside down on her chest and lay back on a throw pillow to catch a quick twenty winks. The glare from the reading lamp seemed to permeate her eyelids, so she switched it off and drifted into a comfortable nap.

Voices from the kitchen awakened her sometime later.

"Let me fix you something to warm you up."

"Just wrap me in your arms—that gets me about as warm as I need."

Nathan chuckled, a low masculine sound.

The ensuing silence spoke for itself. They both seemed a little breathless when the conversation resumed.

"What do you want to do?" Nathan asked.

"Uh…let's just sit together and talk," Jazleen replied.

He chuckled. "You haven't had enough talk from me already? I've been at it for hours."

"I love to hear you talk," she said.

"It's crazy how we never run out of things to say."

"Yeah, strange," she agreed. "But in a good way."

"That is, until I start talking about school, and then you just say nothing at all."

Jazleen hesitated. "It's a part of your life that I can't share."

"Of course you can," Nathan said. "We can share the fun of my senior year and graduation and me going off to college."

"I want to be happy for you," Jazleen said. "But the truth is, I don't want you to go off to college. If you go away, I won't have anybody."

"It's not like it's forever. And if I get into Northwestern, it's not that far away."

She made a huff of disagreement. "You might as well be going to the moon. If you really care about me like you say, you won't take one step off Canasta Street."

Calla couldn't keep listening. It was wrong to eavesdrop on Nathan, even by accident. She knew she wasn't supposed to hear any of what they'd said.

She reached up and turned the light back on. But instead of reading, she set her book on the coffee table and got up and left the room. She didn't speak to them or acknowledge that she'd heard them talking. But they knew.

It had been easy to walk away from the conversation. Less so to get it out of her head. And along with it came other voices.

"She's got your Nathan wrapped around her little finger."

"He's mighty sweet on that girl."

In the following weeks at work, Calla worried about it. Evenings at home, it colored her enthusiasm. College was what she and Nathan had worked for, waited for. Her son was going to graduate with honors. There was so much going on and Calla wanted to be celebrating. But she was worrying instead.

* * * * *

To enjoy the rest of Pamela Morsi's
story please visit
www.HarlequinMoreThanWords.com
for your free ebook.

PREVIEW OF
MERYL SAWYER'S
~ Worth the Risk ~

CHAPTER
∽— ONE —∾

L exi Morrison swept through the doors of Stovall
Middle School along with a gust of spring wind.
She waved at the secretary as she sailed down
the hall to the cafeteria to volunteer in her sister's class.
She hated being late, but it couldn't be helped. Professor Thompson had kept her behind to compliment her
work. It would have been unspeakably rude not to listen,
especially since she was counting on him to give her a
reference once she'd completed her MBA.

"Lexi, there you are," called Mrs. Geffen as Lexi
shouldered her way through the double doors into the
cafeteria.

"Sorry I'm late," she whispered to the teacher. The
second the words left her lips, Lexi realized the room
was silent, which was unusual when over thirty teenagers were assembled in one place.

Then Lexi saw why. At the front of the room was a tall man with dark hair and striking blue eyes. He wore a navy shirt with Black Jack's emblazoned in red on the pocket. He must be the guest chef who was scheduled to demonstrate today.

"Mr. Westcott was just telling us that he learned to cook in the C.I.A.," Mrs. Geffen told her in a voice everyone could hear.

Lexi nodded and understood what he meant, but she couldn't imagine the students would catch on. No doubt they assumed he'd been in the Central Intelligence Agency.

She quickly glanced around the room to locate her younger sister, Amber. Volunteering once a week in Amber's culinary arts class was the commitment Lexi had made to encourage Amber with her studies. This cooking class was an elective and the only subject that interested her. Unlike Amber, Lexi had always been in advance-placement classes and loved school as much as her sister hated it.

She spotted Amber in the front row. Her sister was always so eager to get to this class that she'd probably been waiting for the doors to open. Her honey-brown head tilted slightly toward the guest chef, then turned and caught Lexi's eye. "Hot," she mouthed.

So that's why her sister had been in such a rush to get here. Lexi thought the guy looked arrogant. He was frowning at her. She'd obviously interrupted and he didn't appreciate it.

"Class," Mrs. Geffen said as the group began to whisper, "Mr. Westcott was telling us about his training. Let's listen to what he has to say."

The teacher was short and packed into a moss-green suit that she'd worn almost every Wednesday that Lexi had volunteered.

"Someone asked where I learned to cook," the chef repeated.

Lexi recalled Brad Westcott was the owner and executive chef of Black Jack's, one of the most successful restaurants in Houston. It was also one of the few that didn't purchase produce from City Seeds, Lexi's gourmet-vegetable operation.

"Like a lot of you," he said in a voice that indicated he was at ease with inner-city kids, "I used to think cooking was tossing something in the microwave."

The students chuckled and elbowed each other, especially the boys. Many of them came from Mexico or South America and regarded cooking as women's work. They were in this class because their other elective choices had been filled.

"Then I went into the army," he continued.

That statement got the boys' undivided attention. Many of them would join when they were old enough.

"I was assigned to the officers' mess hall. That's what they call the kitchen—the mess hall. Mostly I peeled potatoes, carrots—"

"What about the C.I.A.?" yelled one of the boys.

"The army is where I became interested in cooking," Brad continued, ignoring the interruption. "When I got out, I had enough money to enroll in the C.I.A. The Culinary Institute of America right here in Houston."

Lexi smiled, but it took a few seconds before the light dawned on the rest of the students. The girls giggled while the boys rolled their eyes or elbowed each other.

Their reactions didn't bother Brad Westcott. "Over half the students at the culinary institute were men. Top chefs in many restaurants are men. Lots of the celebrity chefs on television are men."

The boys seemed more interested. "A good chef can make a lot of money," Brad continued. "Plus, you meet lots of interesting people, especially women."

Now they were impressed. Money was a never-ending concern in the inner city. The word *money* got the boys' attention, but mentioning women didn't hurt. They might try to deny their interest in the opposite sex, but they didn't fool anyone.

"Something to think about," Brad told them with a canted smile that made him look mischievous. "Today, I'm going to show you how to make an easy treat. Has everyone washed their hands?"

Lexi was sure they had. It was required before any class where food was to be prepared, and special monitors at the door checked the students. In addition, the tables had been covered with clean butcher paper to prevent spreading germs.

"You're going to learn how to make chocolate truffle balls."

There were a few snickers from the boys and Lexi groaned inwardly, but not for the same reason. No doubt they thought truffles sounded like a sissy word, even though most of them probably had no idea what it meant.

Lexi knew her little sister adored desserts—especially chocolate.

Amber had been diagnosed with juvenile diabetes when she was just seven. She realized sweets weren't good for her, but she often ignored the doctors' warnings. The girl loved to cook and she especially liked to bake.

Lexi and Aunt Callie had tried to encourage Amber to prepare healthy food, but since Aunt Callie's death, she had become more difficult. She indulged her sweet tooth even though she was aware of the health risks. If a hyperglycemic attack resulted, her blood sugar would suddenly spike, and she would need a dose of insulin or a trip to the E.R.

Amber resented Lexi being named her legal guardian. Lexi couldn't understand her younger sister's attitude. After all, since the death of their parents, Lexi had been more of a mother to Amber than Aunt Callie. Their aunt's death and the judge's decree had merely formalized the arrangement. But at fourteen, Amber believed she was old enough to take care of herself.

Seeming to realize Lexi was thinking about her, Amber turned and flashed playful green eyes that were exactly like Lexi's. Then she turned back to the two boys who would be her partners for the cooking assignment. How could Amber be so sure of herself? Lexi wondered.

Lexi was almost ten years older than her sister and had excelled in school, especially in math. Amber never worried about her grades or about having diabetes. She took everything with an "oh, well," attitude. She didn't seem to realize—or care—that they lived one step from being homeless.

When Aunt Callie died, she'd left them the house. It no longer had a mortgage, but there were property taxes and utilities, plus college tuition, to be paid. Lexi worked two jobs to make ends meet while she attended college. The last thing she needed was for Amber to become ill from an improper diet.

"Do you sell vegetables to Mr. Westcott?" whispered Mrs. Zamora. She was one of the mothers who regularly volunteered to help Mrs. Geffen on cooking days.

"No. I think Black Jack's is more casual, less gourmet," Lexi responded, although she wasn't really sure. She couldn't afford to eat out, so she'd never been in the trendy restaurant.

"That's too bad," Mrs. Zamora said almost wistfully with a glance at the visiting chef.

Lexi didn't need to look at him again to know that most women—not just girls Amber's age—would find the guy attractive. He was tall and powerfully built, with a ready smile and blue eyes that radiated a certain sparkle.

"Black Jack's probably doesn't serve baby vegetables and exotic greens," she told Mrs. Zamora. Lexi was justifiably proud of the unusual vegetables she raised in the backyard behind the house they'd inherited. It was in an older part of Houston where homes had large yards. Most of the neighboring houses had been split into multi-family homes with shared rear yards.

Luckily, Aunt Callie had kept the family home intact and used the yard to raise market vegetables to sell. After her death, Lexi had realized there was more money to be made in smaller "baby" vegetables that could be sold directly to restaurants.

"I was at Black Jack's once," Mrs. Zamora said. "For my husband's company's party. Great ribs."

"Right," Lexi responded, her eyes on the chef. Ribs and steak. Texas food.

Right now, Brad was showing the class how to roll the chocolate mixture into small balls. "Does anyone know what a truffle is?"

Lexi doubted many of the students would, but to her surprise Amber's hand immediately shot up. Brad nodded at her and Amber answered, "A truffle is in the mushroom family. It's brown and grows mostly in deep forests. Pigs hunt them by sniffing them out. They're *very* expensive."

The class laughed uproariously, as if Amber had just told an off-color joke.

"That's right," Brad's voice cut through the noise. "Truffles are hard to find and rare. That's why they're so expensive."

Amber must have read about wild truffles in one of her cookbooks. Why she couldn't devote as much attention to her other studies mystified Lexi.

"We call this chocolate a truffle because it's brown and roundish," Brad continued. "You don't have to roll a perfectly round truffle. Just make them about the same size."

Lexi, Mrs. Zamora and Mrs. Geffen walked around the room helping any students who were having problems. It was a simple assignment. The only ones who asked for help really wanted attention. Lexi often found this true when she volunteered.

After they formed the truffle balls, the class was shown how to roll them in cocoa powder and place them on cookie sheets for cooling in the commercial-size refrigerator. Everyone seemed to be having a lot of fun. Of course, that meant the noise level in the cafeteria shot into the stratosphere.

Brad Westcott didn't seem to mind. He made his way around the room to speak encouragingly to the students. Lexi caught him looking at her several times.

"I hear he's one of the chefs being featured on a television program about rising stars in the restaurant business," Mrs. Geffen whispered as the students lined up to put their cookie sheets into the refrigerator.

"Really?" Lexi said, but she wasn't surprised. Black Jack's had opened to rave reviews and become an overnight sensation.

What Lexi didn't understand was why the chef had chosen to demonstrate chocolate truffles. Mrs. Geffen's class was supposed to feature healthy food.

Many students, like Amber, had chosen culinary arts as an elective because of their previous experience in Recipe for Success back in elementary school. The program had given them an appreciation for growing and preparing food.

"How many of you know about my restaurant, Black Jack's?" Brad asked after the students had gone back to their seats.

Most of the group raised their hands. Lexi considered it tactful of him not to ask how many had eaten there.

Fast-food places were the extent of most of their dining experiences.

"Good," Brad said. "We're known for ribs and steaks, but also for fabulous desserts. I'm sponsoring a contest for middle-school students organized by the Chef's Association. The grand prize will be a thousand dollars and a summer internship with my pastry chef for the student who creates the best new dessert."

"An internship is an opportunity to work alongside a professional," Mrs. Geffen told them. "You learn by doing."

"You won't get paid for your work," Brad added.

There were some moans from the boys, but most of the students were interested. Especially Amber. She was beaming and whispering to the students seated beside her.

Great. Just what Lexi needed. Summer was her busiest season in the garden and her most profitable. She wanted Amber to go to summer school to boost her grades and help with City Seeds in her free time. Spending hours in the kitchen creating a new dessert would be catastrophic for her health and no help in raising the money they needed so much. Besides, as far as Lexi was concerned, the world had too many desserts.

* * * * *

To enjoy the rest of Meryl Sawyer's story, please visit
www.HarlequinMoreThanWords.com
for your free ebook.